SOONER

BORN TOO SOON...
LOVED TOO LITTLE

"Elizabeth, this is Sooner Hawes. I've brought her home to stay with us awhile."

Elizabeth felt the fear beat up at her from inside. She stared at Mac. His eyes held steady. They weren't pleading anymore, just waiting.

My God, he's just up and done it, without explanation, or asking, or even trying to talk me around. She wanted to scream at him that he had no right to—to handle her like this. Not even a baby she might come to think of as her own, but a—a mongrel!

What were you thinking, Mac? All you have to do is force on somebody the opportunity to love, and she will? Couldn't you at least have tried me out on something more likely? She's never heard of a toothbrush, doesn't even know what toilet paper is, and she picks her nose!

Do you honestly think that even in time I could come to love her as my own? That—that dirty, little stranger.

A Girl Named Sooner

Suzanne Clauser

AVON
PUBLISHERS OF BARD, CAMELOT, DISCUS, EQUINOX AND FLARE BOOKS

AVON BOOKS
A division of
The Hearst Corporation
959 Eighth Avenue
New York, New York 10019

ISBN: 0-380-00216-7

First Avon Printing, January, 1975.
Fifth Printing

AVON TRADEMARK REG. U.S. PAT. OFF. AND
FOREIGN COUNTRIES, REGISTERED TRADEMARK—
MARCA REGISTRADA, HECHO EN CHICAGO, U.S.A.

Printed in the U.S.A.

always to Charlie, with love
and to Betty, with thanks
and to Connie
    fine writer, fine mentor, finest as friend

PART I

SOONER

"The sword of the Lord is filled with blood, it is made fat with fatness, and with the blood of lambs and goats, with the fat of the kidneys of rams."

Sooner shivered with the ecstasy of the old woman's pulsing words even as their horrid meaning reminded her of what she had to do. She moved silently across the cabin to the half-open door.

Old Mam sat by the cookstove, the jug cradled in her lap, savoring the devastation of the prophet's vision as much as she was the jug's liquor. "And the unicorns shall come down with them, and the bullocks with the bulls; and their land shall be soaked with blood, and their dust made fat with fatness."

Sooner slipped through the door out onto the stoop and down the steps.

"For it is the day of the Lord's vengeance, and the year of recompenses for the controversy of Zion."

The air of summer-not-quite-come bit through Sooner's thin dress, but the sun had warmed the earth, and she squirmed her feet down into it gratefully.

"And the streams thereof shall be turned into pitch, and the dust thereof into brimstone, and the land thereof shall become burning pitch."

She crossed the clearing to where scraggly brown brush limned the bank down to the creek. There below, the water had receded from its final high rush after the March rains. The willows were lowering their new yellow-green toward the clear current. Sooner had been scared all spring that they wouldn't come back after the January flood. She couldn't remember such high water ever before. Even Old Mam said she couldn't recollect worse.

"It shall not be quenched night nor day; the smoke thereof shall go up for ever."

Heedless of the strands of hair she left in those winter-dry weeds tall enough to catch at her head, Sooner plunged down through the brittle grasses and scratching thistles, and the sound of Old Mam faded. She ran past the little shagbark that, in this the ninth year for both of them, she was beginning to outgrow, ducked under the low thorny branch of the honey locust, and drew up short at the water's edge.

Bird screeched to her from amidst the thorns, and beat his black wings so that the red and then the white beneath flickered. Sooner gave a little giggle and moved close to him.

"Stuck, ain't you! I keep tellin you, Bird. I only could fix that broke wing pretty good. Not real good. You can get up in such places, but you can't get down again!"

Bird preened his ruffled feathers, then hopped delicately from his perch to Sooner's shoulder and submitted while she ran her finger over the crown of his head. He screeched again, walked with cautious deliberation down the arm Sooner held up for him until he reached her wrist, fluttered the shorter distance from there to the ground, and began to peck.

Sooner watched him intently, as if she had no other purpose down here than to see Bird scratching for bugs. Then she caught in her breath and tightened her lips, like Old Mam when William wanted to pull the plow one way and Old Mam wanted him to pull it the other. She glanced up toward the cabin, swallowing against the flurry that stirred somewhere between her neck and her middle. . . . *Sword of the Lord filled with blood . . . blood of lambs and goats . . .* and maybe a muskrat, too?

Wanting to forget what she'd come for, Sooner turned back to Bird. "Where's that Li'l-un?" she asked him. "He ain't doin his job so good, iffen you got to dig for it." Bird paid her no mind, so she couldn't forget. She set her mouth again, looking with hidden slyness upcreek. Not that she could see much. The course curved round a willow clump, and was lost behind old growth. But she knew what was there, waiting for her. The ragged, black, silted-over hollow which Old Mam had this week plow-broken for planting; then, Old Mam's still, set permanently under roof among some sycamores near the water, far enough from the cabin to be safe, and far enough to wring bitter complaint from Old Mam every time she hauled the corn chop to it; and beyond that, the trapping line, Old Mam's line, sets laid now for more than a day and a half, and left unchecked. And since Old Mam was just getting into the glory of her Bible talk with that fresh jug of corn liquor, Sooner knew the traps would stay unchecked—long enough so the animals caught in them would likely starve to death, if they didn't tear and thrash and chew themselves to pieces first. Times when Old Mam wasn't sipping at the jug, she'd lay an oaken piece from off the woodpile across their heads and end it quickly for them. Sooner always made sure to be downcreek then, maybe crooning loudly to herself over a mouse track in the snow, hoping not to hear. But times like this, Sooner could hardly bear the thinking of it, of what was happening up there to the poor little things.

She started upcreek along the bank, and wished she could walk in the water the way she did come summer, and fight to keep from slipping on the bottom stones. It was a game she played with the stones, throwing her arms about so as to end by toppling over

11

into the cool wet. But now was too early for that, and the water would ache her clear to the knees with its cold. Still, it had cleaned itself after the rains, and it was something just to look. In spite of the current, it was like seeing the bottom through glass. *The streams thereof shall be turned into pitch.* Not for the first time, Sooner wondered what pitch was.

If it were summer, the traps wouldn't be set at all. The pelts were too thin then, and the price poor.

Suddenly, she wanted to get there and have it over. Now, where the bank flattened beside the creek from flooding every spring, though the ground was marshy, the woods were thinner and the walking easier and Sooner left the water to cut across a meander. It was quicker. But when she came to the hollow, she followed a longer way, skirting the plowed earth to keep from leaving a sign for Old Mam. Not that it would help. Old Mam would figure it out easily enough when she found the traps sprung. But Sooner kept to the edge anyway just to know that she'd done it all properly.

The turned-up sod smelled good. The sun, caught warm in the hollow, had brought as many bugs to the great moist clods as if they were William's steaming dung, and a flock of crows settled off a ways to quarrel over the rich feasting ground.

When Sooner reached the whitening sycamores back by the creek, the breeze puffed hard at her from on upstream, and carried with it the coughing plaint of a cow with a swollen bag.

Can't be, Sooner told herself. Ain't no cow this side of Bead's Knob.

But as the pleading rhythm sounded again, fear settled on her. She began to run, cutting across another meander to break through blackberry briars to the water's edge.

The big black-and-white animal stood in the quag-

12

mire of mud she had created on the bank, her flanks
heaving, her head tearing from side to side, her eyes
showing too much white, her udders so distended from
her pent-up milk that they barely trembled even with
all her motion. Sooner looked from that dumb anguish
to the cause of it beyond: a spring-born calf, caught
in one of Old Mam's traps. The little one's foreleg,
bloodied and badly torn, was held between steel jaws.

Them bloody swords the Lord has, thought Sooner,
they couldn't do no worse.

The calf's body was awkwardly folded to the
ground. Even if he'd had the sense to try, he couldn't
have reached high enough to suck.

"Soo, cow, soo." Sooner moved in a steady, slow
circle around the skittish mother as the weary refrain
of the animal's distress jerked out of her again. Utter-
ing little coos and chirrups of comfort, Sooner knelt
by the calf and lifted his head, too heavy for his young
outstretched neck, into her lap. Quickly, she reached
across and pried the trap's jaws apart. Already held
half open by the foreleg, the trap's spring pressure was
weak, and it was easy to slide the leg free. A shiver
ran the length of the calf's body. Sooner gathered him
up, one arm around his chest, the other beneath his
rump, and staggered to her feet. His legs dangled helplessly toward the ground, so long they almost touched.

"Sure couldn't heft you far, ole calf." Sooner panted
and shuffled toward the cow. "You're near to big as
me!"

The cow blew her wind nervously, but she stood
for Sooner's approach. The calf's head hung heavy, and
he would not search for the teat. Gently as she could,
Sooner lowered him to bear his own weight. She made
her voice stern, not wanting him to take weakness
from her caring. "Now you listen here, li'l critter—
you got to try some for yourself!"

His legs trembled but held, even the hurt one.

Hastily, Sooner grabbed his pointed face and shoved his soft lips around the nearest teat. There must have been a little seep, because suddenly the calf's eyes closed, his neck strained, and he started to suck.

"There, now," she crowed. "Ain't that just fine? Ain't it?" She dropped to squat on her heels, studying the ragged gash the jaws had made. She picked a burr out of the caked blood. "Wash you off pretty quick, and your mammy can take you home." She looked at the burr sticking to the tip of her finger. "Could've worked its way into you," she said, "and it would've festered sure. I best wrap you up to keep them stick-me-tights offen you." And then she was scared at hearing such a promise. The only wrapping she had was her dress, one Old Mam had done up.

But strength was running down the calf's legs like a spilling of warm milk, and it made her glad. In quick, easy movement, she rose and hauled her dress over her head, leaving herself only the patched drawers bunched around her waist by a drawstring. When she saw the hem of the dress, her scare came back. Old Mam had, as usual, pieced the dress together from one of her own old skirts, making it to do Sooner through a heap of growing. The hem still ran almost clear to where her waist would be.

No help for it, she told herself, and started tearing the dress in half. The old calico ripped easily. She pushed the smaller part into the creek to wet it, turned back to the still nuzzling calf, and with her arms over his withers to control him, she began to wipe at his torn flesh with the cold water. He trembled and the blood started to flow, but that didn't bother Sooner, though the cow shifted about uneasily and tried to butt her head into Sooner's way. Sooner used her teeth to tear the dress some more, then wrapped it around the bleeding foreleg and tied it in place with a last bit.

14

"Now! There you be, ole calf!" She stood up and away from the two animals, and waited. The cow sniffed at the calico, and then moved off through the woods up the bank and away from the water. "Go on home," Sooner ordered, and nudged the calf to follow. The cow looked back, bawled, and the calf bolted after his mother.

Sooner looked down at the sprung trap, resisting as she always had to the temptation to jerk it up by the stake and toss it into the creek to disappear forever.

"Anyways! Anyways! It weren't meant for him, no-how!" It was a kind of rehearsal for when she'd be facing Old Mam.

"Sass and arrygance," Old Mam would call it. "And on top of everthin else!" And she'd reach for the willow switch.

Too naked for April, Sooner felt cold—or was it because of the picture she had of Old Mam?—and she could hear the cow crashing through the dry bushes up the bank, the noise receding toward Bead's Knob.

She wanted to be going with them. That's where those other kids were. Sometimes Sooner wandered up over the hill that way, hoping they'd be there, laughing and trailing their pappy and his plow. When Old Mam plowed, Sooner either had to get William to go where Old Mam wanted, or she had to follow along and dig holes in the rows and drop in the seed corn. Three to a hole, top with a minnie from the creek, and cover over.

She wished she could go with the cow and the calf, but she couldn't. This was only the first trap in the line. There might be other hurt critters—a muskrat or a mink or, where the bait was a piece of shiny tin, a pretty round-eyed coon. And even if none had been caught yet, Old Mam's Bible talk had just started. Better to spring them all so it'd be done with.

She moved on up the creek. Though her pace

15

dragged, her breath was tearing at her throat as if after a run, and the sweat itched down her cold sides from under her arms. It was the thought of that dress, torn up and gone with the calf; the thought of Old Mam with her head full of an ache that dizzied her and no pelts for trading in Switzer this last setting of the year. The anticipated pain from the cut of the switch, arising out of memory but stronger than that remembered, was almost as real to Sooner as what she knew she had coming, and she had to make water. While she squatted, she could look up across to the opposite bank. There was a mound of fresh, crumbling dirt: a groundhog's new tunnel. Babies would be waddling out of that hole before long.

Seven sets in all; six to go. Sooner pulled her drawers up tight between her legs to catch the last drips and started out again. Maybe she'd find all of the traps full and the little things all already dead. But she put down the hope. She never yet had been that lucky, because she never could stand the waiting long enough. She sighed, and kept on walking.

MAC

It was only five-thirty, the sun not up yet, when the phone jerked Mac awake. Harvey Drummond, voice higher and flatter than usual, wailed at him over the crackling line.

"McHenry, that you? He ain't dropped manure since yesterday. You got to come!"

To calm him down, Mac asked who, though he knew.

16

"Royal Master, God damn it, who do you think?" And then a muffled, irritable, "All right, Jane, all right," obviously in answer to a wifely reprimand to watch his language. The Drummond phone was in the kitchen.

Elizabeth stumbled out of bed with Mac and pulled together a hasty breakfast, making sleepy jokes about the sad plight of being a veterinary's wife. "Might as well have married a real doctor," she said. Something like her old self, this morning. So Mac dared, "Maybe you'll start on the garden today, huh?" But the quick dying of her smile, her defensive shrug and low "Maybe" showed him his mistake. He pretended not to see, kissed her lightly, aimed a whack at her backside, and headed out the door. Billy Sanger would be by before school to feed and water the animals. Mac gave the infirmary a quick look around and left for Drummond's.

Things were beginning to stir as he drove through Switzer. Across from the courthouse, Phil was unlocking the door into the jail and didn't see Mac. That building's brickwork needed whitewash, but it would be a while. The county was already so miserly with Phil's salary that he lived in quarters attached to the back of the cellblock to save on rent. Was he just now getting home from Selma's? Surely not. Both he and Selma depended on votes for their jobs, and early as it was, it was late enough to be seen. Anyway, neither of them would be that unkind to the electorate. People were willing to know and yet not know, but no voter wanted to be slapped in the face with it. And who else was there to elect? Selma always ran unopposed, and Phil was an excellent sheriff.

Telfer's Drugs and Sundries wasn't open. George kept banker's hours. But Melvin Cox was up and out and taking the walk to his broiler hatchery. Mac went right by it, but he only waved to Melvin and drove

17

on. No sense to offer him a lift. Melvin was growing a paunch and the exercise would do him good. They were due to play bridge with the Coxes some night this week. Or was it with George and Eleanor? Elizabeth would know.

Elizabeth. *My dear love.* I wish to God there were some way to make things right for you. For both of us.

Forgetting as usual to brake before the railroad tracks, Mac was bucked off his seat and winced to hear the truck protest. No way to treat a good Ford, he told himself, especially since he didn't have a chance in hell of finding money to replace it for another couple of years.

He hadn't left or come back to town this way in nearly a week, so he took notice of the current as he crossed Blue Run and was relieved to see it docile enough under the bridge. It would be a while before people stopped thinking about high water and worrying about it. They'd had quite a winter. There wasn't a piece of running water in the whole county hadn't been in flood.

He turned up the winding, steep hill out of Switzer, and put on speed as he topped the rise by the new overlook the CCC boys were building. On beyond the entrance to their camp, the tarred county road became dotted with potholes. The constant freezing and thawing of every southern Indiana winter pitted all the roads as its legacy to spring. But Mac was hardly aware of the holes, swinging the wheels of his pickup around and back by reflex. Rumor was that the WPA wouldn't be down here to patch things up before June. Mac wondered if he'd be able to drive a straight line by that time, he was getting so used to weaving his way everywhere he had to go. Mr. Roosevelt and his CCC and WPA would be a lot more popular in this part of the country if they'd get their contracts done on time. The world was going to hell in a basket, the county said, because there were always delays. Where would they think the world was headed if nothing was done at all? And yet, each of the two times Mr. Roosevelt had been elected, they had sent up groans of despair. The good old U.S. of A.'ll never be the same again. Which just might be a very good thing, Mac figured. His and Elizabeth's votes were two out of the nine always tabulated in Switzer on the Democratic side of the ledger. They had amused themselves after the election trying to guess who the other seven were, but in conservative Hoosierdom, the secret ballot had a real value, at least for Democrats.

Mac shifted down for a new hill picking up ahead of him. The deep pink froth of the redbuds—Elizabeth always called them fairytale clouds—was scattered through the brown wooded ridges on either side of the road, to get darker and richer as spring jumped into summer, probably around the first of May. And there was a touch here and there of dogwood white. The past week had made a real difference, with the long spring rains over and the hot sun beating down every day. Elizabeth had taken to these hills from the first. After growing up in flat central Ohio, she said, they were like mountains to her, and she loved them.

No matter Elizabeth's fond exaggerations, Geiger County was not mountainous. It was only that the hills folded in on themselves so precipitously that the streams had the rush and echo of rivers, the sky seemed small and familiar, and the villages boasted the tenacity and self-reliance of bigger cities. It might be the poorest farming in Indiana, but it sure was the prettiest country in five states. Maybe over the weekend he'd bring Elizabeth out for a drive.

No, that wasn't such a good idea.

Mac shifted forward again, a straightaway opening up in front of him. They used to drive out on back county roads, looking for the perfect place. Somewhere not too far off the beaten track because of the slushy winters and wet springs, but with a view. A good place for kids. At times, they were so continually pulled on by the unfolding hills that they'd end up clear down on the bank of the Ohio—much too far to be looking for land, but too beautiful to resist just looking. All that, though, was before September, and the operation, when the last hope had been killed. No, she wouldn't see the spring. Even if she'd agree to come out with him, she'd refuse to see it.

It was the same with too many good things in their life, Mac thought. Her beloved garden still lay fallow, and April half gone. And there was that business at winter's end when she'd banned his animal boxes from the kitchen. But the doctor kept telling him that she'd recovered from the surgery beautifully. Lord knows, when it happened she'd been game, and quick to say that after seven barren years it shouldn't come as such a blow.

But it had. It had. Sputtering up again into Mac's mind came the unhurled accusations at old Dr. Stroud. All his reassurances that it wouldn't amount to anything, and might even work the long-awaited miracle. And then that eager-beaver young surgeon up at the med center had just gone ahead and cut everything out of her. The whole shooting match, gone. And with it, the children they'd never have.

He halted the run of thoughts, ashamed. How many times had he reassured the owner of one of his patients, only to go in and find things weren't as he'd expected?

Hell. He shoved his foot on the brake. That was Drummond's lane he'd just passed.

He backed the Ford and turned off the road by the wooden sign proclaiming "Drummond—Registered Holsteins." It was hardly readable any more. Nobody had the money these days for fresh paint, though as Mac looked over Harvey's fields, he was reminded that Harvey was sticking the bad years better than most. And come the county fair, late summer, and that blue ribbon Harvey was counting on, Royal Master's service fees would make frills commonplace for the Drummonds, or so Harvey figured. Mac chuckled. Harvey'd probably sat out the night in the barn, praying for the great fart which had never materialized. But Mac couldn't blame him. Three years running, Harvey had had high hopes, only to have one thing after another defeat his yearling bulls. Last summer it had been old-fashioned hardware disease. A careless hand had missed some rotten wire when forking down hay, and the animal had swallowed a bellyful of it.

As Mac pulled into the yard before the house, Harvey charged down off the front porch like Royal Master himself after a cow in heat.

"Morning, Harvey." Mac stepped down from his high seat and went around back to haul out his rubber boots and bag.

"Took you long enough to get here," Harvey sputtered. "I tell you, Doc, that yearlin's real bad off."

"Well, now, Harvey, well, now—we'll just have a little look and find out, huh?" Mac waved to Jane standing in the kitchen door, dish towel twisting in her hands, and the two men turned for the barn. Small, dark Harvey jittered alongside Mac, a feisty terrier making Mac more aware than usual of his own slow hulk.

The barn was open, as it should be to circulate the air, and it smelled sweet with hay and warm, clean beasts. Royal Master had a large stall to himself, and the hay about his feet was dry and fresh. As Harvey'd said on the phone, too clean. Looked like the young bull was stopped up good. Mac studied him a moment. Ears hanging down, hair rough and on end. Mac ran his hand over the rump. Hot. His temperature was up.

"Get a twist on his nose, Harvey, and make sure

you hold on to it. He may be but a yearling, but he's big enough to crack a couple of ribs, and I've got me a busy day ahead."

Harvey did as he was told. Keeping clear of the restive hind hooves, Mac worked his right hand into the animal's rectum, and found the heavy impaction. Pulling his hand free and crossing to a spigot to wash, he said, "First thing we've got to do is loosen that bowel of his, and maybe that's all the problem there is. We'll need a couple of Jane's washtubs. Fill 'em up with warm water. I've got a syringe in the truck."

Harvey started off at a trot.

"Hey, Harvey." Mac stopped him softly. "Your bull's a fine, strong brute. Don't worry so." Harvey's face relaxed a little, and Mac grinned and began pulling on his boots. "You better haul on a pair of these, too," he added. "It'll be messy."

Forty-five minutes later, the job was finished, and Royal Master, worn out by his own bellowing, bucking protests against indignity, was peacefully munching hay. Mac eyed the back of his stall, an odorous and oozing brown mess, now. "Looks like you've got your morning's work laid out for you, Harvey."

As Mac started cleaning up, Harvey asked him to have a look at one of the spring calves. "As long as you're out," he said slyly, "and I'll be owin you for doctorin the yearlin anyways."

Why was it, Mac wondered with wry amusement, that in time of trouble they all hollered loud and clear in his direction, and then when the trouble was past, they wanted to niggard him on his fee?

The calf was bedded down at the other end of the barn. "Seems like he must've got bit by one of them steel fur-traps, you know?" Harvey was telling. "Come trailin his dam in here, day before yesterday, all bandaged up clean as a whistle. But you might better check him out, Doc."

22

Mac hunkered down in the hay by the calf and explored with eyes and fingers the gashed foreleg. "He'll come along all right. The jaws didn't get the tendons." He swiveled around to look up at Harvey, while his hand went on gentling the nervous baby. "You say he came in bandaged?"

"Yup." Harvey pulled some ragged cloth down off the side of the stall. It was old and faded and streaked with blood, the floral pattern undefinable. "Jane figures it was that girl lives with old Mrs. Hawes, the other side of Bead's Knob. Leastways, I checked my fence up thataway, and found it windblowed."

Mac took the cloth from him, rising to his feet.

"Jane says it looks to have been a calico dress, from the stitchin in it. And I know for a fact old Mrs. Hawes runs a trippin line up Black Willow Creek." Harvey's tone was getting edgy. "I seen her ridin in to Switzer after that sickly-lookin mule of hers with some skins for tradin. Ought to be a law."

Looking up from his study of the sad piece of calico, Mac cocked an eye at him. "Don't need a law," he said mildly. "Only need to keep your fence mended." He started through the barn, shoving the calico into his pocket. "That the Mrs. Hawes supplies Jim Seevey his brew?" Jim had the combined furniture emporium and funeral parlor in town, and transported moonshine as well as corpses in his hearse. "How come you're so certain it wasn't the old lady doctored the calf?"

"Old Lady? Old bitch is more like it. Mean, and stingier than a rat's tail, too. She'd have slaughtered him for veal." Harvey helped Mac gather up his bag and boots and paraphernalia piled in the barn door, and they moved on out into the yard. "Sides which," Harvey continued, "my Judith Ann, she says that kid's got a way with animals. She says she's seen her, times over by Bead's Knob, with a chipmunk stickin out of her pocket, and a redwing, big as life, on her shoulder.

23

Accordin to my Judith Ann, she ain't to school much—ain't to school at all, matter of that. Accordin to my Judith Ann, she ain't even clean."

"She cleaned up your calf well enough," Mac said. He threw his boots over the tailgate. "How old is she, Harvey—the little girl?"

"I think Jane said she ought to be about nine or so," Harvey answered.

Feeling oddly exposed, Mac yanked open the truck door and got in.

"Thanks a heap for comin, Doc," said Harvey, already turning back for the barn and his bull.

Mac gave an absent nod. He was becoming a maudlin ass. Just because a little girl had a way with animals. He twisted the key in the ignition savagely so it almost bent against the lock. Christ, he stank. Not only with Royal Master's fecal smell, which wouldn't wash off no matter how he'd scrubbed, but with his own sweat. He spun the wheels leaving the yard, then halted the truck before turning on the road. He rubbed hard at his short bristling hair to clear his mind. Where to next?

Since he was out of town anyway, he might as well take the day and get on with the tuberculin testing. His appointment as federal inspector added only a pittance to his income, but at least it was money and not just more chickens or eggs or a couple of pounds of beans, the kind of fee he got paid too often. Moreover, it was a job needed doing. Let's see. He ought to check in at Fuerst's and Maurer's and Dunkle's place, too. The Brownsville Pike, that'd be. He turned right, and picked up speed.

A couple of years ago, when Mac was just beginning his inspections, old man Dunkle had pulled a real fast one on him, raising a swelling under the tail of that cow with a pincers so she'd be slaughtered for TB. Dunkle figured he'd get more money from the government than on the open market, and he was right, he had. But since, Mac had worked to get him to keep his barn clean and airy, and to improve the fodder, and most of Dunkle's cows were producing pretty well now. Maybe he could grab some lunch there. Beevy Pike. There was a culvert for Black Willow Creek on Beevy.

*　　*　　*

Mac crossed it about a half hour later. He slowed down, eyes searching for a turnoff. He could feel the calico still bunched against his thigh in his pocket. There was the break; he swung the wheel into the rutted dirt lane, and stopped. The ruts headed uphill and curved around a bend. They were deep in places, still showing damp in the lowest part of the furrows. Maybe Jim Seevey was willing to chance that heavy hearse of his to keep up his supply of moonshine, but Mac didn't relish the thought of getting stuck. It might not even be the right place. He hesitated, his hand on the gearshift, ready to throw it into reverse and go on. And then, the hand reached for the ignition and turned it off.

He got out and stood listening through the cooling creaks of the Ford to the sound of the water off to his left. He started along the edge of one of the damp furrows. An old and twisted and sometime limb-broken apple tree spraddled over the road up ahead, just starting into bud. The rest lining the lane was scrub, through which darted the flame of a cardinal. He rounded the bend only to see the ruts twist back around another. The air smelled fragrant with blooms yet unborn, and now that he was a little higher he could see the sparkle of the creek down the bank. A catbird was mewing its complaint. He went on, and before he reached the second bend, he could notice a smudge of chimney smoke curling up into the blue ahead. He heard the voice as he walked around the

25

curve, and something else—an unidentifiable swish, swish that broke the phrases of the voice.

"I'll teach you!" Swish. "You know"—swish—"what you done cost me?" Swish. "Fifteen." Swish. "Maybe twenty dollar!" Swish. "You don't never learn!"

"Stop it!" The willow switch finished its sweep against the child's legs before the old woman swung to stare toward Mac.

They stood in the dirt yard, the woman and the child, in front of the cabin where the smoking chimney was. The child wasn't trying to get away. She just waited for it, her eyes squinched up, her hands fisted, her thin little legs welting red with the stripes of the switch, even showing a few lines of blood.

The woman, Mrs. Hawes, Mac supposed, suddenly sank to the crooked step, and moaned. "My poor head," she wailed, clasping that frowseled object as if it were about to fly off. The child now sneaked a look toward Mac, and her eyes rounded open. She wore a loose shiftlike dress, too small for her, its material as faded and gray as the scrap in Mac's pocket; her hair was short, but so ragged the old woman must have hacked it off with a corn knife, and its reddish straw color was without a gleam, dull like her skin. High on one cheek a sore ran. She'd either picked at it, or maybe it just wouldn't heal. Diet, the doctor in Mac diagnosed automatically, the beans-and-bread diet of the country poor, and not enough of it.

"What you be wantin, mister? You come for to peddle, I ain't got money for nothin," Mrs. Hawes said.

Mac crossed the little clearing toward them. With her skirt hiked for sitting, Mac could see that the tops of her scuffed workman's boots were unlaced. Her shirtwaist was stiff with grease spots and missing some buttons. Her streaked black hair straggled from the sparse lump of it on her neck. She was stringy-thin, and her brown skin, weathered into a web of lines, clung tightly to the sharp bones of her face. She had the look of Cherokee blood far back.

Her eyes were narrowing at him. He stopped short of her by a few feet. "What did she do, for you to whip her like that?" he asked.

Her mouth twisted. "What's it your affair?" Now, she turned her glare on the child, but the child's gaze never flickered from Mac. "Cost me twenty, twenty-five dollar in tradin skins, that's what she did."

The value had gone up with an audience, Mac noticed.

Mrs. Hawes' voice rose. "Twas my last run till first frost, and she sprung my sets, ever one of em. And lost a pretty new dress doin it. One I stitched up for her special."

Mac remembered the cloth in his pocket. New? Special? Like a sow's ear.

Mrs. Hawes clambered to her feet, her hand tightening again about the switch. "Prevaricator, that's what you are." This beamed at the girl in heavy, doomsday tones full of righteousness. "Givin me them stories of a calf . . . shameless, like to your mammy!" Her arm was drawing back the switch again, and Mac's hand half reached out to stop her.

"It was the truth, what she told you. There was a calf." The switch hovered. Mac continued. "Harvey Drummond's. I just came from there. He—he asked me to stop by and thank her for what she did." He smiled at the child. "The calf's going to be just fine, little miss."

For the first time, something stirred in the small round face lifted to him—relief, pleasure, maybe only a vague interest. It was hard to tell. Was she weak-minded?

But his defense had only sparked more venom in the woman. "Truth, was it? Then that veal belonged to

27

me!" She was sputtering with outrage. "He was tres-passin, weren't he? So he be mine!"

Mac's gorge rose, and his face must have shown it. Her regard of him turned sour. "I done tole you, mister. Tain't none of your affair. Now you get offen my place, afore I take my shotgun after you."

There was nothing for it. It looked already as if he'd only made it worse for the child. His eyes winced from those striped little legs. "It's no way to treat your own granddaughter, even so," he said, his voice low, unable to hold it back.

The woman snorted, staring at him with proud and angry challenge. "I allus done right by her! And I learned her right, too!"

Mac turned abruptly and moved for the truck, feeling on his upper lip the sweat that always broke there first when he was nerved up. For a moment, he was afraid the Ford wasn't going to catch, but it did finally. He backed out, not bothering to check the road. The vision of that old puncheon cabin got in the way. Logs in need of chinking; shutters over the unglassed window hanging askew; to the side, an old Buhr stone mill with a skinny, fly-bitten mule hitched to its swivel; and clinging on at the cabin's rear, a lean-to, probably to shelter the corn the woman ground in that old millstone. And something else, too. A chipmunk had dodged busily in and out from beneath the cabin's sagging front stoop the entire time, quite undismayed by the dreadful scene playing so close by.

A horn blasted behind him. He glanced into the rear-view mirror, hearing the skid of tires. Jim Seevey in his old Packard hearse wanted to turn in at the lane. Mac shifted gears hastily to get out of his way, and drove rapidly on down the road without acknowledging Jim's shouted "Hey there, Doc."

The little girl had just stood and taken it. Lord.

There'd been the lean-to, but nothing else. They didn't even have an outhouse.

SOONER

"Ain't never seed nobody so big!" Sooner breathed the words slowly, full of regret that the wondrous sight had gone.

Old Mam turned where she was staring after the yellow-haired man and looked at Sooner. Sooner felt her stinging legs want to shrink up inside her dress so as not to be there at all. "Ain't you done for me yet?" she asked.

A motor's grind-cough-grind came to them from down the lane.

"Iffen that's him a-comin back . . ." Old Mam started for the cabin. "This time, I'll have me my shotgun."

But Sooner knew from the sound. "It be Jim Seevey," she said.

The black hearse swayed to a stop in the middle of the clearing, there was a loud bang, and then silence. Jim Seevey got out and stood smiling by the door in his black suit, his hat in his hands.

"How do, Mrs. Hawes," he said to Old Mam. Jim Seevey always had his hat in his hands, Sooner thought. Didn't he ever put it on his head? Maybe that's why it was so empty of hair.

"You be a day early," Old Mam told him, "but I got my jugs readied for you all the same."

Now, Jim Seevey sent a nod at Sooner. His eyes drifted down to her legs and she saw him swallow.

"You gonna come load em up or ain't you?" Old Mam asked. She had reached the corner of the cabin on her way round back, and was waiting for him. Her head must be aching her something fierce, Sooner figured. It mostly pleasured her to visit awhile when Jim Seevey came.

Jim Seevey smiled bigger, and crossing the hard-packed dirt to the stoop, he spoke easy and soft. "Why, Mrs. Hawes, I was thinking maybe to set a spell. That is, if you'd have a little sampler to spare." He sat down on the step and hung his hat on his knee. His white shirt, pushed out by his belly, poked through his jacket front and spilled over the belt of his trousers.

Sooner's legs were starting to itch. She looked down and saw one little dribble of blood still dribbling, and she caught it on her finger and licked it for its taste. The big man had come clear from the other side of Bead's Knob to tell her the calf would be fine. He didn't need to. Sooner had known that already.

Old Mam was studying Jim Seevey the way she did when she suspicioned somebody. She walked back and up the step past him with nary a word and went inside.

Jim Seevey winked at Sooner. She giggled, scrunching her shoulders with it so as not to be heard, and winked back. She couldn't do it to look right yet, but each time he came he showed her how all over again. He shook his head at her and winked again, and she winked back again, and then Old Mam came out with a cracked Ball jar half full of clear reddish liquor. She plunked it down next to him, and sat in the rocker with the split cane seat and watched him. He tipped the jar to pour free into his mouth, then heaved a fine, deep sigh.

"Mrs. Hawes, I swear it's the best run of whiskey you ever boiled up."

Old Mam gave a sniff.

He held the jar to the light and jiggled it a little. "Never saw such a bead to compare! Nor such a color!"

"Tain't like that white lightnin what comes cheap and eats out your gizzard," Old Man said, sounding proud. "I age my shine. And in charred kegs, to boot. Some say as hickory bark colors up pretty good. But I say that's cheatin." She began rocking the rocker. "You offerin me a price better than three dollar to the gallon?" she asked.

"As good as," he said, and he raised up the jar again.

Little One came running from beneath the stoop, right between Jim Seevey's feet, but the man didn't see for pouring whiskey. Sooner bent over and scooped Little One up. His cheeks were pooched out with last year's sunflower seeds from his hidey-hole under the cabin. She put him in her pocket, hoping he'd drop some seeds there so Bird could share.

Old Mam rocked and bided. Jim Seevey caught his breath, and said, "We got us a new market, Mrs. Hawes. And I can sell more than the ten gallons you like to give me."

"How's that as good as?" she asked.

"A bird in the hand, Mrs. Hawes. Never know when the excise might turn up."

Old Mam sniffed again. "You know, same as I do, the longer my corn likker's done aged, the more it brings me. Near to four dollar by fair time, and better yet in November. What I give you to sell in spring and summer, that's just to keep a-goin on."

Jim Seevey's smile disappeared, and his chin shook a little. "It's been a hard winter, Mrs. Hawes. Seems everybody but me can walk into those county offices and come out with New Deal money. But do they spend it for proudful funerary services? Not so's you'd notice. Anymore, I can't even buy my caskets on consignment. No siree, I got to put out hard cash for each

31

and every one. I need that money now, Mrs. Hawes, not in August or next fall. And the CCC boys, why they're truly beggin for a taste of your good whiskey."

Old Mam sat rocking, her mouth working in and out. Sooner went to the other side of the hearse and drew round fat faces with smiles in the dust on the black paint.

"All I want's, say, fifteen jugs instead of ten? Then, maybe another fifteen around June, and you'll still have plenty held back for the fair."

"I tell you, Jim Seevey, I wouldn't give you listenin time ceptin for Sooney just doin me outa twenty dollar on my skins."

Sooner peered over the fender to see Old Mam's mouth still working in and out.

"She did that? And your own kin, too!"

Old Mam snorted as she had with the big man before. "First that other fella and now you," she said. "She ain't no kin to me. But I allus done right by her, even so."

"You surely have, Mrs. Hawes, you surely have. The other fella . . . Doc McHenry, you mean. Fine man."

"Interferin busybody, more like it."

Jim Seevey was standing up, holding out money to Old Mam. "Forty-five dollars, Mrs. Hawes. You gonna turn it down?"

Old Mam rocked forward, slapped her hands on her knees and stood up, too, and took the money. She counted it, then tucked it in her skirt and came down off the stoop.

Sooner ducked down behind the fender again, and drew some legs and then some arms on one of the faces. Little One was quiet in her pocket.

"I got to tap the barrel for the extra five gallon," Old Mam was saying, "but you might's well start haulin the rest. Sooney! Come out from behind that machine and help!"

Jim Seevey followed around back of the cabin, and Sooner followed after him. With the sun higher in the sky every day, Old Mam had already moved the four aging barrels from under the manure pile to under the shock so they wouldn't get too hot. She pulled the heap apart to get to the one with the tap, opened it, and held a jug to catch the spurt of liquor. Jim Seevey and Sooner went to the lean-to for the jugs already filled and stoppered with corncobs, and began carrying them to the hearse.

"Ain't no kin," Old Mam had said. Sooner had heard it before, but different then. A man's voice, and a face with black hair that bobbed up and down when he laughed, and his white teeth had flashed like shiners jumping for flies.

"She ain't no kin of mine, Mam. Don't you believe it." Jason had laughed as Old Mam had choked over a gulp of whiskey. He was sitting across the table from her and sipping, too, and the kerosene lantern that Old Mam almost never lit burned yellow between them, giving a strange life to the night. "That Marcy," Jason said, shaking his black head, still laughing between his words. But Old Mam just stared at him over the jug. "She done played us both for fools, Mam. Had me so hot and bothered, I couldn't wait to find the preacher. And wasn't a month later, she tells me she's been studded already. But not by me, Mam. Hell, she'd never've had me to the preacher atall if she'd been that easy with me, and she knowed it." He drank deep and wiped the back of his hand across his mouth.

"For shame, boy! That ain't decent talk! And afore your own mam!"

"What'd she do, Mam? Come trekkin in here, whinin an cryin and layin it to me? And you took it for true, and been granma-in it ever since?" He burst out laugh-

33

ing again. "That Marcy! Played us both for fools!"

Jason had come only the once and with morning was gone. But he had Old Mam to haul her money box out from behind the stove and strip it bare for him, first. Jason had put Sooner up on his knee that night, running his hand wrongways across her hair. "Just like to her mammy's," he said. But then he laughed in his high way, and close up his face looked to feel like Old Mam's quick-bread dough, so Sooner slid from his hands and for the rest of that time kept herself to the dark beyond the lantern light. She'd been littler then, and not hard to lose notice of. But she'd puzzled over him for a long time after.

"What was that you was sayin," Old Man asked Jim Seevey between his trips to the hearse, "bout money comin outa them county offices?"

"WPAers, and PWAers, and folks flooded out, and I don't know what all," Jim Seevey said, smiling again now. "Why, I wouldn't wonder you couldn't get some for yourself, you put your mind to it, Mrs. Hawes. Mr. Roosevelt, he likes givin out money, deserved or not."

Old Mam raised up from the barrel, and looked at Jim Seevey, suspicioning him the same as earlier. "Mr. Roosevelt. You sayin *he* be over to Switzer?"

"No, no, not sayin anything like that, Mrs. Hawes. But his New Deal money surely is. And if anybody's deservin, you are. Look how you do for this here child, and her not even kin to you."

He picked up the last jug but one, and that one Old Mam was still holding to the whiskey spigot. He waited until she stoppered it with a cob and took it, too, and they walked to the hearse together. Sooner spied Bird sitting on William's rump, and she crossed to him and reached in her pocket, waking Little One from his sleep; but he'd dropped some seeds there, and she held them out for Bird to peck at. She heard the doors slam and the hearse roar and then go squeaking and grinding off down the lane. She waited, not daring to look around to see if Old Mam was coming with the switch.

"Sooney? You get on with the corn choppin, hear? I've some things to think on."

Slowly, slowly, Sooner turned her head to peek over her shoulder, and saw Old Mam move out of sight on her way to the stoop, and then heard the rocker start up. Somehow, miraculously, what she'd had still coming was over. Always, afterward, it was best to do what she was told.

She walked forward alongside William to his head, and took hold of his ear, and tugged at him to start the circle around the millstones. Flies lifted lazily off his face, and one settled down below Sooner's knee, where there was still some sting. She stamped her foot, and William jerked his head up and jingled his harness. The millstones moaned on the corn between, and the sun was warm as she and William walked round and round and round again.

MAC

Almost home, now, and he was tired. He'd found one tuberculin cow, which always disheartened him. Fuerst's herd would need careful watching for a while, the local physicians warned about the milk, and the commander out at the CCC camp, too. A notice would have to be published in the *Bugle*.

But it was more than that. He hadn't been able to rid his mind of the picture of the little girl. It had stopped him only three miles down the road from Black Willow Creek, to search his pockets for enough money to take the edge off that old woman's switch. But he'd only found three dollar bills and seventy-one cents in change, so he'd gone on, hoping she'd had satisfaction enough already. Nor had he been able to get rid of the nagging worry about Elizabeth. Between this and that, thoughts of Elizabeth were always there. How would she be, tonight?

The truck slowed itself down, rolling as if with reluctance along two sides of the county courthouse and around the corner onto Court Street, where they lived. And it was as always when he caught a coming-home glimpse of the house. No matter his mood or his fatigue, his spirits were lifted.

One of those white clapboards built in the late years of the nineteenth century, it sat proudly back from the catalpas lining the street. A veranda spread across its front to a green-roofed cupola on the southeast corner, there was a fanlight over the door, and altogether it promised graciousness and good kitchen smells and security.

Mac had been born in the large bedroom above the cupola. Through the winters of his childhood, his father's rabbit hounds had lolled before the fire while Mac labored over his homework at the round table in the center of the living room. Summertimes, he had swung on a rope hung from the oak in the side yard, and he'd formed and disbanded several secret societies in the sanctuary of a tree hut in the wild cherry at the back.

His father had been a county judge, with his office toward the rear of the house, a convenient block and a half from the courthouse square. When Pop had died, Mac's mother had been gone four years and more. The house, the office, and the stable on the back alley all had seemed the perfect solution for a newly graduated veterinary doctor and his wife. Pop's office, with its separate entrance, became Mac's. The stable was easily converted to a roomy small-animal infirmary. Most important, Elizabeth had liked all of it, the high ceilings, and the broad windows framed by the smaller diamond-shaped panes, and the curving banister that ran up the stairs in the large center hall. The walnut dining-room table and sideboard, the old hickory bedstead in the front bedroom, the little odds and ends his mother had treasured, had become dear to Elizabeth, too.

From the beginning, she had fallen into all the activities women pursue in small towns as if she'd been born to it, and that had surprised Mac and delighted him. Columbus, Ohio, wasn't a particularly sophisticated city, but the university was, and the university had been Elizabeth's world all of her life until she married Mac; her father taught English up there. Elizabeth had dropped out of OSU one year short of her degree the June Mac had received his DVM, and Mac doubted that the professor would ever forgive him.

Nor did she chafe too much at the communal sharing of everyone's private affairs. It was the social scene she railed at the most, albeit good-humoredly. They'd go to a party, and barely be a half a block on their way home before she'd explode. "Babbitts, that's what they are! Girls on one side of the room, boys on the other, as if we were still in seventh grade. Straight out of *Main Street*. It wouldn't matter so much, except it's always the men who have the interesting conversations!"

Or she'd say, "I heard you, over in the corner. Discussing Roosevelt and the Supreme Court. But the minute I try to join in, wow, change the subject, boys!"

Elizabeth had been weaned on politics, and loved a hot debate. Only thing was, her temper was apt to carry her away so that she said things she didn't mean. Then for days afterward she'd be plunged into remorse.

Politics was a thing they had in common, for Mac's father had held strong opinions, too, and unpopular ones. He'd always said he was glad his judgeship was appointive because he couldn't have got himself elected in a million years.

"As for *we girls*, it's nothing but kirche, küche, and kinder. You sure can tell this place was settled by Germans!"

"Swiss," was Mac's automatic rejoinder.

"It's the same thing."

"It is not." Then, solemnly, "Switzerland is a nation of tall mountains, clear waterfalls, and Alpine flowers, while Germany—"

"Oh, shut up!" And she'd punch him in the arm and break into the laughter which had been close to the surface all along.

And now, after some seven years, her settling in was as complete as his. Every spring, she planted flower beds to edge the office walk and the base of the veranda. At least, she had until this spring. And Mac's books had made deep inroads into his father's legal library on the shelves of the office. Mac kept intending to crate the law books and ship them up to Bloomington to the law school, but somehow he never got around to it. And though Mac's practice was leaning more and more toward large-animal medicine and a barn would be useful, and though they used to take those leisurely Sunday drives looking for a country place, Mac never came home in late afternoon without taking pleasure from the sight of their house. Even this afternoon.

Creeping the truck down the alley, never sure when some kid was going to dive through the privet and under a fender, Mac pulled up under the overhang he'd extended out from the stable roof. He looked across the yard to the office. She still hadn't touched the garden. The barking, mewing, twittering welcome

38

of his patients from inside the infirmary picked him up a little. There were still a few minutes left before he had to go in.

He checked out the cages. Billy had come after school and cleaned the litters. He was doing his job pretty well. Mrs. Freemont's beagle, as rheumy with age as his doting owner, just might be encouraged to hang on for another year. He responded with his first sign of eagerness to Mac's caress, and his coat had taken on some life. The canary which that little four-year-old from down the street had brought in, the boy's face wretched with tears and dread, the bird in shock from a broken wing, was hopping jauntily from perch to swing to oyster shell, and even piping a little.

Mac stripped to shower down in the stall he'd rigged up at the back of the infirmary, and dressed clean in the clothes Elizabeth always laid out for him, and started down the walk for the kitchen. Though the sun was past setting, the house was dark.

Mac could remember times when Elizabeth had burned up bulbs in what used to look like every room in the house to welcome him home at the end of the day, and the light streaming across the lawn had seemed to announce glad tidings of the gaiety that awaited inside. It was this inner laughter in her that had first captured him. He remembered the evening they'd met, walking her home across campus, when she'd suddenly swung his hand high, taking off from the momentum of it to spin, dancing around by his side, her face shining up at the dark sky. Just because everything smelled so good, she'd said, and because at last spring had come.

Now, each day he approached the little back porch with lessening hope for the return of what had been. And tonight, when he opened the back door, he saw what he'd known he'd see: Elizabeth seated at the white enameled table, lost in sad imaginings, her body quite still, her head bent so that the back of her neck looked bare and vulnerable. Dinner was steaming on the stove, the house would be clean as a pin, but the Elizabeth he used to whirl about in his arms, both of them jubilant just to have each other, wasn't there any more.

The kitchen was redolent with lamb stew—mutton, really. Last year, they would have joked about it. She turned late to greet him, with that shy, forever questioning and scared-of-the-answer look, Do you love me, Mac? Do you still love me? All his intentions to re-create their old delight seeped out of him as out of a leaky tub. But he smiled a quick reassurance, and would have bent over with a kiss, only she suddenly gave a little exclamation of guilt and jumped up to switch on the kitchen light. Wanting to forestall the stumbling self-reproach he knew she would offer, Mac turned for the icebox. It was a refrigerator, with the coils crouched on top, but neither of them ever called it anything but an icebox. He pulled out two bottles of beer. When he turned back, she was facing him and he could see that she had expected to turn from the wall switch into his arms. The light from overhead threw the lower part of her small, gently pointed face into shadow, so that her eyes alone reflected what she was feeling: eagerness—disappointment—acceptance. He and Elizabeth froze there, looking at each other for a fleeting moment, but it seemed like one of those breaks in time that copy infinity; or rather, thought Mac, as if they were two children fixed to the ground after spinning out in a game of statues. He cut it off by setting the beer on the table to start across to her. Only, at the same time, she moved to the cupboard to reach down a couple of glasses, asking brightly, "Have a good day, honey?"

Three opportunities missed in the last minute and a half to give her what she needed. Not missed. Lost. Maybe not to be recompensed. This thought followed

40

by a spurt of resentment that he should be made to feel guilty.

"Good enough," he answered her, keeping his tone easy, scrounging through the table drawer after the bottle opener.

"You've got some messages on your desk. Four, I think. And Mrs. Freemont called. Not to bother you, she said." Elizabeth quavered her voice in not unsympathetic mimicry of the old lady. "Just to ask after Boncy." It was echoes like this of the old Elizabeth that kept Mac trying to understand. Elizabeth sat down at the table. "So . . . tell me!"

Mac opened the beer, poured out two glasses, sat opposite her, and recounted his day. She hungered over his words, laughing in the right places, murmuring her understanding, her face, framed by the wavy brown hair, pretty and seeming to be full of life—piquant, Pop had called her when Mac had first brought her home. And the awkward, reaching, unfulfilled moments of before began to recede. Except that, for some reason he had no desire to explore with himself, he deleted from his account the incident at Black Willow Creek.

* * *

He'd been reminded, when he'd taken out the beer, of some slide work he had to do. The blood specimens were keeping cold in the little rack he stored in the icebox. After dinner, he went back to his office, where his microscope was set up, and began preparing smears.

Elizabeth had gone upstairs to work on the curtains. She'd been sewing them for weeks now, but he'd stopped joshing her about it. She didn't tease very well these days. It seemed to frighten her.

He bent over the scope. Anaemia. It figured. Jackson would have to supplement the swill he fed his hogs, just as he'd warned him to do months ago.

Always now, that fear in her. He could see it in her eyes, hear it in her voice, feel it in her body when he held her. But of what? Certainly not him. She knew he didn't blame her for a barrenness she couldn't help. And he was sure she didn't blame herself. She'd never been a foolish woman.

He sat back from the scope with a sigh. Then, remembering, he reached in his pocket and pulled out the piece of calico belonging to the little girl. He'd transferred it to these trousers when he'd changed, oddly loath to throw it away. She'd torn up a precious dress and faced a whipping to succor a calf. And Elizabeth wouldn't even keep his animal babies in the house any more. Always there had been a box or two sitting on the floor by the stove, full of newborns or, in other seasons, maybe a coon dog whimpering from an encounter with barbed wire. It was warm there, and easy for him to keep an eye on. And one night, he'd come home to find them exiled to the infirmary, Elizabeth's sweet gentleness with them gone from her. She'd shrugged and attempted a laugh and said she'd be damned if she was going to be one of those childless women everybody pitied, like Mrs. Freemont with Boney. And she'd refused to discuss it further.

Mac pushed the calico to the back of a desk drawer and placed another slide under the scope.

He kept trying to get Elizabeth to talk, but she wouldn't. Or couldn't. The one time he'd pushed it so far as to bring up the question of adoption, she'd cried out, "I can't do it!" and the exchange had ended with what was usual nowadays: "I'm sorry, oh, I'm so sorry, Mac . . ." He'd been left saddened, and sure he had only compounded things for her and had helped neither Elizabeth nor himself. He had needs, too, damn it. Wishes of his own, and hopes. He wanted children in his house. At least, one child.

Well, whatever was wrong with Cy Crawford's

high-stepping trotter, it didn't show up in his blood.

An exercise in futility, his trying to understand Elizabeth. He just seemed to bog down in complexities, totally unable to analyze cause and effect. He needed to talk, even if she didn't. But there was only Phil, and with Phil everything always had to be simple or he got irritated.

"Time for bed, Mac." Elizabeth's voice, soft and coming from the doorway, startled him. He looked around quickly. She hesitated on the threshold as if feeling unwelcome, looking slim and taller than she really was in her long robe, and lovely. The brows straight, dark, and she thought too heavy; the eyes dark too, almost black, and moody; the upper lip just a tad short; the lower lip so full it begged to be bitten; each breast so small it barely pushed out the robe but fitting his hand like a pouring of summer wheat.

"Will you be along soon?" she asked. "You've had a long day."

He nodded, finally. She smiled a little, and then turned away. Mac went on staring at the empty doorway. The old Elizabeth would have come in and put her arms around him and told him in no uncertain terms that he'd worked long enough and that she wanted him in bed right now.

Abruptly, Mac stood up, doused the office light, and went out to the infirmary to make his rounds. This hour was always a quiet time with the animals. He moved from patient to patient, filling a water bowl here, checking a warm nose there, changing a wet dressing or resettling a splinted limb, jotting down notes for himself on the charts attached to the outside of each cage. Then, he locked the door and walked back through the still spring moonlight into the house.

SOONER

The full moon silvered the new leaves, the bare barks, even the dirt before the cabin, and the only sound was Old Mam's rocking chair. Sooner sat on the step, where Jim Seevey had sat earlier, scratching lines in the dust at her feet with a stick to see if she could make them out afterward. She could, no matter how wiggly she drew them or what direction they ran, the light was so bright.

Old Mam had been silent ever since Jim Seevey left, even over supper, and now she was sitting and rocking again, one hand folded over the other in her lap. Once in a while, she made a little noise between her lips, and gave her head a short nod. When she did that, Sooner would sneak a look up from her scratching, just to see, but Old Mam still went on rocking.

Sooner always liked the face she saw up there in the moon. And she liked to be able to stare and stare as she never could at the sun. She reached out to the light, turning her hand back to palm to back again, wondering at its coldness. Did everyone see the moon the same? Those kids over at Bead's Knob, was the moon the same for them? At the same place in the sky? Were the tree shadows creeping as fast there as here? Bead's Knob was a pretty far piece, so Sooner couldn't be sure.

She stood, and put her arm around one of the smoothened rail posts, and swung herself back and forth. A screech owl grieved in the apple tree, and something rustled off through dry grass in fits and starts. A rabbit, most likely.

One time when she'd gone up to Bead's Knob, the boy and girl were alone, climbing the fence and jumping down off a stake, shouting and with their arms spread like birds flying. Sooner had wanted to do it too, but when she'd run to the fence stake, they stared at her and giggled. The girl told her she smelled bad. And the boy said it was their fence and their stake and they didn't want her hanging around, and he picked up a clump of dirt and threw it straight at her. Afterward, Sooner had tried jumping off the stoop rail with her arms spread, but it hadn't felt the way it had looked when the boy and girl were doing it. Any more, when Sooner went up there, she just scootched down where the weeds were tall enough so nobody could know she was there, content to watch the boy and girl, admiring how it was to be them.

Maybe it would be different for her in moonlight. Maybe that little moment between jump and fall would last longer without the yellow weight of the sun. She scrambled up the rail, and leaped off with her arms spread wide. But she forgot to shout, so it didn't count. She jumped again, crying out like the screechie, and landed so hard she went forward on hands and knees. But the jumping still didn't feel the way she knew it ought to.

Behind her, the rocking stopped. "What you doin, chile?" Old Mam got up, her hand at the small of her back, and peered over the rail at Sooner.

"Nothin," Sooner said, straightening to her feet.

"It's past time for bed," said Old Mam. "And I done decided I be goin to Switzer, come mornin."

Switzer was so far, the moon had to look different there, Sooner thought. She raised her face one last time to the light, and then followed Old Mam inside.

ELIZABETH

Elizabeth was awake and waiting naked when Mac slid into bed beside her. She had been staring through the window at the moon, thinking not about it, thinking about him. But when he came across the room, she closed her eyes and turned her face from the cold light so that he could think she'd gone to sleep if he wanted to.

He didn't want to, for he slid his arm around her, brushing the already hard tips of her breasts with his palm. She responded to him at once, clinging to him silently, wanting to relax so that he wouldn't have to fight the tightness in her. He ran his fingers lightly down her back, trying to help her, she knew. She moved her cheek in rhythmic passage back and forth across the heavy flesh of his shoulder.

"Forgive me, Mac."

"Don't talk nonsense," he said.

He didn't understand. And she didn't want him to. He believed it was the one thing. But it was something else. Still, she dug her nails into his back. "Please. Please."

What was she pleading for? Forgiveness, really? Love? But how could he put a positive value on a void?

He raised her face and kissed her and forced her mouth open for him. She rolled to her back, and pulled him with her, wanting the weight of him full on her, letting him know her impatience. She reached for him before he was ready, so that he grew into her hand.

No more, the slow loving they used to make for each other. No more, that sweet beauty. She was afraid to chance it, that it wouldn't be there for her; needing the release to prove it could still happen.

"Mac . . . come in now, *now* . . ."

She shuddered as he pushed into her, rising violently, almost lifting off the bed to meet him, denying him his tenderness.

He finished it for both of them, giving her the release, and quickly as she wanted it. Then, when he would have held her awhile, she turned her back to him to hide her tears for what she'd lost because she no longer dared seek it.

Life had been pulsed into her to die like water in a desert. And it was as if the desert were growing inside, up from dead womb to deadening heart, a weight of sand trickling through an hourglass; so that she carried always lately the suspicion that in trying so hard not to care, not to hurt, she had killed a portion of herself that could never be reborn. Even more, she was frightened that Mac would find her out.

Pop McHenry always used to say the world was divided among the givers and the takers, and that the only way to live was to be a giver. But maybe she couldn't, any more; or would never be able to again.

Mac wanted to adopt a child. He tried hard not to keep bringing it up, but she knew he wanted to. How could he not, being Mac? But what if she agreed, and then found she couldn't love it?

She caught her fist to her mouth to stifle the sound of fear, and stiffened with listening. Had he heard? No. His breathing was even, slow. He was asleep.

She shifted to her stomach, and grabbed the pillow in her fists. The round of thought never ended. Maybe she should leave him. At least, then, he'd have a chance at a family. But the image of herself without him . . . no, she didn't have courage enough.

Or love him enough, Lizzie? the voice asked. That damned secret, intimidating voice of hers. Somehow, it had the sound of truth that would not be silenced, like the admonishing voice of her mother when she was little. She had always been called Elizabeth, so that when her mother meant to sound severe, she'd used the hated nickname. Just the reverse of the way it had been with her friends. Peggy's mother, annoyed, always called her Margaret, so that Peggy grew up hating the name, and refused to answer when anyone else used it. But Elizabeth's mother had to do things differently.

It used to burn Elizabeth up, and her mother knew it. She'd laugh and say, "It's my strike for freedom, darling. If everybody's jumping into the lake, I won't. But if nobody else will, then I can't wait to!"

If Elizabeth were to talk to her mother now, she'd doubtless tell her she was a fool and to stop fighting it. "Be the only childless woman in Indiana," she'd say. "Enjoy it! Flaunt it! Lord it over the others, and laugh at them! You're freer than they are, don't you know that? Be glad!"

Glad. Was that truth? Or was the truth what she feared? That she couldn't love anyone, even Mac.

Oh, Lord, what matter the release, quick, complete, if there was no deliverance?

In one swift motion, careless of Mac, Elizabeth curled on her side into a tight ball. Old man Freud would call it wanting the security of the womb. Her hands and feet were cold. She slid her hands to under her arms, and wished to God she'd go to sleep. Every night it seemed to take longer.

SOONER

Come morning, Old Mam was so fidgety to get to
Switzer they had to eat cold pone for breakfast.
Afterward, she put her hat on her head to keep off
the sun, picked up her switch, and said, "Help me to
hitch up William to the cart, Sooney."

While Old Mam hauled the little cart into the side
yard, Sooner untied the mule from where he sheltered
under the lean-to. On the way, leading him, she peered
into the hopper which fed the millstones. "Corn ain't
all chopped yet," she offered.

"No matter," said Old Mam. She scanned the sky.
"Blue-dry like it is, corn will keep." She grabbed William's harness to pull him to the cart, but as usual,
the mule balked. "Goldarned fly-bit idiot, you come
on!" She pulled harder, and then flicked the switch at
his backside. William skittered and balked again, and
Old Mam flicked the switch again.

Sooner felt it as if on her own legs, yesterday all
over again. Oh, William, she thought. Do like she
wants.

"What you just a-standin there for? I done tole you
to help!" Old Mam was glaring at her.

Sooner ran forward, reached up to William's head to
take hold of the harness. She rubbed his soft, gray nose
until his eyes stopped rolling back, and then led him
easily around in a turn and backed him to the cart. She
kept him there, standing her ground with difficulty as
William gently butted the back of her neck, pleasuring
herself in his snuffling warm breath, while Old Mam

hooked the traces. But she let Sooner put the bit in his mouth. Then Old Mam clambered up on the narrow seat, plumped herself down, and jiggled at the reins impatiently.

"Come on, chile! Get on up here!"

"I'm a-goin with you?" She couldn't believe it. To Switzer? She hadn't ever been, not once. Old Mam always said she couldn't be bothered. And after, she complained because William took twice as long on the trip as he should have, and said that next time Sooner would have to go, too. But when next time came, Old Mam always still couldn't be bothered.

Quickly, before Old Mam did a turnabout, Sooner climbed aboard. Old Mam slapped the reins at William, but he didn't budge. Her eyes slid around to Sooner. Sooner chirruped, and the mule ambled forward. As they came around the front of the cabin, Little One darted under the stoop. Old Mam hauled back and William stopped.

"Go get that useless critter of yourn." Sooner stared up at Old Mam. "And where's that redwing you allus got peckin round? Get him, too!" But Sooner sat quite still, her eyes fixed on Old Mam's face. What was meant? Old Mam never had any truck with her little things.

"Well, go on! They might better see what all I got to put up with, doin for you!" Then, more to herself than to Sooner, "Might even get me enough, won't have to set up no more with the corn likker furnace! I'm a-goin to work it somehow so's I don't have to winter here!"

Sooner scrambled down and ran to the stoop. She crouched, holding open the big pocket in her dress, checking to make sure there were plenty of sunflower seeds in it, and made small sucking sounds. Little One peeked out, then ran into the pocket. Sooner stood up and looked all around the yard. Bird wasn't anywhere to be seen. She listened, and thought she heard a screech from over the bank, but all redwings called like that. She started across to the bank, flicking her eyes toward Old Mam, scared she might get left if she took too long. But Old Mam was sitting quiet, her eyes closed, her mouth working in and out the way it did with Jim Seevey. William was flopping his ears at the whorl of tiny bugs around his head.

It was Bird. He was perched in the little shagbark that didn't grow. She ran down, held out her hand for him, and then let him walk to her shoulder. Old Mam had somehow got William going, and the cart was rolling onto the lane. Sooner had to make a jump over the back to get on the cart in time, and she crawled forward to the seat.

*   *   *

The trip took a while. Two cars and a truck passed them on the road, honking their horns so that each time Sooner jumped, and Little One, peering over her pocket to see, disappeared back inside. But William just plodded on. When he was going downhill, anyway. When it was uphill, Sooner had to get out and croon and tell him how fine he was to keep him going. Old Mam never stirred. But as they came near to Switzer, she slapped her knee and chortled and said, "Sooney, I got it all worked out. With Jim Seevey wantin my corn likker early like he does, added to what I figure Mr. Roosevelt's owin to me, why, ain't no need to seed this summer's corn, even. You and me, we can go to Flordy right now, iffen we want!"

"Flordy?" Sooner couldn't recollect any place hereabouts named like that. "Where's it at?" she asked.

Old Mam waved her hand in the air. "It's south a ways," she said. "Hear tell it's warm down there all the year round." She was sitting up straight, smiling. For

51

the first time since she'd sprung the traps, Sooner felt sure that Old Mam wasn't fussed at her any more.

A couple of farm wagons with their horses, broad-hoofed and the sun bright on their wide haunches, were tied up at a building on the edge of town. The milk depot, Old Mam said. And there were more cars than Sooner'd ever seen before; and all the dust-free streets running into each other kept surprising her.

Away down one, far at the end, she could see a funny little wooden house, sitting high up and floating on its base as if on water. It was the color of wild mustard, and had scallops all around it. Old Mam called it the station for the Southern Railway.

"Is that where you got onto the train, that oncet?"

"Yup."

"You was a-goin all the way to Louisville, wasn't you," Sooner said, glad to remember so much of what Old Mam had told her about it. "Only you never got that far." Sooner always wondered how trains were. She'd never seen one.

After the station, it was the houses that she looked and looked at the most: big and bright, with two stories, and every one full of windows with folks behind the curtains. There were so many houses, and so many folks inside them.

Old Mam halted William in front of what she named the courthouse. Its gray limestone front was the biggest thing Sooner had ever laid eyes on, all fancied up, too, with curlicues and round white balls on long poles. For lighting at night, Old Mam told her irritably, as though Sooner had ought to have known.

Old Mam got down from the cart. "You set, you hear? Just set there and wait." And she went off up the wide stoop and through the big double doors. Sooner thought she was almighty mettlesome to go up those big steps so unscared.

Bird fluttered down from the footboard to the hard

gray path where people walked. Cee-ment, Old Mam had called it. He pecked at it once, and hopped straight in the air. Sooner giggled at his surprise.

"He's dumb!"

Sooner turned and looked down by the side of the cart. A boy was there, about her size.

"No, he ain't," she said, patiently. "He just ain't used to it, is all."

"How's come you to know so much?"

"'Cause he's mine."

"Yours! No kidding?" There was a pause. "He doesn't have a cage! How's come he doesn't fly off?"

"He got his wing broke oncet."

The boy looked at Bird a moment, then back at Sooner. "What good's he, then?"

Sooner blinked, then swiveled around back to face front, ignoring the boy. But she knew he was still there, waiting for an answer. The thing was, she didn't rightly have one. Bird was—was Bird, that's all.

"How's come you aren't to school?"

School. She'd heard the boy and girl up at Bead's Knob talking about school sometimes. They went there. She'd puzzled over that a lot, but when she'd asked Old Mam, all Old Mam had said was that folks only needed schooling for Bible reading, and she could learn Sooner that good enough. But somehow she never did seem to get around to it.

The boy was waiting again. Sooner wished he'd go away, asking all those dumb questions. Then she thought. "How's come you ain't to school yourself?" she asked back.

"It's lunchtime, dummy!" And giggling, the boy ran down the street.

Sooner watched him go. She wished—she wished she could figure what school was, and maybe go there, just once. She jumped down and scooped up Bird and climbed back into the cart. "Why do you have to be

53

good for somethin, anyways? Just like to Ole Mam, that boy! Should've ast him what he's good for—outside of astin dumb questions!" At the thought of saying that to the boy, she smiled.

Old Mam clomped down the steps and heisted herself back into the cart. "Nobody to home in there, ceptin one lady goin clackety-clackety on one of them machines. She says tain't Roosevelt money, but county, we're after. And that we got to go to the sheriff." Old Mam slapped the reins at William and he started walking.

Sooner had heard Jim Seevey talk some about the sheriff. "We don't throw it in his face, Mrs. Hawes," he'd said to Old Mam, "he'll leave us be. Old Phil likes his mountain dew, just like the rest of us!"

"We ain't got no corn likker for him," said Sooner, now.

"You keep shut bout that, Sooney! We don't know nothin bout no corn likker. Hear me good, chile—we don't know nothin bout it!"

"Yes'm."

William turned the corner, and there, across from the courthouse was a small brick one-story building, its windows barred and without curtains.

"This time," said Old Mam, "you be comin with me." She wheeled William around in the street, and let him stop of his own accord near a skinny maple tree. She got down from the cart, tied the reins to the tree, and looked at Sooner. "Come here to me, and bring that bird, too."

Sooner stood before Old Mam, while Old Mam licked her fingers and tried to slick back Sooner's spikey hair. Old Mam eyed her then. "Iffen you hadn't gone and lost that new dress like you done, you'd look right nice, Sooney. Come on."

She went to the door of the brick building, and walked in. Sooner was at her heels, Bird perched on her shoulder. A man, seated at a great brown table inside, looked up as they entered, and slowly, he got to his feet. He seemed about to say something, but Old Mam spoke first.

"How do, Sheriff Rotteman. I got me a forrester chile. Leastways that lady over to the courthouse just named her so. And I want the money for doin for her. This here's her." She shoved Sooner forward. "I figure she's worth bout ten dollars a month for seein to."

The sheriff opened his mouth and took a breath, but Old Mam talked right through. "And I been figurin, on the way into town. Her mammy dropped her on me near to nine year back, now. Summer-hot twas, but I don't mean to argue none over two times ten. I done count up twelve months in eight year, and added in nine more for up to now, and it comes out one hunnerd and five, total. That brings it to one thousand and fifty dollar this here county's owin to me—not disregardin this month, you unnerstan."

The sheriff waited a little, then seemed to decide Old Mam was done. "You'd be Mrs. Hawes from out Black Willow Creek, right?" The sheriff moved around the table toward them. "Do you mind if we close the door? Flies are really swarming, after this last week." He closed the door. "Maybe you better sit down, Mrs. Hawes." He smiled at Sooner and eyed Bird, then walked on back to sit down behind the table again. Old Mam sat down, too.

"Now what's all this about the little girl being a foster child? Seems to me I've always heard she was your granddaughter."

"Tain't so," said Old Mam. Her voice sounded the way it did when she wasn't prepared to take any back talk from Sooner. "A young gal brung her to me. Skittish and cheapened up, she was, with powder and scent. Oh, she done *said* the babe was my boy Jason's —a sooner babe cause they wasn't married yet for the full term. And she had the marriage lines to show for it. But some later, when my Jason, he come visitin, he says she done had him and me both for fools. He say Sooner ain't no kin to neither of us." She was looking at Sooner, now.

With the door closed, the big room smelled dampy-like to Sooner, the same as William's shed after winter. But there was also a smell of coffee, and she could see a pot steaming on a shelf in the corner. Something else smelled, too, but she wasn't reminded of what it was.

"But I done for her, anyhow. Like she was my own, as you can see from lookin."

Sooner saw that the sheriff's eyes were on her legs. She glanced down quickly, wondering if some flies were stuck there. The sheriff didn't seem to take much to flies. But there was nothing she could see on her legs excepting the dried-up tracks where the switch had cut too deep.

"Course, I wasn't all the fool Jason done made out. I was a-arguin with that gal when she just up and left Sooney there on the stoop. Even pondered awhile takin the babe down to the creek and drownin it like any kitten. Howsomever, I ain't done it. And she growed up just fine, as you can see. So I come to get my money." Old Mam sat back in her chair with a sigh.

The sheriff's eyes moved over Sooner once again. His mouth puckered in at the sides, and he picked up a brown stalk from a small dish on the table and clamped his teeth down on it. The end that was sticking out looked charred.

"How much did you say? One thousand and fifty?" The sheriff talked around the stalk.

"Yup. I heard they was New Deal money a-plenty you be givin away here in Switzer. But the courthouse lady, she said it got to come to me from the county."

"The courthouse lady, huh?" It was mighty peculiar, Sooner thought. The sheriff looked hopping mad, and sounded like it, too. Was he mad at her? He was staring at her kind of that way.

"Mrs. Hawes . . ." he cleared his throat. "Mrs. Hawes . . ." Suddenly, he snatched the stalk from his teeth and gave a hard shout of laughter, so without warning that Sooner jumped the way she had at the horns out on the road.

"I'll be double damned," he said. "And Selma ought to be."

"Ain't no call to be usin words like that afore the chile," said Old Mam. She looked like Bird ruffling his feathers.

The smile died from the sheriff's face. "All right, Mrs. Hawes. If that's the way you want it, I'll take it for the truth. The little girl is a foster child. In which case . . ." He leaned back in his chair, turning the stalk round and round between his fingers, watching it turn. When he went on, he sounded different, his words sounding somehow akin to Old Mam's Bible talk, but quicker. "In which case, there will have to be an investigation as to whether you are providing her a proper home, before the county will be willing to place her with you. Much less pay you anything."

Old Mam's face was wary. "What's it mean, that there investigation?"

The sheriff took a deep breath and stood up. "It means, Mrs. Hawes, that you've got to leave—Sooner?—here. It means that this county's not about to pay you one red cent. So you can just go on back home, now."

Old Mam rose from the chair where she was sitting, her nose reddening the way it did when she was beside herself with Sooner. And, as often when it happened, Sooner had to make water.

"You ain't cheatin me outa my money thisaway!"

"No money. No Sooner. Go on home, Mrs. Hawes.

I'll be out to see you in a couple, three days. Then, we'll see."

"You can't do me like this!" Old Mam's voice was high and angry.

The sheriff walked toward her, and when he spoke his voice was very soft. "I'm the sheriff, ma'am. The law. I can do you like this, and I'm doing it." He stepped to the door and opened it, standing aside so Old Mam could go by.

But she glared at him and then stepped to Sooner and got a grab on her arm and started hauling her toward the door. The sheriff moved into the doorway and Old Mam had to stop. Sooner felt the need inside get worse. Old Mam's hand had a shaking in it.

"Maybe I don't get no money! But Sooney belongs to me!"

"Seems to me," the sheriff said, "seems to me you just finished saying as how she didn't."

Old Mam let go Sooner's arm and looked down at her, and her fingers reached as if to touch Sooner's cheek, a thing she never did. "We make do, her and me. We make do just fine, and allus have." Sooner had never heard Old Mam sound just so. It was uneasy-making, and Sooner wanted to back off from her, but she couldn't take a step. If she did, she'd wet down her legs and puddle the floor.

"Yeah, you see to that, don't you," the sheriff was saying. "With what? A willow switch, is it?"

Old Mam swung around to him. "You wouldn't lay hands on a poor old lady and a puny chile . . . no, you wouldn't!" And she swept her arm up and across his chest so that the sheriff stumbled back against the door. "Go on, Sooney," she said, "run for the cart!"

Sooner stood tightening her legs together, holding in for fear of shaming herself. Old Mam raised her hand high, this time aiming at Sooner. "You do like I tole you!"

The sheriff caught Old Mam's arm and hung onto it. "That does it. Get out, old woman!" He shoved her toward the door, but Old Mam fetched up short and spun around back.

"Ain't a-goin nowheres withouten that chile!"

The sheriff stepped close to Old Mam, vasty oak shrinking up a stunted weed tree. "She stays here, Mrs. Hawes. That's what she wants to do. She hasn't budged. And if I were you, and I had me a little still hid away somewheres, I think maybe I wouldn't argue."

The red went from Old Mam's face, leaving her looking bloodless. She turned and marched through the door to the cart. She grabbed up the switch and marched back toward the sheriff.

She wouldn't use the switch on *him*, would she? Sooner crossed her legs to hold in what was now a terrible need.

"You're havin yourself some good time with this old lady, ain't you!" Old Mam's chin lifted, and her mouth set in a tight line. "You answer me this. Seein as she's a forrester chile, who's to take her in but me? I know how you'll do. Come tomorrow or the day after you'll be bringing her out to me, and not a penny to show me for all I done for her. Well, you give her here, now!"

She was drawing back her arm again, and Sooner stopped her breathing at what was happening. The switch whistled at the sheriff's face, but he ripped it from Old Mam before it hit him, and she came at him like a wild cock, and yelling. The sheriff looked slow, and he talked slow, but he wasn't. He doubled the switch over and cracked its spring, all the while holding Old Mam off. Then he grabbed Old Mam by the elbows, and raised her from the ground as if she were a nothing like Sooner, and carried her before him, kicking and yelling, and sat her down in the seat of the cart. He shoved the reins at her and slapped

William hard across the withers. William started out of his doze at a real pace, and Old Mam was fighting with the reins as the cart rocked around the corner out of Sooner's view.

The sheriff came back inside, slammed the door, and halted, looking at her crossed legs. She felt Little One stir in her pocket down there and wished he wouldn't.

"Was that why you wouldn't run when she told you to?" He sounded tired. "Didn't want to stay at all, I bet." But he smiled, one corner of his mouth turning down with it. "Don't worry about it. She's right. I'll probably be taking you back tomorrow. And maybe she'll go a little easier with her switch from here on out."

Sooner just looked at him, shifting her weight.

"You got to go that bad?" He strode by her quickly. "Come on, then. I'll show you where."

He opened a door at the back of the room and went down a hall. Sooner managed to follow him, grabbing her drawers up tight. There were barred little rooms on either side of the hall, all empty. At the end were two doors. He opened one of them.

"Here you are," he said.

She walked to his side in the doorway, and looked in.

"Well, you hadn't better just stand there." He turned away as if to leave her, but stopped, watching her face. He smiled a little. "Look," he said. "It's all right. You sit on that bowl. And then when you're done, you pull that chain up there."

"You mean I got to do it inside the house?" Sooner was horrified. "But that's dirty!"

His eyes closed for a moment. He sighed. He smiled again. "Yup. That's the way it is, I'm afraid." And he pushed her over the threshold and closed the door on her. She could hear him mumbling, as his footsteps hushed with distance, "Sweet Jesus, I wish somebody'd protect me from my better impulses!"

Sooner did as he'd said to. The noise when she pulled the chain scared her, and she ran out of the little room, thinking she'd done it wrong for sure. But peering back in, she could see that the rushing water didn't spill out as she'd thought it must, and she walked, then, instead of running, back along the hall to the room at the front. She didn't quite reach it when she heard the door to the street open, and she stopped where she was, and leaned her head sideways so to see into the room.

A lady was stepping inside. She had white, white skin, and hair orange like carrots skinned tight back from her face. Sooner hadn't known people came in those colors. The sheriff was back behind the table, and he looked up at the lady, not smiling, as she said, "I know it's early for lunch, but I'm dying to know. How did you get rid of her?"

"I figured I had you to thank for it," the sheriff said.

She gave a giggle, closed the door, and moved to the table, where she sat on the edge and reached out one finger to touch the back of his hand.

"You're not really mad," she said, with a little smile just showing.

"You don't know the half of it," said the sheriff. "Selma, I don't know what gets into you, sometimes. How sneaky can you get, siccing that old bitch on me!" He sounded really mad to Sooner, but he didn't pull his hand away from her touching him.

The lady laughed. "A real dilly, wasn't she? But I wasn't just playing you dirty, you know. If she was telling the truth about the little girl, it'll be up to you to get her named a ward of the county. Come and eat, and tell me what happened."

Bird, having sat on Sooner's shoulder all this while,

suddenly fluttered to the top of her head, and screeched. The lady spun toward the hall doorway and saw Sooner. "My God," she said.

"Yeah," said the sheriff. His eyes shifted from Sooner to the lady to Sooner again, and suddenly he leaned back in his chair, put his feet up on the table, and crossed his arms over his chest. "Come on in, Sooner, and meet the lady you'll be staying with tonight."

Sooner walked into the room and stopped again, and put her hand in her pocket with Little One and held on to him.

The lady was staring at the sheriff. She jumped to her feet. "Oh, no you don't, Phil Rotteman! You're not going to land her on me! Talk about sneaky—"

"Hey, now . . ." the sheriff's voice was quiet, and he looked over at Sooner. "Not fixing to land you on anybody, Sooner." He winked at her, and he did it much easier-looking than Jim Seevey. "You and me, we'll just have us a fine time here, tonight."

"Now, Phil. Don't make me out to be so mean." The lady looked at Sooner, too, and smiled at her. "I'd be glad to have you, honey. It's just"—she looked back at the sheriff—"you are sneaky, and you know it. I haven't forgotten the way it was with those spotted hounds of yours. 'Just keep 'em for a little while, Selma darlin', till I find a place for 'em in the country.' And before I knew it, you had a kennel building in my back yard. Those hounds are still there! First them, next this little girl, and quicker than pickup sticks, you'll be moving in, and we'll be one big happy family!"

The sheriff stood up. He was grinning. "Such a thing never entered my head. But it's a pretty good idea, at that."

With the sheriff standing, Sooner could see that the lady was almost as tall as he was, and bigger around by half. She sure seemed peppery.

The sheriff turned his grin on Sooner. "Why don't we all go over to Cy's for lunch, and you two can get to know each other."

The lady sniffed, just like Old Mam. "What for? So she can worm her way into my affections? Well, I'm here to tell you, you're the only worm I want in my life, and sometimes even you get too much. Like right now." She started for the door.

"Selma?" The sheriff looked as if he didn't know whether to laugh or not.

The lady opened the door. "I'll bring you a couple of hamburgers," she said.

What's a hamburger? Sooner wanted to ask, but didn't. The lady spoke so fast and so hot and bothered that Sooner had the feeling she'd never get the words more than half out before the lady'd be talking again.

She was still standing in the open doorway, her eyes now moving down and up Sooner. When she spoke this time, it was more softly than before. "She is kind of cute, isn't she." But then, "Phil, I swear, you're as wily as my daddy was a fisherman. There's no trick you wouldn't pull to get a ball and chain on me!" And she left, slamming the door behind her.

"Well," the sheriff said, "it was worth a try, anyway. So . . . you stay here, tonight, Sooner." He looked quickly around the room, his mouth thinning into a line. "Thing is, what do I do with you until then?"

Sooner shrugged up her shoulders, and thought about it a minute. "We could play checkers," she said. "Ole Mam, she splained me how, till she wouldn't play with me no more. I'm real good at checkers."

MAC

He'd already told Elizabeth not to have lunch for him, and when office hours were over around eleven-thirty, he walked uptown. It was another bright day. Elizabeth's white and yellow jonquils, the bulbs left from last year, were kept company by tulips and hyacinths in yards on down the street. Phil usually wandered over to Cy's Grill shortly before noon, sometimes with Selma, sometimes not. Today, Mac intended to get there before she did. After last night, he was more than ever determined to reason it through. He was no boy in first rut. He wouldn't lay it all out for Phil. But Phil liked things simple, and maybe that's what was needed, simplicity. To untangle the maze. Just putting it into words might help.

Elizabeth had shocked him, last night, with her desperate intensity, and turning away from him afterward. And he had shocked himself. As he'd entered her, he'd found himself dragging up from memory, deliberately dragging it up, the vision of those two cats he'd seen out back in the alley. The male taking his pleasure over and over again, the female with her eyes closed, purring, screaming, purring again. Their softness and abandon. He'd wanted to feel it. And then, not dragged up but coming whether he wanted it or not, there was a picture of Selma. Phil's Selma. Welcoming flesh, easy, pliant. The shock of it had nearly wilted him.

Why Selma? What did he want with Selma Goss, for Christ's sake? Why not Elizabeth, at least as she used to be? His sensual Elizabeth, who liked to explore and play games with sex, to laugh and forget herself in ecstasy. Hell, they'd both been so eager before they were married, he'd been sure she'd never make it to the altar a virgin. And she damned well wouldn't have, if he'd owned a car in those days. What was happening to that Elizabeth? And what, in the name of God, could he do about it?

He rounded the corner to the jail, and saw Selma just going up the courthouse steps. Had they already had lunch? Well, anyway, at least he'd have Phil to himself.

Phil ought to marry the woman. After all these years of convenience, he owed it to her. Though maybe the convenience was more hers than his. It had been going on since high school, the two of them the one steady romance everybody took for granted; and even then, Selma was saying she didn't want to be tied down. It had sounded brave and independent, coming from a girl in high school. But she was still saying it, according to Phil, and now it seemed a silly pretense. She was tied down by her job as Clerk of Courts, wasn't she? And as far as Mac knew, she never considered not running for reelection every three years. Women and logic. As Phil liked to say, "Oil and water, they don't mix."

Mac walked into the jail, saying, "Hi," then stopped. A little girl was seated cross-legged on Phil's table, bending over a checkerboard to move a piece, while Phil watched, his dead cigar drooping from his mouth. It was the little girl from yesterday. A redwinged blackbird perched on the back of Phil's swivel chair, and a chipmunk sniffed his way about some lunch bags and crumpled paper napkins on the table top.

Phil looked up and grinned. "Here's the fella who'll know."

As before when she'd seen Mac, the child's eyes were slowly widening on him.

"What's good for redwings, Mac? To eat, I mean? We've run clear out of sunflower seeds."

"Well, I—" Mac found he was blank. He came all the way into the room. "Hello again, little miss."

"You know each other?" Phil asked.

"We met, yesterday," Mac said, and he smiled at her, trying to keep from looking at her legs.

"Oh?" Phil sounded noticeably cool. "You wouldn't be the one gave the old lady her big ideas about New Deal money, would you?"

"What? What are you talking about?"

Phil leaned back in his chair. The redwing screeched and fluttered clumsily to the table top.

"We'll finish the game another time, Sooner. You go on out on the step and watch the cars for a while."

She scrambled down from the table and backed slowly toward the door, not looking away from Mac even for a moment.

"And take your two friends with you." This in aggravation, as Phil pulled out a handkerchief and wiped the table clean where the redwing had deposited a splash. The handkerchief looked as though it had seen similar service before. The child collected the bird and the chipmunk and started again for the door.

"Corn," Mac said, finally not blank. "Dried corn. It'll feed both animals."

She now had the door open, peering around it at Mac, and the words burst out of her with a great wonder.

"First time I done ever et ketchup! The lady, she showed me how to do with it." And then, wistfully, "Sure wisht I could drip that ketchup over everthin!" She went out, closing the door behind her very carefully.

"She can talk," Mac said. "I wondered, yesterday. What's she doing here, Phil?"

"Mrs. Hawes came roaring in here with her this morning. She claims Sooner isn't her kin and that somebody owes her ten dollars a month for keeping her. Starting with one thousand and fifty for the past nine years."

Phil's voice was flat, and Mac decided to believe him. He wouldn't put anything past that old woman. Not kin. That's what stuck in his mind.

"Not kin?" he asked.

"She swears to it."

"And you saw those beat-up legs and became a patsy, huh?"

"Yeah, sure." Phil said it wearily, but then he chuckled. "The legs and that greedy Mrs. Hawes. The gall of her, my God. Even went after me with her switch!"

Mac pulled a chair over, swung it around, and sat down. "What're you going to do with her, Phil? Sooner, I mean. Lord, what a name. Sooner."

Phil blinked a little at his seriousness. "I figured to keep her here a day or so. Maybe throw the fear of God into the old bitch." He took a kitchen match from the box on the table, relit his cigar. "That is, if I can stand baby-sitting her menagerie that long." He drew on the cigar and continued. "Legally, I suppose she could be sent to Naptown. There's a state children's home up there. But she just wouldn't survive it, you know? Hell, she's like a wild Indian. Can't even read. I asked her, and she said, 'Ole Mam, she jist never gits around to showin me.' God knows she's not adoptable, Mac. She'd spend the next eight, ten years institutionalized, if she didn't die from lack of fresh air first. Life with Mrs. Hawes may not be sweet as honey, but"—he sighed—"it's a hell of a lot better than that Indianapolis orphanage, I can tell you."

"Yeah," Mac said. "Yeah." He stared at Phil puffing

away at his cigar, not really seeing him. What did he want to say? I'll take her? *I'll* take her. God. He'd come down here to talk, and now this. Thinking to find simplicity to untangle the maze that was Elizabeth. Well, here it was. Real simplicity. What would she do?

Elizabeth, what will you do if I—

"How long *could* you keep her, Phil?"

"To tell you the truth," he answered wryly, looking at the handkerchief bunched on the table, "the sooner I take Sooner back to the country, the happier I'll be."

"I mean, could you keep her longer than that? Until something's decided legally?"

"I told you. It's been decided. I'm taking her back. Tomorrow morning, more than likely."

"Damn it, Phil! I'm asking if you could hold Mrs. Hawes off awhile! Could you?"

Phil studied him. "Kind of revvin' your motor a little, aren't you? What is it, sympathy or guilt?"

"Huh?"

Phil leaned across the table toward him. "You have the means. You and Elizabeth could offer any child a great deal in lots of ways. You both deserve a child. But you don't decide it like this, Mac." He sat back again, muting his tone a little. "Besides, the way I heard it, if a woman adopts a child, she wants it brand-new. So's it's more like her own. But that one out there —Mac, Elizabeth'd go through the roof if you took that kid home!"

Mac heard him out with increasing resistance. His hands were clenched over his knees. He tried to smile, doubtless showing this old friend more bitterness with it than he meant to. "Probably. Probably she will. But would that be so tragic? It'd be better than—" He stopped and hauled in his breath.

Phil's eyes were narrowing at him speculatively. No; his gaze was shrewd. Phil could be hellishly perceptive.

"What did you come down here for, Mac? You don't often have time to waste in the middle of the day."

Mac looked away from him. He couldn't answer him now. He set himself. "How long could we have her? Just to see?"

"You can't use a child so!"

"Use her?" This time, he met Phil's eyes steadily, and he was dead earnest. "No more than she'd be using us. Even if she ends up back at Black Willow Creek . . . even if it's only for a few days or—or a few weeks . . ." Lord, the hope rose up so quickly in him. "How could it do the child any harm? Did it ever hurt anyone to see new things? Learn new ways?"

"If they have to give them up afterwards, you can bet it hurts!" Phil sounded hard and angry. "Do you have any notion at all what you'll be asking of that little girl? You and Elizabeth . . . all of us here in town, our life is like something from another planet to that little girl!"

"Phil . . ." Mac was sweating, and the words came hard to find, hard to say, but the need was so great. "You know how I found her, yesterday? She'd doctored a calf of Harvey Drummond's. And doctored it well. And when I saw her, with that yellow hair, and so mistreated . . . All right, I'll say it all. I want her. I hope to heaven Elizabeth will, too, but—*I* want her."

Phil wasn't looking at him any more. He spoke heavily. "I guess I could put Mrs. Hawes off. With legal double-talk, or something." Now, he raised his eyes to Mac's. "Because one thing, Mac, I'm going to make sure of. The way back to what she knows has to be left open for Sooner. For a while, anyway." There was a long pause. Finally, "But it's up to you to give her the how and why of it. Elizabeth, too."

It was settled. Mac rubbed the sweat off his upper lip, got up, went over to the door and opened it. She was crouched on the step, her arms wrapped around her knees, the bird on her shoulder. Not a pretty child, with her skinny, marked-up legs, and that hair going every which-away. She cocked her head to look up at him, and smiled. How had he ever thought she might be weak-minded?

Elizabeth . . . it's not just for me, Elizabeth. I want it to be right for you.

"Ain't never seed nobody so big!" Sooner said.

He smiled back at her. "Come on back inside," he said. "We've got some talking to do."

ELIZABETH

Once in a while, it was nice not to have Mac home for lunch, but not two days in a row. It left too big a hole for her to fill, so that thoughts from last night could rise up in her mind over and over again.

Her hands trembled as she folded up the curtain she'd been feeding through the Singer. Think about them, she told herself. Bright and crisp, they'd be; not all of lace, like the old ones now nearly in shreds which Mac's mother had hung, but pretty. She'd found the perfect thin white muslin for them right over at Wick's, even the lace for the edging, and hadn't had to go clear up to Paoli, after all. The lace didn't look machine-made, either. She peered at it closely, again. Well, not very, anyway. Not from a distance.

She smoothed the muslin carefully, her hands steadier now. They should have been finished weeks ago. But some days when she would get out the material to pin or baste, thought would catch her unaware. A half hour or an hour later she'd come to, having sat there with the stuff in her lap but nothing done. It was the same with working up the flower beds. Every morning, she planned to go out with a trowel and mulch, and come three o'clock, when it was too late, she'd start up from her chair. Dinner should be underway; or, what was it she'd been going to have for dessert?

The courthouse clock bonged out noon, startling her. She'd been at it again. Such a stupid, fruitless waste of time. She shoved the curtains into their drawer.

She didn't feel much like all the trouble of heating up the leftover stew, just for herself; but there ought to be something in the icebox for a sandwich, cheese or something.

There was, and she fixed it, warming the breakfast coffee at the same time, and took plate and cup into the living room, where her book was.

What do people do who don't read? she thought. What would I do?

What are you going to do, Lizzie? the voice asked. All the rest of your life? Grab for a book every time the thinking gets a little rough?

Oh, shut up, she told the voice crossly. So if I want to, yes!

She sat down and curled up in the big chintz chair by the window, found her place in the book, and began reading, crumbs spotting the pages as she ate into her sandwich. And the print jumped and blurred together with the crumbs.

She'd been proud of the way she'd taken it, last fall. But through the winter, things kept battering at her, reminders everywhere of the lost dream. The world was full of parents, and all wanted to share their child problems with her. She'd even said something like this to Harriet Cox, not long ago.

71

Harriet had laughed. "It's your own fault, you know. You're always so interested. And seem to care so much."

Elizabeth had been surprised. It was the last thing she would have said of herself. But she guessed it was nice if others wanted to think it. Only, it made it hard, sometimes.

She heard her own small click of self-disgust, and flipped back the page of the book to reread what she had just finished reading.

Mac would enjoy this book, she told herself, determined that if she had to think, it would be about other things. Mac wasn't the reader she was, but she'd gotten pretty good over the years with her recommendations, at least of novels, and then he'd read straight through, unable to put the book down until he'd finished it. No one would ever take him for a thinking man. When she'd first met him, at that Deke picnic up at OSU, she hadn't judged him for one, either. He'd sat through an evening of political argument, quiet, listening, not saying much, and it wasn't until later that she'd discovered he was as opinionated as she was, but lacked her urgency to speak her mind. They'd seemed a million miles apart then, she and Mac. He was big and rangy and slow-moving, talking in his soft Hoosier drawl of sick animals over at the university clinic and of hunting coons down home. She, the faculty-bred child, was full of her mother's brittle wit and a habit of intellectualizing everything.

She remembered the first time he'd taken her to visit the veterinary clinic. She could still see him, holding a jet-black kitten so tiny it left room in the palm of his hand, caressing it with a single finger and talking to it with logic. And now, when compassionate townspeople brought him hurt wild creatures, an owl or possum, rabbits sometimes, even an occasional buzzard, he named them on the spot: George and Harry; Sam,

Helen, Tom . . . He didn't shoot any more, but he never missed the annual fox hunt. For the sake of the run it gave everybody's dogs, he said. And the fox always won free, anyhow.

If ever a man was born to have children, Mac was.

His gentleness, the openness in his face, the suggestion of innocence in the way he accepted the world around him, seeming odd and charming somehow in a man five years older than she—even that first evening, these things had tugged at her. She had found herself singing inside just to be with him. There was a lift, a sense of ease, of comfort. And when he'd taken her hand, and the spark had caught them both so unaware . . .

Elizabeth slammed the book closed. To hell with Margaret Mitchell and her Ashley and Melanie. They were no help at all. And she shouldn't be eating a sandwich. Ever since the operation, she'd been putting on weight, and in all the wrong places. The least she could do for Mac would be to keep her figure. The phone rang.

It was Eleanor, asking what time they were expected for bridge tonight.

"Seven-thirty," Elizabeth said quickly, as if she hadn't completely forgotten about it.

Eleanor immediately went on to the subject of the church supper next week. Elizabeth knew she'd talk forever, so she scrambled for the rest of her sandwich and finished it while she listened and made appropriate noises.

It didn't take Eleanor long to leave the question of whether to fix chicken and noodles or her special devil's-food cake. "What a winter it's been! We've had one cold after another in this house. Honestly, the germs they bring home from school. If it isn't Tommy, then it's Mike, and then it hits all of us, one after the other."

73

It was at times like this that some bitchy remark would pop into Elizabeth's head, and one of these days, Elizabeth was sure it would just pop out. Like a cheerful "Want to switch problems, Eleanor?" But she knew Eleanor meant no harm. None of them did. It was only that anything said about children seemed to strike her like an accusation. "Why don't you adopt a little baby?" she was sure they wanted to ask. "That poor, sweet Dr. McHenry! So deprived!" If it was what they were thinking, they were absolutely right.

Eleanor was still rattling on, now about a quarrel between Mike and Tommy over a game of marbles. Eleanor had had to break it up, and "there they were, suddenly both allied against me, the great ogre. Really, those kids!"

Elizabeth cut in. "Look, Eleanor, let me call you back, huh? I think I hear somebody at the door."

She sat for a moment over the phone after she hung up, longing to be somebody else. At least Eleanor didn't live on their block. She wouldn't know Elizabeth had lied. But there *were* steps on the veranda. It was really kind of funny, she hadn't lied, after all. She got up to go to the door, already opening.

Mac stood there, a couple of packages from Wick's under his arm, just looking in at Elizabeth, strangely, as if he were pleading, or— He stood aside and said, "Go on in, Sooner."

A little girl stepped into the house, and of all things, she carried a blackbird on her shoulder. She was the scruffiest-looking child Elizabeth had ever seen, she was sure. And the dirtiest. Mac came in after her and closed the door.

"Sooner," he said to the child, "this is Elizabeth." He looked at Elizabeth again, setting his jaw as though asking for a haymaker right in the teeth. "Elizabeth," he said. "Elizabeth, this is Sooner Hawes. I've brought her home to stay with us for a while."

Elizabeth felt fear. She stared at Mac. His blue eyes held steady. They weren't pleading any more, just waiting.

My God, he's just up and done it, without explanation, or asking, or even trying to talk me around. She wanted to howl at him that he had no right to handle her like this. Not even a baby she might come to think of as her own, but a *mongrel!*

"Don't, Elizabeth."

She blinked at the sharpness of his voice. Oh, no . . . she hadn't said it aloud, had she? Why could she never learn to think before speaking? She looked quickly at the child, but the little girl showed no reaction. There was no point in hurting her. Elizabeth didn't want to hurt her. Maybe Mac just—knew.

"Understand, Elizabeth. It's settled."

She looked back at him, startled. He didn't speak so, to her. What was this challenge? She felt it like the thrust of his arm. He was suddenly looking a very big man, standing there laying down the law in his own home.

Come on, Lizzie, the voice said. You know he's been bringing waifs and strays home all his life.

Elizabeth's gaze moved again to the child, and over her. Sooner, was that what he'd called her? She didn't retreat from Elizabeth, didn't edge toward what must seem to her Mac's towering and probably comforting presence. She held still, alone, with that bird on her shoulder, her eyes fixed on Elizabeth except for little fleeting moments when like fidgety sparrows they darted about the room, to return to fix again on Elizabeth. Dirty. Too thin. That hair, and the spot on her face. Hardly a threat to anything, really.

The fear began to quiet itself.

Nobody could be expected to love such a child. And nobody would find fault with Elizabeth, not even Elizabeth, if she couldn't.

Good heavens, the Telfers, and bridge here tonight. Elizabeth took a deep breath. Face that when the time comes, she told herself firmly.

She smiled down at the child. "Hello, Sooner," she said. Sooner ducked her head shyly. To Mac, Elizabeth said, "She could do with a bath, couldn't she."

He tried to hide his surprise, and then his relief. "Yeah. She sure could." He took a deep breath, and grinned, holding out the packages. "I, uh—we stopped at Wick's on the way home, got her some things." He started toward the kitchen. "Come on, Sooner. Let's go out back to the shower, and—"

"Mac," Elizabeth interrupted, "she's not one of your animals. There's a perfectly good bathtub upstairs. Here, give me those." She took the packages from him. He looked thunderstruck, as if he thought the battle was all won. Well, it wasn't. "How long"—her lips began to tremble; she compressed them and pushed the question out—"how long will she be staying here?"

He didn't answer, just held her eyes for a long moment and began rubbing at that yellow hair of his in the small-boy way he had when making up his mind about something. It was as good as an answer, to Elizabeth. He hoped the child would stay for good. Incredulous anger was churning up inside her; but then he said, giving a little, "Let's just take it day by day . . ."

Elizabeth sighed and turned toward Sooner, and stopped. "What's that in her pocket?"

"That's Li'l-un," Sooner said, her voice piping and eager. She reached into the pocket and pulled forth a chipmunk, cupping it in both hands, holding it out for Elizabeth to see.

"Oh." Suddenly, the whole thing seemed quite mad, insane for him to come home blithely trailing a Little Orphan Annie like this.

"Have you got any more little friends like him

76

tucked away?" Elizabeth asked, feeling on the verge of hysterical giggles.

"No'm," Sooner answered.

"Uh, huh," said Elizabeth. "Well, you give Little One and the bird, too, to Mac, and then you and I'll go upstairs."

When Sooner had deposited her pets on Mac, Elizabeth took the little girl's grubby hand and moved her toward the stairs. Halfway up the flight, she called down to Mac, still watching them, "We'll talk, afterwards." She continued with Sooner on up the stairs.

The big, white bathroom, with its high, four-footed tub, opened into the hall. Elizabeth led Sooner in, closed the door, and set the packages on the floor in the corner.

"Now then," she said, and looked at the child expectantly. But Sooner was staring about her with what had to be a wondering curiosity.

Keeping her voice gentle, Elizabeth asked, "Sooner, have you ever had a bath? All over?"

"You mean, wash everthin all to oncet?"

Elizabeth nodded.

"Come summertime, I get into the creek," she said. Her eyes, Elizabeth noted for the first time, were an odd kind of tawny color, and there was a little frown of concentration on her forehead. "Course," she was saying, "that's only in the summertime. And Ole Mam, she gets fractious iffen I forget and go in with my dress still on me. Summer past, I made me a real raft. But I done looked, after the rains, and it weren't there no more."

Well, thought Elizabeth, once she gets started, there seems to be no stopping her. Not so slow-witted as she looks?

"Any other time"—Sooner obviously wanted to be helpful—"ceptin summer, that creek water, it's mighty cold, don't you know."

77

Elizabeth dropped the plug into the drain and turned on both taps over the tub. "That's the nicest thing about a bath," she said, as comfortably as she could. "You don't have to worry about whether it's summer or winter."

Sooner was watching the water gush out. "Just like that sink the sheriff's got," she offered. "Only bigger."

"The sheriff?"

"Yes'm. Over to the jail, where I been."

The jail? Elizabeth decided to ignore that for the moment.

"Let's get you undressed, huh?"

She reached out to help the child, hauling that thing she called a dress over her head, letting it fall to the floor. Sooner stepped out of her drawers by herself. Elizabeth gathered up the discarded clothes and threw them in the wastebasket, but with a momentary qualm. The woman Sooner called Old Mam must have made them, and though they were ragged and faded and poor, they'd been sewn with care. The stitching was as even and fine as any of Mac's mother's.

A pity the woman didn't feed the child with equal care, Elizabeth thought grimly. Now that she stood there naked, Elizabeth could see the ribs outlined, and what she had thought were simply dirt streaks or briar scratches on her legs were quite something else again: peculiar diagonal welts, some of which looked sore.

Elizabeth turned off the water. Sooner wasn't tall enough to climb over the high edge. "Here we go," said Elizabeth, and she lifted the child up and stood her in the tub. She weighed hardly anything at all. Sooner's eyes widened abruptly, glued to Elizabeth's face. She began to shiver.

Why, the poor thing, Elizabeth thought. The warm water's got her frightened half out of her wits.

"Am I gonna smell good, like to you?" the child asked, stuttering it out.

"Even better! We'll wash your hair, too, so you'll smell good all over."

Another moment, and Sooner screwed her eyes closed and squatted down in the water. Elizabeth got her legs straightened and knelt by the tub with a washcloth in one hand and the bar of soap in the other. She hadn't known two feet could get so filthy.

She began the washing, dipping the cloth in the water, and squeezing it out over the child's body. Beneath her hands, she felt the shivering stop, the muscles ease, and Sooner's eyes opened.

In the beginning, their voices had resounded off the tiles, seeming enormous. As if by agreement, the two of them had ended by speaking so softly that the things said were transformed into intimacies. Soap turned the clear delicacy of the child's body skin to satin under Elizabeth's fingers. She felt she was floating in a cocoon spun of warm water and steam and flowery soap smell, bound together by the child's eyes, catching hers sometimes, and never leaving her face. Slowly, the child took on an air of sleepy contentment.

Like a nervous bride seduced by her husband-lover.

The image startled Elizabeth for its sensuality. Why that thought, now? It couldn't be the same, this closeness with a child. But she knew it was, for both of them. Sensual. Almost sexual.

Their eyes caught, and Elizabeth laughed, low and amazed. Sooner reached a wet finger to her face, streaking it with suds, bemusing Elizabeth.

Was it a mutual seduction, then, each of the other, like a love at first sight?

No, it couldn't be that easy. Not for her, Elizabeth, who was dead inside. It was only that she'd wanted so much to feel alive; and wanting it had made it seem to happen. Anyway, it meant no more than what she'd felt last night with Mac: the quick release a physical thing without significance or hope for her.

79

Or are you rationalizing it away too hard, Lizzie? asked the voice. *Because you're scared to commit yourself and become vulnerable?*

Elizabeth stiffened by the side of the tub. That was absurd. Vulnerable to *this* child?

Sooner had stiffened, too, shivering and frightened again. She lost traction and slipped beneath the water. At once, Elizabeth hauled her up, sputtering and with soap in her eyes. Elizabeth finished the bath briskly, emptied the tub, and had to repeat the whole process. This time, she scrubbed toes, fingernails, and even the backs of Sooner's heels with a brush, and still wasn't satisfied. She wondered acidly how many baths would be needed to wash that ground-in dirt away. Sooner wouldn't be here that long.

They fell into silence as Elizabeth dried Sooner down. Oddly, into Elizabeth's mind came her dream children. She'd banished them months ago. The boys yellow-haired, like Mac; the girls small and dark, like her mother. Bright, pretty children, and loving. Children of her world. How did Mac think Sooner could ever be a substitute?

When she opened the packages she saw that somebody at Wick's had done well by Mac. Brown oxford shoes, two pairs of socks, two pairs of cotton underpants, a slip, a nightgown, and a very pretty blue-and-red plaid dress with a white collar and a great big bow which she fluffed out after she'd tied it about Sooner's waist. She combed the wet uneven hair as best she could, and caught it back off Sooner's face with an old silver barrette of her own. It really was too heavy for the overfine wisps, and doubtless would slip out before the day was through.

She ought to have one of those lightweight children's barrettes, Elizabeth thought. Powder-blue, maybe, or white. And some play clothes, too. Stupid! She pulled herself up short. She won't be here that long!

Sooner lifted the full skirt up and buried her nose in it. "Smells different, don't it," she said. "Ain't never had nothin new, afore."

"And you smell different, too," said Elizabeth. "Come take a look at yourself."

They went together into Elizabeth and Mac's bedroom, where there was a long mirror on the closet door. Elizabeth felt her throat tighten as she watched Sooner, with her turned-up nose and mercurochromed legs, approach her own image as if it was the most beautiful thing she'd ever seen.

What must she be thinking? Elizabeth wondered. Maybe she's never seen herself at all, before. Does she feel changed?

Sooner took hold of her skirt and spread it as wide as it would go. Then, she turned up the hem and inspected it anxiously. "Ain't gonna do me for much time," she said. She touched the barrette in her hair, looking at Elizabeth's reflection. "Elizbeth?" she asked. It was the first time she'd spoken the name, and she gave to it a soft elision that was pleasing. "Now I'm smellin pretty, can I go to that there school with all them other kids?"

School. Well, *she* seemed sure it wasn't to be day by day. Oh, Mac!

The child put a finger up her nose. Would she stick it in her mouth, or wipe it down her new dress?

"Don't do that!" Elizabeth said sharply.

She grabbed a hanky out of a drawer and thrust it at Sooner. "Use this," she said. "I don't know about school, Sooner."

She heard the difference in her voice and winced at it, and then felt ashamed at the bewildered look Sooner gave her. Sooner couldn't help it; she didn't know any better.

But you do, Lizzie. So if you can't do anything else, at least be kind.

Shame, Elizabeth thought, ought to be experienced only in the awareness of others. Because, if only you yourself know it, who will do the forgiving?

She made herself smile and held out her hand. "Let's go show you off to Mac," she said. And then, this time with more promise, "And we'll see about school."

The hospital-sharp, animal-rich smell wrapped them round as they entered the infirmary. Sooner made a small sound, and Elizabeth looked down to see her halt just inside the door, her eyes moving slowly around from cage to cage, but whether in amazement or disquiet, Elizabeth couldn't have told. She'd had those two little wild pets. Would she be disturbed at the closed-in feeling, at the lack of freedom? Was that pity on her face as she looked in at the brown woolly monkey and Mrs. Freemont's beagle, one seemingly as exotic to her as the other?

"The sheriff, he tole me bout Mac, that he doctors up critters. But all shut in like they are . . ." She raised a confused face to Elizabeth.

"It's the best way, Sooner. Really, it is, at least with tame animals." Mac had come from the back, some pieces of wood in his hand. "If they were to run around loose, they might fight, or hurt themselves." He looked at Elizabeth, gesturing with the wood. "I thought maybe she could keep the redwing with her in the house if I fixed him up with a perch."

Elizabeth's anger started to assert itself. Quickly, Mac looked Sooner up and down, then smiled his pleasure. "Well," he said, "don't you look like something, now! Pretty as a picture!"

Sooner smiled a slow-coming smile that lit up her face. Elizabeth felt her heart lurch, which only made her madder. "Mac," she said, as matter-of-factly as she could manage, "we were going to talk, remember?"

They went back to the house, to Mac's office, permitting Sooner to be in the infirmary alone, Elizabeth with trepidation, but Mac apparently with none. He'd told Sooner to leave the animals in their cages, and he said he figured that was enough.

Hah! thought Elizabeth. We'll see.

"Now," she said, settling herself into the leather chair before Mac's desk, "you'd better tell me what this is all about."

She heard him out without interrupting him once, all through the stumbling account of yesterday, and the old woman with the willow switch, and finding Sooner today in Phil's office. Mac didn't sit down as he talked. He wandered erratically around the room, picking up and fiddling with things he probably hadn't touched in years.

When his voice seemed to have finally trailed off to a full stop, she asked the only really important question. "Why?"

He didn't answer.

The calmness she had been pretending to was deserting her. "Is this some kind of test or something?"

He turned and looked at her with puzzlement. She spun around in the chair away from it, her hands clutching each other in her lap. She struggled to keep her voice even. "Day by day, you said. All right, Mac. I'll look after her. Keep her clean. Dress her decently. But don't expect anything more."

"Elizabeth . . . she needs us. And you need her as much as—"

She swung back toward him so abruptly that he stopped. How could he! He made her feel pitied. For a moment, she almost hated him.

She rose. "What were you thinking, Mac? All you have to do is force on somebody the opportunity to love, and she will? Couldn't you at least have tried me out on something more likely? She's never heard of a toothbrush, doesn't know what toilet paper is, and she picks her nose!" Elizabeth caught herself back, realizing that what she'd just said had nothing to do with anything. And then the rest spewed on out of her. "Do you honestly think that even in time I could come to love her as my own? That dirty little stranger?"

"Why not?" His words came flat, with a pushed-to-the-wall stubbornness. "Since when are there reasons for loving? There aren't. Only reasons not to. And then you go on loving in spite of them."

He couldn't be talking about Sooner—how could he know what she'd felt with the child, bathing her? He had to be talking about Elizabeth and the reasons he was finding not to love her any more. It hadn't been real, anyway, what she'd felt upstairs. It was only something wanted: a dream; and the child was wrong for it! No, he couldn't know. He wasn't God. Though he seemed to think he was, full of his wisdom and faits accomplis.

"You're so sure," she said, hearing the sarcasm ugly in her voice, but not caring. "Good old mother instinct, is that it?"

Swept anew by fear, her eyes went hot and swelled with tears. Mac hated to see her cry, but she couldn't keep them from swamping in. "Well, don't blame me. Don't blame *me!*"

"Blame you for what? What are you talking about?" The stubbornness was gone; he sounded helpless. She stood there, unable to answer, her breath caught in her throat, looking into his round, open face, so earnest and eager to understand her. She yearned to tell him everything, everything about herself, and he would laugh at her self-suspicions and make her laugh, too. But supposing he recognized the truth in it? No. Better to be glad that he didn't understand, that he go on thinking the trouble was only because of the child and had nothing to do with her. Was all that she'd said and thought about Sooner excuses? Never mind. Let them stand and be her shield.

There was an eruption of noise. Barks, screeching, and the sound of shattering glass came from the infirmary. Mac jumped to the same conclusion she did, that Sooner had turned all his animals loose. He looked crestfallen, poor innocent, and she hadn't the heart to say I told you so. Together, they ran for the infirmary. The racket inside was deafening. But at first glance, it seemed that in spite of their frantic noise, all the animals were still caged. Sooner was cowering back against one wall, her hands over her ears, her eyes fixed upward. Elizabeth looked up, too, and saw perched atop a cupboard that cute woolly monkey Mac was treating for a cold. It was the cupboard where Mac kept empty jars and phials and beakers, and one after another, the monkey was hurling them at the cement floor, obviously delighted by the explosive results.

Elizabeth looked back at Sooner, whose eyes were now turned pleadingly toward the glowering Mac.

"I only went for to let him hole onto my hand," she wailed, "but he run loose from me—so quick!"

There was a crash nearly at Elizabeth's feet, and she skipped back from the flying glass. Mac strode forward to reach for the monkey, and had to dodge a flying bottle. Big Mac, befuddled by that tiny creature. Elizabeth's gaze returned to Sooner, and Sooner was looking at her, and their eyes held. It was as before, a moment engrossed and out of time. Both had been close to tears only minutes ago, but now they giggled, standing there in all the din, with Mac exasperated, and though they both tried very hard, they couldn't do a thing about it. They just went on looking at each other, she and Sooner, carried away by their helpless giggling.

...a haunted house" "look," ...said. They were all ... corner of the playground, and Scooter had been ... watching them.

"... mouse over by the ... rocks," Sally ... spooky, and there's a witch inside."

"... room," said Jean, "... somebody, if you don't ...

SOONER

That first day, the day she came, was the only day Sooner was scared. She liked taking the bath, with Elizabeth there, and being all warm and wet at the same time. But then the room took that sudden chill, and the shivering started up again. It made her remember how Elizabeth had looked downstairs when she'd stepped inside the big house, and that made her think of Old Mam and her saying to the sheriff how she'd come near to drowning the babe that was Sooner in the creek, and she slipped down in that slidy washtub and went under. But Elizabeth pulled her out so quick, Sooner figured she wouldn't do what Old Mam said. And after the ruckus in Mac's infirmary, when she and Elizabeth laughed so hard, she stopped being scared about anything.

Mac finally got hold of the creepy-crawly monkey and put him back in his cage, and the other animals hushed their noise, and while she and Elizabeth picked up all the broken glass, Mac began to think it was funny, too. Sooner like the way Mac laughed. It started kind of low, and then burst out of him, full and rocking like a live thing, and his eyes got all crinkled up at the corners.

Afterward, though, her own laughter turned back to almost crying. It was because of Little One. Mac had put him in a cage, and Sooner was sure he didn't want to be in there.

"Maybe your tame critters ain't sorried by it none," she said, "but Li'l-un, he's sorried somethin fierce."

89

Mac came over by her, his voice gone all soft and quiet. He said, "Little One isn't used to cars, Sooner. Let loose outside, he might get run over on the road."

Sooner looked in at Little One and knew it wasn't right for him to be in there. It brought an ache to her throat, and she had to sniffle up her nose. Elizabeth dabbed at Sooner's face with a hanky from her own pocket; Sooner couldn't ever remember what had happened to the one Elizabeth had given her in the house.

"Don't wipe your nose on your arm," she said to Sooner. Then to Mac, "Be consistent. The chipmunk isn't exactly tame, you know. And you did say the cages were for tamed animals."

"It's up to you, Sooner," Mac said. "If you want to take a chance on the cars . . ."

"Li'l-un, he's almighty quick," Sooner said. "He'll get along."

And so she got to take Little One outside, and right away he found a hole low down in the trunk of the oak tree and made himself a home in it. But Sooner watched him to be sure. There were lots of acorns around the oak so he didn't have to forage far, and the sound of the motorcars spooked him. The minute he heard one coming, he popped down his hole.

Elizabeth kept watch with her. Mac was finishing up Bird's perch. He came out with it, Bird clinging to it, about the time Sooner reached certainty that Little One would get along just fine. Right then, with Mac there, Elizabeth suddenly caught in her breath.

"The Telfers," she said to him. "They're coming for bridge tonight. I better call it off."

"Why?" he asked her.

Elizabeth's eyes turned away from Sooner. She opened her mouth, and closed it again.

"Everyone in Switzer'll be talking about it before long," Mac said. He smiled. "And you know how

Eleanor likes to be in on things. Why not do her the favor?"

"We aren't sure there's anything to be in on. Are we?" she asked. He was silent, looking at her. "Anyway," she finished, "it's so late I don't know what I could fix for dessert."

Must be special, that bridge tonight, Sooner thought, for Elizabeth to fix dessert. Old Mam only did it near to Christmas, and then she'd make sugar pie. Sooner's mouth watered, thinking of it.

"You could do sugar pie," she said to Elizabeth.

Elizabeth was surprised. Mac reached out and mussed Sooner's hair, almost dry now after that shampoo Elizabeth gave it. "Haven't had a sugar pie since I was little like you," he said to her.

"I've got your mother's old recipe somewhere," Elizabeth said. "But it always sounded too simple to be good."

"Oh, it's good," said Sooner. "Want I should show you how to do with it?"

"Well . . ." Elizabeth said. She smiled. "I guess you can read out the recipe to me, if you want." She started for the house.

Read? thought Sooner.

"Elizabeth," Mac said.

Elizabeth stopped and looked back at him. Then, she closed her eyes a moment. "Of course. Naturally. She can't read." She sighed another big sigh. "I should have known." She smiled at Sooner again, but this time it was an odd kind of smile, as if part of her was missing in it. "Well, then. Come along and show me, Sooner."

"I'll see to Bird for you," Mac said. "Until the pie's in the oven."

As Sooner followed Elizabeth toward the back door, she thought about reading. Old Mam had said you could learn reading in school, but Elizabeth had said only "we'll see" when she'd asked if she could go there. Sooner figured out now that "we'll see" meant yes, because reading sure mattered lots to Elizabeth, she could tell. She gave a little skip before she went up the back steps. She wanted more than ever to go to school, to learn reading for Elizabeth.

* * *

When the folks named Telfer came, it was after supper, and Sooner had already had her piece of sugar pie. It was as mouth-watering as Old Mam's since Sooner had remembered just right how to do with it. And after that, Elizabeth had taken Sooner upstairs to a big room she was to sleep in all by herself in a high bed. She had made her clean her teeth again with that little brush and had helped her into the ruffly night-shift that was soft and came clear to Sooner's ankles. And that was how she was, down in the parlor, when those folks came.

They didn't see her at first over by the couch because they took off their coats in the hallway. When they did see her, all the talking and laughing stopped, and they stared at Sooner. Mac came across the room and put his arm around her.

"This is Sooner Hawes," he said. "She's here to stay with us."

"For a while," Elizabeth said.

The lady, Eleanor, said, "No wonder you hung up on me and never called me back! I bet Mac was bringing her home right then." She whirled and hugged Elizabeth. "How marvelous!" she said. "How simply marvelous of you both to take an older child instead of a baby. Older children are so hard to place, they say."

"It isn't like that, Eleanor," Elizabeth said, pushing free of the other lady, and sounding the way she had when she'd told Sooner to use a hanky. "Not at all."

92

"I done showed Elizabeth how to do with sugar pie," Sooner told them. "Did you know they got a stove don't need stokin? And ain't no need to tote water, neither. And they's a box right there in the room, keeps cole as good as any root cellar. And all them lamps, they give off light with nary a match. Look how it does." She ran to the wall and flipped the thing Elizabeth called a switch, down and up, down and up, and the lights obliged by going off and on, off and on. "Did you ever see the like?" she asked those Telfers.

She stopped talking, and all of them were looking at her. Maybe she shouldn't have flipped that switch so fast. Maybe it was hard on the lamps.

The man, George, cleared his throat, and it sounded loud as Old Mam's shotgun in the quiet. "Elizabeth," he said, and then he cleared his throat again. "Elizabeth, I have to hand it to you. You're every bit as remarkable as Mac has always said you are."

Elizabeth looked at George, and then at Mac, and then at Sooner, biting her lip as if she'd hurt herself.

"Well," said Mac, and he clapped his hands together and rubbed them and picked up a chair to carry it to the round table in the center of the room. "Let's play cards, huh?"

The Telfers moved to the table, too, all silent now, but Elizabeth came over to Sooner. Her chin was held up high. Like William's straining at the bit, Sooner thought, and that was strange because Elizabeth had never seen William. Elizabeth reached out a hand to her, but never quite touched her.

"They're going to love your sugar pie, Sooner." She bent quickly to Sooner's ear, and whispered, "I sneaked a bite, and it's scrumptious." She turned, now, and gave Sooner a little push. "Stay up and watch awhile. You can see fine from the couch." And she

93

went to collect a chair from the dining room for the table.

So, Sooner sat on the couch and watched. She hadn't known how to think about bridge when Elizabeth explained it while they were fixing the pie. It had recalled to Sooner the time Old Mam went on the train to Louisville only never got there. Walker Hawes, Old Mam's man in olden days, had found some card-playing fools just like him on that train, and he'd rendered up to them every bitter cent he'd had in his pockets, so Old Mam had told, and they'd had to get off that train in New Albany and come back to Black Willow Creek flat broke. And all Old Mam had to show for going to Louisville on the Southern Railway was the straw sailor hat she'd ribboned the flowers to with her last piece of velvet. Blue straw flowers, she'd said they'd been, to match the velvet, and she'd dried them special, just for going to Louisville. Ever after, Old Mam had told Sooner, she'd known that cards were the tools of the devil. But as far as Sooner could see for looking now, they were only little pieces of shiny paper. Nor was the devil anywhere around. At least, she didn't think so. It was warm in the parlor, but not fiery warm the way Old Mam said it was down in Hades where the devil lived. It was warm, and the slip-slap-slip of the cards, the nonsense murmurs of the grownups made her sleepier and sleepier.

She felt herself lifted up, and buried her face away from the light into Mac's shoulder, and knew he was carrying her upstairs to the high bed. He set her down on it, and bent over and put his lips to her forehead, and covered her up with bedclothes, and left her there with the door ajar so she could hear the low voices from downstairs.

That bed was something. She sank into it until she thought she'd go clear down to the floor, and all of a sudden she was wide awake. Bird was resting on the perch on the table by the bed, his head tucked under his wing. He took to his perch straight off, she thought. Why couldn't she take to her new bed the same way? She squirmed around, and moved from side to side, but no matter what she did, the bed felt so soft she was scared to fall asleep for fear she'd sink in and stop breathing and not even know. Finally, she crawled out very quietly so nobody would hear, and dragged the fuzzy blanket with her, and curled up with it on the braided rug.

She found herself back in bed in the morning. They must have put her there, only she couldn't remember it. But it was very nice because when first light came, she leaned over the edge and with Bird saw the sun move across the braided rug, lighting it up one braid at a time, making the green, then the red, then the brown, then the green again, all bright as could be.

Afterward, she had to use soap on her face and brush her teeth again. Twice a day, said Elizabeth, though it seemed a mite foolish to Sooner.

When breakfast was done, with its eggs and piles of toast and butter and jam, enough to make a body sick if she didn't have care, Sooner and Elizabeth carried out the dishes. It was a lot of walking, first to set the table, then to clear it, just to eat. It had happened last night, too. Maybe it would happen every time.

She stood and watched while Elizabeth ridded up the dishes and began washing them. Elizabeth didn't take to it overmuch. She was full of sighs and frownings, and said she hated it.

"I can dry," Sooner offered. Elizabeth studied her a minute, then handed her a towel. "Fact is," Sooner said, reaching for the first saucer, "I could wash em for you, too. I done it for Ole Mam." She reached out and touched the spigot running hot. It did it upstairs, and it did it downstairs. "Tain't no chore, doin dishes with that kettle you got allus bubblin inside the walls. Why, the soap come outen a box like it was water itself!"

Elizabeth turned from the sink to stare at her. Then she leaned back and stared all around the kitchen, and smiled. "You're right. It's no chore at all." Quickly, before Sooner knew it was coming, Elizabeth reached and pulled her into a short hug. Sooner didn't have time to do likewise. Elizabeth stood back, again. "It must be wonderful," she said, "to find marvels everywhere you look. And they're there, if we'd only stop to notice." She smoothed Sooner's hair out of her eyes. The hug had made it come loose from the barrette. "Thank you, Sooner."

Sooner stared up at her. Old Mam never hugged her like that, nor touched her, either.

I done *give* somethin to Elizabeth, she thought, having to tell herself so to believe the glory of it. First time I done give somethin to anybody, ever.

Elizabeth smoothed the hair back again. "Tell you what," she said. "After we finish the dishes and make the beds, we'll go downtown and buy you a new barrette."

They went to the same big store where Sooner had gone with Mac, with the wooden floors that shook and the queer pipes that popped out little baskets after a swish that kept surprising Sooner, and they found the same lady to do for them. They bought two barrettes, in case she might lose one, the lady said, both made like little bows. And then, while Elizabeth was waiting for her change, the lady shook out from its folds a sunsuit for Sooner to see. It had a big apple stitched on it, and Sooner touched it with her finger, it was so pretty. Elizabeth touched it, too. "Oh," she said, "isn't that cute?" And before Sooner knew it, Elizabeth had bought her that sunsuit and one other, and some more of those soft-feeling underpants, and a red sweater, and another long shift for sleeping in, and some hankies, too, smaller than Elizabeth's, with blue polka dots and a face painted on that Elizabeth called Shirley Temple—all, all for Sooner's very own and smelling of the new smell.

The last thing Elizabeth let Sooner choose all by herself. It was a toy boat, painted blue and with a candle inside it, and Elizabeth told her that when the candle burned the boat would go putt-putt around the bathtub. Elizabeth said she would be taking a bath every night before bed in Switzer, and that the boat would make it fun. But Sooner knew the boat couldn't make it like that bath was yesterday, with Elizabeth.

While they were in the store, Elizabeth often called Sooner by name. When they were leaving, with all those packages in their arms, the lady at the store began to turn very pink; and as if she were mad about something, she said, "I'm speaking out of turn, I know, but I got to say it! The way you call your little girl is something shameful!" And she spun around and walked off back into the store.

"But she isn't—" Elizabeth started to say, and then she closed her lips tight. She glanced down at Sooner and moved on to the street door.

"Don't seem to me you call me shameful-like," Sooner said, trotting to keep up with Elizabeth. "Different from how Ole Mam does, but not shameful."

"That isn't what she meant," Elizabeth answered, and wouldn't say any more about it.

There was plenty to talk about, anyway. All the new and different things in the stores along the way home; and what's this street called; and who lives in that house, and that one over there?

"Goodness!" said Elizabeth to Mac at lunchtime. "She's wearing me out with all her questions!" Mac just grinned.

They did up the dishes again—there sure were lots

97

of dishes to do in Switzer—and then Elizabeth told Sooner to go play by herself. "I want to do some sewing," she said. But when Sooner saw the big whirring thing Elizabeth called a singer that did the sewing for her, she had to ask how. Elizabeth tried to show her, and then shooed her from the room. "Enough is enough!" she said.

Sooner stood at the top of the stairs, wondering what to play at. Out at the creek, she'd know. Except that more than likely she'd be helping Old Mam plant the corn. Behind her, in the room for sewing, Elizabeth was working the singer. Downstairs were all those things that Elizabeth had pointed to yesterday and had said she mustn't touch for fear they'd break: vases, and bowls, and even plates hanging on the wall. If she played down there, not even touching them, they might break. But on the wall along the staircase there was nothing at all to worry over.

She thought about jumping down the stairs, but what she really wanted to do was skid down them on the banister. It would be better than sliding on the mud after a rain into the creek, because the banister went so much higher. Only maybe Elizabeth wouldn't like that. She couldn't be sure, so she started leaping steps instead. She tried two steps at a time, and then found out that by holding onto the banister she could leap as many as three. She was thinking again of those kids up at Bead's Knob. But no matter how or where she tried, Sooner discovered, she couldn't make it feel the way it had looked for them.

All of a sudden, the singer stopped and Elizabeth came running. "Stop that banging!" she said. Sooner held very still halfway down the flight looking around and up at Elizabeth at the top of the stairs. Sooner hadn't seen that face on Elizabeth before: an angry face. Would she take a switch to her? When Old Mam looked like that, she'd sometimes send Sooner out to find the switch herself. Just the right one, she'd tell her. But Sooner couldn't remember any willows near the big house, so maybe Elizabeth wouldn't.

She didn't. Instead, as puzzling as it had been that first time in the bathtub and just the same, there was a strangeness between herself and Elizabeth, and the stairwell went cold. The anger wasn't in Elizabeth's face any more, but she wasn't smiling, either, not even the hiding smile. She just said, "If you *have* to jump down stairs, Sooner, please take off your shoes." She turned and went back into the sewing room, though the singer made no sound for a while. Sooner shivered. She didn't want to get whipped, but why hadn't she been, with Elizabeth all that angry? Sooner remembered the way Elizabeth had hugged her this morning, and how warm she'd felt with it. Sooner couldn't figure Elizabeth out. She'd have to think on her, some. The thought cheered her. She always had been one for puzzling out things. Old Mam had used to take her down for it until Sooner started keeping her puzzlements to herself. She'd long ago decided that it pleasured her more to ponder than to know.

The singer was going again. Sooner sat down on a step and did what Elizabeth said. She took off her shoes, and then thought what a fine idea it was because those new shoes felt very heavy on her feet. But she didn't *have* to jump again. She could slide on the banister. It would be quieter for Elizabeth. She tried it, sliding down and then running back up and sliding down again, silent in her socks. And even though she kind of missed the noise her shoes had made jumping, the sliding was faster and lots more fun.

Then, in the middle of a slide, a picture came to her of the way those kids had spread their arms like birds flying. With a shout, Sooner spread her arms— and toppled off onto the cabinet which stood under the stairs. No vase stood on it, so nothing was broken.

And it was worth the hurt, for again Elizabeth came running, and this time she kissed Sooner. To make it well, she said, and she smiled a *whole* smile. To Sooner, seeing it, it was the difference between the moon and the sun. And the kiss brushed against Sooner's skin with the softness of a squirrel's tail, only better, better than anything she'd ever known. She felt it move through her clear to her middle, where it lay hot and fluttering like a little bird. She longed to hold on to it, and she kept reliving that hurt over and over so to remember the kiss that came after.

That night at dinnertime, Elizabeth told Mac what had happened, and he said he'd rig up a swing for Sooner in the oak tree. It's where he used to swing, he said. Elizabeth told about other things in the day, and Mac told his things, and Sooner thought that all the talking was just fine, especially when she was asked to tell things, too.

Later on, when Elizabeth brought in the chocolate pudding, which Sooner found she liked almost as much as ketchup, Elizabeth said she had an announcement to make. Her face was bright, as if it were a thing to celebrate. She said she'd been thinking about it all afternoon, and she'd decided Sooner should have a new name.

"Don't be ridiculous," Mac said, and he reached for the cream to pour onto his pudding.

Elizabeth stopped a moment before she sat down again at the table, and the smile disappeared. "It is not ridiculous, Mac. Even the girl at the store today made a comment."

Sooner was watching both of them, much taken with the idea of a new name, especially if Elizabeth wanted her to have one.

"The implication isn't all that common, Elizabeth," Mac was saying, now sounding very crochety. "The girl's probably country. But nobody'd think twice about it, in town. You didn't. Anyway, what're you trying to do, make her over completely?"

Elizabeth looked at Mac what seemed to Sooner to be a long time, but he just ate his pudding. Elizabeth swallowed hard, though she hadn't a thing in her mouth, and she laid down her spoon and went to the kitchen.

"Eat your pudding," Mac said to Sooner, finishing his.

So Sooner did, wondering about the queer silence. But what she wondered about most was what her new name would be if she could have one.

She was still thinking about it when Elizabeth tucked her into the too-soft bed and said good night. Elizabeth had that friend named Eleanor and the sheriff had his lady named Selma and there were those names in Old Mam's Bible: Ruth and Esther and Jezebel.

Sooner turned and turned again in the bed. She listened for sound from downstairs, but there was none. It was strange, because Mac and Elizabeth had had so much to say when she'd been with them at the dinner table. One more thing to ponder, the same as Elizabeth was.

Keeping very quiet, Sooner scootched from between the smooth sheets, and pulling the blanket after, she curled up on the rug. Now she felt right.

She counted over the day, and remembered how Elizabeth's hands had been, cornering the sheets when she'd made the beds, so quick and right with nothing wasted in the way they moved. She remembered the things carried home from the store, each one refolded now and laid in drawers. She remembered skidding down the banister, and the kiss that came after. To-morrow, there'd be a swing, and she knew she'd like it because Mac used to swing when he was little. She remembered how she'd given Elizabeth something in the kitchen after breakfast, and remembered the glory of then. She figured it had to be the best day in all her life. She began searching her mind for something else to give.

The next morning, she was still on the rug when Elizabeth came in to wake her up. It sorried Sooner to have missed watching with Bird the sun cross the colors of the rug. Elizabeth was fussed to find her out of bed again. That night, instead of leaving her after tucking her in, Elizabeth drew a chair up to the side of the bed, and opened a book, and began to read to her. Sooner went to sleep right in the middle of it, so that the next night, Elizabeth had to turn back and read some things all over again, or so she said. And this is what she did every night after that. She read lots of things, and from the Bible, too. The New Testament, Elizabeth called it, because Sooner asked Elizabeth, one day when it occurred to her that Elizabeth might know, what pitch was, and brimstone, and told her about Old Mam's Bible talk. Elizabeth seemed kind of angry at it, but never did explain. She just started reading to her the soft words in her soft voice at night, and they made Sooner feel warm and petted, and she never had to leave the bed for the floor to get to sleep again. Every morning she and Bird could watch the sun cross the beautiful rug.

Beautiful was a word she'd never heard until Elizabeth used it one day when May came in, and she was talking about the catalpa trees all over town that had white clumps of flowers crowning each branch. Mac called them those trashy catalpas, but even he liked them, he said, in spring. They made Sooner think of the apple tree at the foot of the lane. She wished she could see it come into bloom. But it wasn't a sadness to her, because of the catalpas.

In fact, there was only one sadness in being away from Black Willow Creek, and that was her worry for William. He'd be missing her, Sooner was sure.

Old Mam never would put up with his stubbornness, and he was getting old and slow. Once or twice she tried to think how it would be in Switzer in the summertime. She wouldn't be able to cool off in the creek nor play the slipping game on the bottom stones, but Switzer wasn't like Black Willow Creek in so many ways, maybe it wouldn't matter.

She spent lots of time in the infirmary, sometimes with Mac and sometimes alone, and she was always careful how she went about opening any of those cages. She helped Billy Sanger when he came after school, and if he forgot she would clean the cages by herself. Mac said she did such a good job he was thinking of firing Billy, and that made Sooner feel very proud.

Mac took to calling her Puss, and when they were together he would flip her hair or tweak her nose, and those things always made her giggle. At the end of a day that he was gone, she would listen for the truck and run out to him, and he would swing her up and whirl her around, laughing and hugging her. She was puzzled, the first time, when he stopped, and looking toward the back door he set her down. Sooner turned, and saw Elizabeth standing there. Then she smiled at them, the smile Sooner thought of as the one she smiled to hide behind because some of her wasn't in it. Evenings after that, Elizabeth wouldn't be at the back door, and the whirling and the laughing would go on and on. But it was Elizabeth's hug Sooner longed for. She would have liked to ask somebody about that: why it was you wanted most what you had the least of.

Hardly a day passed when Sooner didn't name names in her head. She had more names to try, now, for she'd learned that Elizabeth had friends besides Eleanor. JoAnn and Harriet, for two. And there were those pretty names out of Elizabeth's Bible, like Mary

103

and Martha and Miriam. Of course, Sooner knew right along the new name she really wanted. Elizabeth. But she never quite dared name herself that.

Saturdays, she and Elizabeth and Mac would all three get into the truck and go off somewhere with their lunch packed in a basket. Sometimes Saturdays were swell, and sometimes they weren't. Swell was a word she'd learned from Edwin. He came from down the street and had a canary with a wing that had got broken like Bird's.

It was Mac who thought up a picnic, and to begin with, Elizabeth didn't want to go. She said it was a lot of work, and that there were jobs to do around the house, and besides it always rained on picnics. But Mac had no truck with that.

"Pshaw!" he said, like Old Mam. "Sooner and I'll fry the chicken, won't we, Sooner. And there's not a sign of rain. It's a beautiful day, and a beautiful spring, and you're going to see it," he said to Elizabeth, and he mussed her hair, but she didn't giggle the way Sooner always did.

Elizabeth still didn't want to go on a picnic, but after Mac banged the frying pan on the stove getting it ready, and started spattering grease, Elizabeth told him he was the winner. "For this round, anyway," she said, and she shooed them both out of the kitchen.

That Saturday, they had their lunch in Marengo. Afterward, they went over to a place where steps led down right into the ground. Lots of people were gathered there, and some girls and boys all about Sooner's size. A lady kept trying to bunch them up, making Sooner think of a bobwhite mother with her covey of chicks. Elizabeth told Sooner, when she asked her, that it was a school group, and that the lady was a teacher.

The kids were laughing, and running, and once a boy shoved into Sooner, but when he looked at her, he said, "I don't know you," and ran back to the others. Then a man came and said the tour was going to start, and the teacher called out, "Everybody find his buddy and hold hands!"

"What's a buddy?" Sooner asked.

"That's a friend to be with, and she keeps an eye on you, and you keep an eye on her, just to be safe," Elizabeth said.

"Just like us," Mac said. But Sooner knew it wasn't, because all the rest were in two's, and they were three.

The man led the way down the stairs, and into a big cave right under the hill where they'd eaten. It was cold and spooky the way the kerosene lanterns threw moving shadows into the blackness. The other kids were quiet, until one of the boys howled like a wild dog, and they all started screaming, and the buddies clung together, their arms around each other.

"They're silly, aren't they," Elizabeth said.

Why did she say that? Sooner wondered. Wasn't that what buddies were for?

Up on top of the ground again, all those kids got lined up, still two by two, to get into a bus. As it drove away, Sooner could hear them singing.

But the three of them didn't sing in the truck going back to Switzer, and without all those kids, it was very quiet. Sooner remembered how loud it had been with them in the cave, so that the man who talked couldn't do it very well. But he did tell some about the underground river. And looking up at the dark ceiling, Sooner had finally figured out what pitch was, so she decided to be glad she'd gone to Marengo Cave.

"I know!" said Mac, giving Sooner and Elizabeth both a start. "Next week, we'll have a picnic on the river."

"That'll be nice," Elizabeth said. "Won't it, Sooner?"

105

Sooner only nodded her head. But between that Saturday and the next, she thought a lot about going down to the river for their picnic and guess it would be nice, as Elizabeth had said.

One time when Edwin came over, she told him about it.

"My big sister's going on a picnic, too," he said. "She's having a birthday party, and they're all going on a picnic."

"What's a birthday party?" Sooner asked him.

"That's when you invite people, and they all bring you presents. Let me be on the swing, now," he said.

"Iffen I bring one of them presents," Sooner said as she got off the seat, "can I come?"

"Nope," said Edwin, climbing onto the seat. "I can't either. My mother says it's only for kids in school."

Saturday morning, Sooner was in the kitchen with Elizabeth, putting things in the basket just right as Elizabeth handed them to her, and then they went out the back door to the truck, so it wasn't until they drove down Court Street that she saw all the kids in front of Edwin's house. Every one of them had a box tied up with ribbon.

Presents, Sooner thought. That's what they are. I sure'd like to see what all's inside them boxes.

She turned around and knelt on the seat to keep looking at them through the back window until the truck turned the corner.

It took a while to get to the river. When they did, they picked a grassy spot high, high above it, and sat on a blanket there, and ate their fried chicken. Every time a car passed, Sooner thought maybe it was those other kids. But it never was.

The river shined in the sun like Black Willow Creek, only it was much wider. The bank below them was steep and with no path down to the water that Sooner could see. The river curved in a sweep, so

106

that it seemed to run right under their feet and out again. Mac called it Horseshoe Bend, and across was Kentucky, he said, the fields lying low and spread out like the patchwork quilt she and Old Mam slept under on coldest nights. When the wind blew hard from Kentucky, it brought the sweet smell of good bluegrass. Mac said so, though Elizabeth poked him in the arm, and said, "Oh, come on!"

And then Mac started talking about how in the winter past the bank of Horseshoe Bend had caught the water up when it flooded, and how the town below named Leavensworth had been washed away.

"Leavenworth," Elizabeth said, her voice sharp but laughing, too. "Stop saying it with an *s*. You Hoosiers! It isn't spelled that way."

Sooner recalled that she'd worried that the cabin would be washed away by the creek in January, but Old Mam had said it never had nor ever would because her Walker, he'd had care to build above the high-water mark.

"Them folks at Leavenworth," Sooner said, thinking to not say it with an *s*, "how's come—"

"*Those* folks," said Elizabeth.

Sooner kept forgetting about that, all the different words Elizabeth wanted her to use.

"How's come what, Puss?" Mac asked.

"How's come they didn't put their places up here, stead of down there?"

"Because they weren't as smart as you are," he said. "But they learned, and they're building a new Leavenworth"—he said it slowly, tipping his head and raising a brow, and grinning at Elizabeth so she'd know he hadn't said it with an *s*—"not far from here, way above the river."

"With that New Deal money?" Sooner asked.

"How do you know about New Deal money?" Elizabeth asked, looking very surprised.

107

Before Sooner could tell her about Jim Seevey, Mac said, "Because she's so smart."

Not as smart as all them—*those* school kids, I bet, Sooner thought. They can read. And they have birthday parties and presents and buddies.

"Can I go to school?" she asked.

Mac and Elizabeth looked a long time at each other, then Elizabeth turned her head away and looked down at the river.

"We'll see, Puss," Mac said. He leaned over and tweaked her nose, and then began packing up the picnic basket to go back to Switzer.

So, on days that weren't Saturday, Sooner went on watching the school kids from the front window of the house after breakfast. They had their books strapped up, and they carried little red and blue pencil cases. She'd watch them go to and fro at noon, and then back home again in the afternoon, when she'd stand on the lawn as they'd go by, but they never talked to her much. The girls walked close together, whispering, and the boys were always throwing one another to the ground or tossing a funny-looking ball, their knickers humming as they ran.

In between, on those days, when she wasn't in the infirmary, she'd help Elizabeth set the table for lunch, or swing in the yard. She liked the swing even more than she had the banister, especially after she got used to feeling upside down inside. In fact, she got so she wanted it, and would swing as high as she could just to feel it. If he was working out back, Mac would sometimes come and give her a big push. When Elizabeth would come out and work in the flower bed, Sooner wished Elizabeth would push her, too, but she knew pushing wasn't much fun. She had to push Edwin, because Elizabeth said so. Edwin was only half as big as she was, and it was dumb.

Once, she asked Billy Sanger about school. All he

108

said was that he hated it, but he never really told why. Since Billy could be mean to Mac's critters and pull their tails, Sooner didn't like him very much, anyway, and she just kept on hoping for school someday. But Elizabeth would still only say, "We'll see."

One afternoon, though, it changed, for after saying that, Elizabeth said, "Oh, Sooner!" and sighed. And then, she sat Sooner down at the living-room table with a big sheet of paper and a pencil, and began showing Sooner letters. So she could read for herself, Elizabeth told her. It was fun all right, but all the other kids learned reading in school. So she finally had to switch her mind around on that "we'll see." It couldn't mean yes, after all.

MAC

Over the squee-squaw of Sooner on the swing and the dull clatter of Elizabeth doing the supper dishes, Mac heard a car door slam. The sound of the swing died. He set aside the book, and opened the door to see the sheriff's car out front. Mac moved along the veranda until he could see Phil talking to Sooner.

She was still seated on the swing, her legs tucked back under her, ready to push off again. Phil went around back of her, and hauled her backward and high, and then let her go with a push. She squealed with delight, and stuck her feet straight out in front of her, pulling on her arms to sail as far as she could. She loved the swing. On her return, Phil gave her one more push, and came across the lawn and up the steps to Mac. He took off his hat and smoothed back his hair.

"Wonderful what decent food can do," he said. "I bet she's gained ten pounds, and her hair has a shine to it. Quite a change."

Mac nodded, studying Phil uneasily, wondering why he was here. Mac had done his best not to push Elizabeth beyond the day-to-day understanding they'd made when he'd brought Sooner home. He had the feeling that if things were just let run on, habit might make the decision for her. Was Phil looking for that decision tonight?

"Can I talk to you and Elizabeth for a few minutes?" Phil asked.

It sounded as if that's what he was here for, all right. But there was nothing to do but invite him in.

"Sure," Mac said, and he turned and preceded Phil into the house. "Sit down. I'll get her. How about some coffee?"

"Only if you've got it made. I can't stay." He perched on the edge of the couch, seeming very much on official business. Mac hesitated.

"I can probably find a free afternoon, next week," he said. "If the weather's any good, how about we pile your hounds into the truck and give 'em a run over by Lukemayer's place?"

"Fine idea," Phil said. He grinned. "They need it, all that winter fat to get rid of."

Elizabeth was drying her last batch as Mac entered the kitchen. He went over to the pot on the stove and hefted it. Plenty left. He got down cups and saucers. "Phil's dropped by," he said.

She set down the half-dried pan and looked at him.

"He takes sugar," Mac reminded her.

She set out a tray and put the sugar bowl on it, while Mac poured coffee, and they loaded the cups on the tray together. He picked it up.

110

"Where's Sooner?" she asked.

"Still out on the swing," he said. So she feared the same thing he did.

He moved ahead of her toward the living room. Phil stood up as Elizabeth followed Mac in. She hadn't taken time to remove her apron.

"Hi," Phil said.

"There's some cake left, Phil. Would you like a piece?" she asked.

He shook his head, smiling, and they all sat down and Phil helped himself to sugar. "Like I told Mac, I can't stay. Just before I came over, I had a call from the CCC. The commander's raising hell with me." He caught himself. "Sorry, Elizabeth." He sighed, and took a long gulp of coffee. "Good. Sure is better than mine."

"Why's the commander angry with you?" Elizabeth asked.

"His boys've latched onto a supply of bootleg." Phil chuckled wryly. "He figures it's my fault. Laid into me for not doing my job." He looked at Mac. "I'd guess Jim's trying to make hay while the sun shines, but I can't overlook it. A little easy whiskey, that's a convenience for everybody, and if it keeps the temperance ladies happy to vote the county dry . . ." he shrugged. "But once the federals get riled, and riled at me, too, we'll have the excise down on us in no time. And that means trouble all around. So, I've got to go see him—tonight, before he tries selling any more out there." He drank some more coffee.

Mac wished to hell he'd get to it, whatever he'd come for. Mac felt as if hidden dynamite was about to explode, and they weren't prepared. He and Elizabeth were hardly talking at all, these days, except when Sooner was with them and things could seem at least to be easy and right.

"What's too bad is that the commander didn't call

111

me earlier," Phil was going on, at last. "I haven't any proof that Mrs. Hawes is Jim's moonshiner, but it's pretty common knowledge. And this trouble out at the CCC camp would've given me some real ammunition to throw at her this afternoon."

Mac glanced at Elizabeth to catch her eyes flickering away from him, and the squeak of the swing came loudly from the yard.

"I'm not here to pressure you two, so don't look like that," Phil said, in that soft way of his. "You've gotten this far along, but I know it takes time. For all three of you." He smiled. "Though I just inquired with Sooner, and she seems pretty content. I asked her if she wants to go back to Black Willow Creek, and you should have seen her face fall. She finally said, 'Ain't yet seed the full moon here in Switzer!' Any minute, I thought she'd start crying."

Mac took a first long sip of coffee, grown cold now, hoping to hid his relief. It might sound a silly excuse for Sooner to give, but at least it was an excuse to stay. He'd never had the courage to ask her himself. And he imagined Elizabeth hadn't asked her, either, though maybe for different reasons. He resolved to remember to let Sooner stay up, next full moon.

"The thing is," Phil was going on, but hesitantly, "well, I said it to Mac when you first took Sooner in, Elizabeth. I want to leave the way open for her to go back home—it must seem home to her, no matter how it looks to us. And I can't do that, once she's been declared a ward of the county. Of course, when—or if—I know you all want to make this arrangement permanent, it'll be simple. A hearing in chambers, and that's that."

Mac could feel Elizabeth stiffen halfway across the room from him.

"I meant it when I said I wasn't going to pressure you," Phil continued easily. "But the old woman is doing it to me. I've been telling her right along that she'd just have to wait awhile. That I haven't made up my mind whether to make application to the court or not. And then here she comes, busting in on me a couple of hours ago, full of fight and saying she's got to have Sooner back for choring."

Elizabeth made a small noise. Mac saw she was sitting straight up in her chair, her face indignant. "How does that show feeling? If all she thinks of her is that she's some kind of slavey or something!"

Phil smiled at her placatingly. "All country kids are expected to chore, Elizabeth."

"Well, yes, of course. And she does chores, here— sets the table, and makes her own bed . . ."

Mac had to smile. "When she's reminded enough."

"Yeah, well, anyway," Phil said, "I've been talking big with Mrs. Hawes about my investigating things. Which I'm not, but—I do know she's never sent Sooner to school. This afternoon, I got rid of her by pointing that out." He grinned a bit. "I told her she'd been breaking the law all these years, and she left right smartly." The grin died, and Phil took a deep breath. "But I know, because I've driven by here daytimes and seen her out there on the swing— I know she still isn't going to school. And when Mrs. Hawes finds that out, which she could, easily enough . . . well, it puts me square in the middle, doesn't it."

Mac knew he mustn't answer Phil. Because things weren't at all right and easy, yet; not for any of them; not by a long shot. No, this time it had come from Elizabeth. He looked over at her, waiting, and he was suddenly full of the conviction that everything hinged on this.

"Yes," Elizabeth said, her voice sweetly mild. "Of course, it does put you in the middle, Phil. I'll see about it right away."

In the release of tension, Mac wanted to shout his love for her.

Phil was rising to leave. They saw him to the door. And then, before Elizabeth followed him down the veranda steps to bring Sooner in for bed, she murmured as if Mac weren't there: "After all . . . school will be out in no time."

SOONER

The day after the night the sheriff came, Elizabeth took Sooner to see the principal of the school. Sooner could hardly believe it. Elizabeth had said "we'll see" for so long that Sooner had stopped asking.

Her hair was a little longer, now, since it was near the middle of May, and Elizabeth trimmed it to even it off, and had Sooner put on the plaid dress with the white collar, and they polished up her shoes.

They walked over in the middle of the morning. There were lots of kids in the yard, and Elizabeth said they were having recess. Some of the girls were hopping over twirling ropes. Sooner'd never seen that before, and though she tried very hard, she couldn't make out the sayings they were shouting to keep time with. Anyway, Elizabeth pulled her on up the steps and inside.

School was big, like the store, with wooden floors, too. But there were long hallways, and lots of rooms, and a smell of its own.

The principal smiled at Sooner, and then listened while Elizabeth explained. "She can count, Miss Varney," Elizabeth said, "and even add and subtract a little. And she's learning the alphabet now, and can almost print her own name."

Though she hadn't told Elizabeth yet, every time Sooner practiced printing S-O-O-N-E-R, she thought what a waste of time it was, because before long her name wouldn't be Sooner any more, if she could just make up her mind.

"I know school is almost over," Elizabeth went on, "but she's really so eager to come. I thought maybe she could just sit in on a class until the end of the term. I'm sure she'll behave herself, even though most of it'll be way over her head."

"As long as she enjoys it, I see no reason why not," said the principal. "There's only two and a half more weeks, after all. Let's see—she's nine, you said. That would put her in fourth grade, but—well, under the circumstances, I think third might be better. I'll speak with Mrs. Henderson. She teaches third grade. But of course she'll be agreeable. Sooner can start right in tomorrow morning."

As they were leaving, Miss Varney said to Elizabeth, "I must tell you, Mrs. McHenry, what a wonderful thing it is that you and the doctor are doing. It's terrible when a child is permitted to be so deprived."

"Oh, no!" Elizabeth answered quickly. "You don't understand. We—*I'm* not a do-gooder at all. It just sort of happened, really."

But the principal only smiled and patted Elizabeth on the arm. "Modest, too. We could do with more like you in this world, Mrs. McHenry! Aren't you a lucky little girl, Sooner!"

At which Elizabeth took a deep breath and walked Sooner down the hall and out the door. Outside, she muttered, "First Eleanor, and then Reverend Campbell, and now her. And all it does is make me feel guilty!"

But Sooner was just feeling lucky, the way that Miss Varney had said. Tomorrow, she'd be walking to school with the others, and walking home again, and whispering with those girls maybe, and maybe she'd even see those kids from Bead's Knob. All the way home she hung on Elizabeth's hand and pretended she was skipping rope, as Elizabeth called it. And she reminded Elizabeth that she needed a pencil case. She wanted a green one.

But the next morning, it wasn't quite like that, Sooner discovered. Because Elizabeth insisted on walking her to school, to help her find the right room and everything, Elizabeth said. And all the way, she kept telling Sooner things. She was to raise her hand real high for the teacher to see when she wanted to go to the bathroom and the teacher would show her where. Elizabeth had already told Sooner to say it that way: go to the bathroom, instead of saying, like Old Mam, to make water. And Sooner was to be sure to use the toilet paper, and did she have her hanky with her? And she mustn't speak in the classroom unless spoken to, but she mustn't be afraid of asking the teacher questions, either. And the teacher's name was Mrs. Henderson. Hen-der-son. And all she *really* needed to remember was just to do whatever the other children did. And Elizabeth would be waiting at eleven forty-five to bring her home for lunch.

"I can find my way," Sooner said. "Sides, all them other kids will be there to walk with."

"Maybe so," said Elizabeth, "but I'll be here anyway, just for today." And by that time, they were at school.

The teacher met Sooner at the door to the room, and led her to a desk of her own. Then, after the bell, she had Sooner stand up and tell the class her name. It looked like an awful lot of faces to Sooner, but she did see one she recognized, the girl from over by Bead's Knob. The teacher called her Judith Ann. Sooner noticed her, because when she stood up, Judith

116

Ann leaned over and said something to another girl, and the teacher had to tell her not to talk.

By the time recess came, Sooner was getting tired of trying so hard to sit still. They had had arithmetic, but it was with double numbers and Sooner couldn't figure it out. Then came penmanship. While all the rest practiced what the teacher said were push-pulls and ovals, Sooner printed S-O-O-N-E-R. She didn't mind, because that morning she'd completely forgotten to choose a new name to try for the day. Elizabeth had said she mustn't talk in class, so she didn't, but all around her she could hear giggles and whispering.

When the bell rang, everybody ran outside, and Sooner ran after them. One of the girls—her name was Jean—had a long rope for skipping, and right away she and another girl began to turn it and the others lined up to go through. Sooner got at the end of the line, jumping a little in place so that when her turn came she'd remember how. But it looked harder than she'd thought, because they did other things at the same time.

"Teddy bear, teddy bear, turn around;
Teddy bear, teddy bear, touch the ground;
Teddy bear, teddy bear, tie your shoe;
Teddy bear, teddy bear, twenty-three skidoo!"

That's what each called out in turn, as one girl would run out and another would run in.

Judith Ann came up late, and pushed Sooner out of line. "That's my place," she said. "Anyway, there's already too many!"

Sooner stood where she was and watched, feeling each jump each girl made in her own legs, wishing she could jump, too. After a while, Jean suddenly thrust her end of the rope at Sooner. "You can turn if you want." Sooner ran forward and took the rope, and Jean moved to the front of the line, shouting, "My turn! My turn!"

Turning the rope had looked easy, but it wasn't. It wobbled, and went two curves at a time, and everybody groaned.

"I told you she was dumb," said Judith Ann. "If she can't even write her own name!" She grabbed away the rope. "I'll do it!" she said. And the rope spun around, hitting the ground again and again with a fine slap, and Jean began jumping.

"I know, I know!" said the girl at the other end:

> "Rooms for rent,
> Inquire within;
> When Jean moves out,
> Let Sooner move in!"

Sooner wasn't sure what was meant. Jean had run out. The others were all nudging each other and giggling. Finally, one of them shoved her into the center of the rope. "Well, go on, if you want to so much!"

The rope came around, and Sooner jumped, but somehow it whipped into her legs instead of hitting the ground. It stung like Old Mam's willow switch, and Judith Ann and the girl at the other end both doubled over with laughing. Sooner kept jumping even though the rope didn't move.

"That's mean," a girl named Sally said. Sally had long black hair, and Sooner had seen her in class rising up from her seat and tilting her head way back and smoothing her hair down so that when she sat again she was sitting on the ends of it, and then she would tip her head forward and the hair would spring free. Sooner wished she could do that, but her hair wasn't long enough, she knew, and it wasn't black, anyway.

"Let me go again," Sooner said now. "I can do it!"

"No, you can't! No, you can't! Dummy! Get out of the way!" the others said.

So Sooner spent the rest of recess watching and jumping in time with the others, hoping that they'd see how high she could go, but nobody seemed to notice.

Elizabeth was waiting at lunchtime. Judith Ann always brought her lunch with her, the way all the county kids did, Sooner had learned, and she was opening up her lunch box on the steps as Sooner came out. Judith Ann watched Sooner go to Elizabeth, and said, "I bet you came after her 'cause you think she might run off!"

Run off? Why should she run off? Sooner looked up at Elizabeth, puzzling over this, to see that she was smiling at Judith Ann. "No," Elizabeth said. "Of course not."

"You gonna 'dopt her?" asked Judith Ann. "She's awful dumb, you know."

Elizabeth stopped smiling. She took Sooner's hand, and they started toward the street. "Come on, honey," she said. "I've got lunch waiting." When they got to the sidewalk and turned for home, she said, "Now! Tell me all about it. Did you skip rope the way you wanted?"

"It's hard!" said Sooner. And she talked all the rest of the way home about those push-pulls and ovals and double numbers. It wasn't until lunch was over that she remembered to ask what 'dopt meant, but Elizabeth told her not to pay any attention to that Judith Ann Drummond and just to forget about it, and she let Sooner walk back to school by herself.

In the afternoon, they had some geography, and there was art, and singing, too. Sooner liked singing, once she could remember the words. At recess, the others didn't jump rope for very long, because Jean asked, "Who's brave enough to go past the haunted house with me, after school?"

"I am! I am! I am!" three of the girls answered. One of them was Sally.

"What's a haunted house?" Sooner asked. They were all in a corner of the playground, and Sooner had been standing by, watching them.

"It's that house over by the railroad tracks," Sally told her. "It's spooky, and there's a witch inside."

"Holy cow," said Jean, "you *are* dumb, if you don't know about the haunted house!"

Sooner didn't ask what a witch was, though she wanted to.

Jean was still talking. "Neat. We'll all meet at the side door when the bell rings, and then we go to find sticks." But she wasn't looking at Sooner when she said. it. Could Sooner go, too? She wasn't sure.

After school, she watched where Sally went and followed her, and that way she found the side door. She'd wondered ever since recess if Judith Ann would be going, but she wasn't there, just Jean and Sally and two others, named Marjorie and Phyllis.

Sally saw Sooner come up. "Can she come?" she asked the rest.

Jean shrugged. "I guess so."

So they all went down the school steps and to the street and walked right through town. Somehow, the other four were in a little bunch or two by two, giggling and whispering, just the way Sooner had seen girls coming home from school, and she had to walk behind, kind of skipping from side to side to see if she could get into the bunch, too, but she couldn't. Anyway, they'd said she could come, and she was as brave as they were, going to the haunted house.

They turned down a street Sooner had never been on, and the girls spread out, looking for sticks, so Sooner did the same thing. But she watched to see what sticks the others found so she'd get the right kind. Her heart was beating very hard because she was scared she wouldn't find one at all, and then they'd tell her to go on home. Finally, everybody got a stick, even Sooner.

"Gee, you got a neat one!" Marjorie said, looking at Sooner's. "Want to trade?"

So she changed sticks with Marjorie. And then the others all ran giggling farther down the street, and Sooner had to run fast to catch up with them.

Since Sally had said it was near the railroad tracks, Sooner wondered if maybe Old Mam had been mixed up, and if maybe the haunted house was that funny-looking station, but it wasn't. It was at the end of the street, sitting behind a high picket fence made of iron. The house was tall and dark brown, and the windows looked black and without any curtains that Sooner could see.

The other girls stood huddled together, peering between the pickets but not touching them.

"Is she anywhere around?" Phyllis asked, her voice low and not giggly any more. She must mean the witch, Sooner thought.

"She's inside, dopey," Jean said. "She's always inside, *guarding*—you know that." Then, she said to Sally, "You first."

"Why me?" Sally asked, her eyes big. "You go first," she said to Marjorie.

"I dare you," said Jean, looking at Marjorie.

"Well, I double-dare you," Marjorie said back.

"That's not fair," Jean said.

"Yes, it is!" Marjorie and Phyllis and Sally all said. "You've got to go first, now!"

Jean turned and looked at the haunted house, and shivered, and the others kept saying, "Double-dare, double-dare!"

"Promise to come right after me?" Jean asked. Everybody nodded.

She took good hold of her stick. "Remember," Phyllis told her, "you have to hit every one, or the witch'll grab you!"

Jean started to run very hard, holding her stick out so that its tip hit the fence, and it made a big clatter all the time she ran. Before Sooner knew it, the others were all running after Jean and doing with their sticks what Jean did, until the fence rang with the noise.

Sooner looked hard at the haunted house, but couldn't see the witch anywhere, and she ran, too, holding her stick out, and watching to make sure it hit every picket. The stick almost flew from her hand, and she had to slow down. The fence was still clattering from all the other sticks when she started, but toward the end, her stick was the only one. She reached the end of the fence, proud she'd done it, and glad the witch hadn't grabbed her, and then she saw she was alone. Where were the others? Had the witch grabbed them? Sooner looked down the cross street and caught a last glimpse of Sally's red skirt going out of sight around the corner beyond.

All at once, Sooner felt a quivering beneath her feet and a rumbling which grew and grew. The witch was coming to grab her, she was certain, but she couldn't run away. She spun around to stare at the haunted house, and then something screamed and roared behind her. She spun around again, and saw it: big and black and moving by her on its silver tracks. It wasn't the witch. It was a train. She didn't know how she knew it, but she did. It was a train, with people waving at her from inside high-up windows. That train was something. It rumbled on and on, and the wind blew, and smoke came out of a stack from the front of it, and it was something wonderful. She stood and watched it all go by, waving her stick back at the people, and after it passed she waited a very long time, hoping another would go by. But it didn't.

She wasn't sure how to get to the house on Court Street, so she decided to go back to school and go from there. That meant she had to pass the haunted house and its fence again. After looking all over for the witch and not finding her, Sooner set herself the way Jean had, and held out her stick, and ran as fast as she could. She touched every picket just fine, and made a big clatter, and when she was done she kept on running all the way back to school.

She had started from school for the house on Court Street when Elizabeth came toward her.

"Sooner! Oh, Sooner, I've been so worried, where have you been?" She crouched down in front of Sooner, and held her by the shoulders. "I've nearly lost my mind, looking for you," she said, giving Sooner a little shake, and Sooner thought Elizabeth was going to hug her, but she didn't.

"I done been to the haunted house," Sooner said, almost crowing with it. "And I done just what them others did, and the witch, she didn't grab me, and there was a train!"

There was a moment, and then Elizabeth stood up, and sliding her hand along Sooner's arm she took Sooner's hand and threw away her stick.

"Don't you ever do that again!" she said, pulling Sooner back along Court Street. She sounded mad. "From now on, you come straight home from school, before you go anywhere else!"

"Can I go see the train again?" Sooner asked.

"We'll see," said Elizabeth, still sounding mad. Sooner hoped this "we'll see" wouldn't take as long as the one for school had, but she had the feeling that it might.

* * *

Always after that, Sooner came straight home from school. But that meant there was never anywhere to go, later, because Jean was the only one who walked home Sooner's way, and Jean was always with somebody else. Anyway, Jean didn't have to come straight home. She said her mother didn't care.

Every morning, Sooner went to school believing that today would be different. She learned some about how to add double numbers, and the teacher let her do Palmer method when the others did, and Judith Ann and Jean stopped calling her dumb because the teacher told them to. But it never did get different, not really, even though Elizabeth bought her a skipping rope of her own, a stripey one, and even though she jumped with it every day in the schoolyard thinking the others would see how good she was. Sometimes, she'd get tired jumping by herself, and then she'd just watch. Once she went over to the corner by the building to see the boys play marbles, but they sent her away because she was a girl. And every afternoon, she walked home from school by herself.

Most times, when she'd get there, the house smelled like heaven—or at least like what Sooner reckoned heaven ought to smell like—with cookies Elizabeth had cooling just out from the oven. No matter how often Elizabeth warned her, Sooner never could wait long enough and would end up shifting that first hot cookie very fast from hand to hand to keep from getting burned. Elizabeth always called her a greedy little girl, and then they both would laugh. Sometimes there was gingerbread, and that smelled best of all. It got so Sooner's mouth began watering before she'd be halfway home, and she tried to think about that instead of how she didn't have anybody to walk with.

After cookies, Elizabeth would make her go outside to play—for the exercise, she said. Sooner would go swing, or, if Edwin didn't come over, she'd bring

Bird outside to peck around. She tried to talk to Little One, sometimes, but Little One was pretty uppity these days, what with that big oak tree all to himself, and he didn't always come when she wanted. And pretty soon, she'd go back inside and dress up the doll with the china face Elizabeth had got for her when she'd bought the skipping rope, or she'd get out her pad and her green pencil case and sit at the round table and practice the alphabet.

And in a while, Mac would come stomping through the house from the infirmary, shouting, "Where're my two girls!" and if Elizabeth was at the table too, helping her, Sooner could watch how her face would become more beautiful than ever. Mac would pick Sooner up out of her chair and boost her toward the ceiling and she would squeal because it was so high. Sometimes, he would tickle her until Elizabeth made him stop. Sooner loved the weary feeling she got in her middlle from all that giggling. And sometimes, he would be a big bear, and growl, and nuzzle her cheek with his scratchy one so that she'd have to try to wrestle free. She always forgot he could scratch because his hair was even yellower than hers and didn't show on his face. Her surprise would make him laugh, like thunder so close to her ear, but it was nice.

Dinner was always the talking time. And when it was over, Mac got to taking Sooner onto his lap and they'd listen to the radio together. The radio was in the cabinet she'd fallen onto from her banister slide, and she was gladder and gladder she hadn't busted it.

All these things made it so that clear through until Sooner walked there the next morning it always seemed that school would be different for sure tomorrow.

*　　*　　*

At last, one day it was. Late in the afternoon just before school let out, the teacher was talking about animals, and she asked who had any unusual pets. One boy talked about this garter snake he'd caught. And another said he had a real box turtle. Sooner thought and thought, and finally she raised her hand, and said she had Bird.

"So what?" a boy spoke out of turn. That was James. He said, "Lots of kids have canaries."

"He ain't a canary," Sooner said.

"Isn't," said the teacher. Then, she asked, "What kind of bird is he, Sooner?"

"He's a redwing," Sooner answered, "but he's all black, ceptin for unnerneath his wings."

"You mean he's a wild bird?" the teacher asked in surprise.

"Yes'm."

"And you keep him in a cage?"

"Oh, no'm! Wild critters, they don't take to cages. He's got him a perch for inside. Outside, he's just loose."

"Why don't he fly off, then?" another boy asked.

"Doesn't he fly off," said the teacher, just the way Elizabeth was always doing with Sooner.

"Cause he—" Sooner stopped, recollecting that boy by the courthouse that day. If she told them about the broken wing, they'd think Bird wasn't worth much. "He just *doesn't*, that's all," she finished, pleased she'd thought to say it right.

After school, when Sooner came out on the step, some kids were waiting to walk home with her. She wished one of them was Jean, only Jean had to go to her cornet lesson. But one of them was Sally, and one was Phyllis, and there were three boys, too—five whole kids! They wanted to see the wild bird that wouldn't fly off, they said.

That was the nicest walk ever, home from school. Sooner carried her skipping rope under her arm, and Sally told her she thought it was real pretty. Much

126

prettier than Jean's, she said. Jean's was only old clothesline.

When they got home, Sooner ran ahead up the walk and into the house, shouting that she'd bring Bird out. She was halfway up the stairs when Elizabeth came from the kitchen.

"Hey," she called up to Sooner. "How about saying hello when you get home?"

"I got some kids with me," Sooner said, breathless. "They want to see Bird." And she ran on up the stairs. When she came back down, Bird on her shoulder, Elizabeth was still at the foot of the stairs.

"After you show Bird off," she said, "bring them inside. The cookies'll be done by then."

Sooner hardly heard her. She ran past to get outside quick before those kids went home.

"Looks just like an old crow!" Paul said. But then, Sooner made Bird flutter his wings, and they saw the white and red underneath. Bird walked down her arm, the way he always did, and dropped to the ground and began pecking.

"You sure he won't fly off?" James asked.

"Yup," said Sooner, very pleased.

"Bet he would if he got scared," Sally said.

"No, he wouldn't," Sooner said.

James suddenly made a dash at Bird, but Bird only ruffled up his wings and hopped away a little.

Sooner giggled. "See?"

Laughing and shouting, they all began making dashes at Bird. But he only skittered back and forth out of their way.

"He isn't scared," said Sally. "He just thinks it's fooling, and that's why he doesn't fly." She threw her hair forward over her face and bent over to see how far she had to go before it touched the ground.

"Hey, I've got a nickel," Phyllis said, reaching into

her pocket. "Let's go to Telfer's and get some shoe-laces. I like licorice!"

Sooner didn't have a nickel. They would go off, and she'd have to tell Elizabeth the kids didn't stay for cookies.

"He is *too* scared," she said. "I'll make him scareder, and you'll see."

She ran to the driveway next door, hurrying so they wouldn't leave without seeing, and came back with a gravel stone. She threw it to land near Bird.

When Bird still didn't fly, Samuel said, "Let me try," and he went to the gravel and grabbed up some, and began throwing it at Bird. And then they all did that. Everyone was giggling and hopping up and down, and nobody was leaving for those shoelaces, and Sooner knew that Bird wouldn't fly because he couldn't, so she got some more stones, and she threw, too. Their aim was getting better and better, because Bird was getting tired. But though he fluttered and fluttered his wings, and got up into the air a little sometimes, he didn't fly. And instead of just throwing one stone at a time, first the boys and then the girls began tossing whole handfuls of gravel at Bird. He crouched down and tried to draw in his head and fluffed up his feathers and closed his eyes.

"Boy," Phyllis said. "He sure is something!"

"You're lucky, Sooner!" said Sally.

"Crazy bird," said Samuel, "won't fly, no matter what!"

It was exciting and scary at the same time. Even though she was beginning to feel kind of queer inside, with them all closing in on Bird and throwing harder and harder, Sooner did it too. They'd all walked her home from school, and they were all laughing and playing at her house, and each day she'd hoped they would, and now they were, and they weren't leaving at all.

128

Little puffs of dust lifted out of Bird where the gravel stones hit. He rose from his crouch to skitter away, but the kids used their feet and hemmed him in and made him skitter back. He opened his beak and uttered no sound.

Fly, Bird! Sooner pleaded inside. Please fly! Please fly! She pleaded inside and threw stones and giggled and ached with wanting the stones to be hitting her and not him. He skidded once onto his breast while trying to run. Ragged, broken feathers, color dropping from them like pollen, started to fall from his wings.

Sooner's giggles sounded in her own ears higher and higher, and she jumped up and down faster and faster, and her legs felt odd and shaky, and her breath kept catching back in her throat.

Bird ran in a circle. Suddenly, he stopped and stretched up, up, his black eyes seeming to look straight at Sooner. Then he toppled over and lay still.

"Sooner!" It was Elizabeth's voice from the veranda, cutting through the awful silence. "What on earth are you doing?"

Elizabeth ran down the steps and bent over Bird. The others just stood and let the gravel trickle through their fingers from behind their backs. Nobody was laughing any more. Elizabeth picked up Bird, and faced Sooner.

"He's dead," she said. "What kind of child are you, to kill your own pet?"

Sooner stared up at Elizabeth. Dead? Bird, dead? As she heard the kids run away, the shivering started from deep inside her.

"Go to your room," Elizabeth said.

Sooner looked at Bird, lying so still on Elizabeth's upturned palms, and she knew suddenly that her cheeks had been wet for some time. She reached out for Bird. Her fists were full of gravel. She opened them, watch-

129

ing the stones fall to the grass until her hands were empty. Then she went into the house.

From the window in her room, she could see out back, see Elizabeth take Bird to a place under the wild cherry and dig a hole with her garden trowel. When she laid Bird in the hole, Sooner saw her stroke his head with her finger, and Sooner wished she could do that. But her hands had been full of that gravel, and it was gravel that killed him.

Shivering so that her teeth chattered, Sooner watched Elizabeth cover Bird over with dirt.

It's cold down in there for Bird, she thought, under that tree and all.

It was very quiet downstairs, though she heard Elizabeth come in the back door. She wondered if Elizabeth would come up, and she stood by the window waiting a long, long time. Surely now she'd get switched. She was so certain of it, she could almost feel the sting on her legs. Maybe if she got switched, she'd have to think about the sting and not about how cold it was.

But Elizabeth didn't come, and Sooner finally went and lay on the bed, and looked at Bird's perch. It stood empty and small without Bird on it. Bird wouldn't be there tomorrow morning to watch the sun cross the braided rug. And she wouldn't ever again hear him screech to her from the low branches of a tree.

Those kids walked her home and they weren't going to stay if she didn't show the way Bird wouldn't fly, and she didn't tell them he couldn't.

She stretched her hand out to the perch, remembering the feel of his feet on her arm as he'd march up it to her shoulder, remembering the quiet times when nobody else was there when he'd reach his head to her and make the funny little sound that was only for her.

The truck drove in the alley and stopped. Mac was home. She heard the door bang closed, and then heard Elizabeth call to him, and then their voices came up from the kitchen, but Sooner couldn't make out the words.

Mac would know, now. How would his face be? Like Elizabeth's when she came out of the house and saw Bird? Or worse, because of Sooner's always being with the animals in his infirmary?

The voices were getting louder, coming through her open door and not up from the kitchen any more. They were in the living room.

"It was horrible, Mac! She's nothing but a savage!"

"Keep your voice down," Mac said, very quiet but mean, sort of. As if he were mad at Elizabeth. But Elizabeth hadn't killed Bird. She's used soft hands, and had buried him.

"Well she is!" Elizabeth said, sounding mad, too, and the way Sooner would sometimes, when she was trying not to cry.

"What did she say?" Mac asked. "Did she explain it?"

"I haven't talked to her," Elizabeth said.

"You just left her up there by herself? To think about it, all by herself? She's only a child, Elizabeth!"

"That doesn't excuse her—what she did! And why do you even try to? You, of all people! I tell you she was doing it, too. And laughing!"

There was a tremble in Sooner's legs as if the jumping had just now stopped, but the rising into her throat wasn't laughing.

"Wait for me in the office," Mac said, and in the silence afterward, Sooner heard steps on the stairs, Mac's steps. She didn't want to see his face. Quickly, she turned over and closed her eyes, not to look.

He stood in the doorway. She could hear his breath-

131

ing, and she knew he was there. She tried to stop breathing herself.

"Sooner?"

She felt his hand on her shoulder, on her hair, on her cheek.

"Puss, are you all right?"

Couldn't he tell she was asleep? She squeezed her eyes as tight-closed as she could, and wished he'd hurry and go away. She didn't want to see him looking at her. She didn't want to see them looking at each other, either, not looking the way they sounded together, downstairs. She didn't want to see that, ever. She was shivering again.

She heard him sigh, then heard the slippery swish of the comforter and its weightlessness was over her. She heard the door close; he was gone. She opened her eyes and peeked around to make sure.

Bird ought to be where the sun could warm him, on the bank of the creek, maybe. She remembered the way. You went around the courthouse, and by the milk depot, and after a while there was that stand of cedar, and then three more hills, and the cutoff, and then the lane.

She turned over beneath the comforter and stretched her hand out to Bird's perch again, and pretended he was ducking his head to preen his feathers and that soon he'd come walking up her arm.

ELIZABETH

Elizabeth had obeyed Mac and gone to his office to wait for him, indignant and with a sweeping fury. Had

132

he lost his mind? Or maybe he just hadn't believed her, Elizabeth, when she'd told him what had happened. He had never put up with cruelty in anyone. Was he so taken in by Sooner that he'd forgive her anything?

She sat down in his chair, suddenly glad to sit. She had been pacing the living room, waiting for him to get home, stopping now and then to listen for a sound from upstairs but there wasn't any. Mac's office clock told her she'd been quite a while pacing, feeling close to nausea at what she'd seen.

When she'd come from the kitchen with the plate of freshly baked icebox cookies in her hand, she'd heard the shouts and laughter of the children, and she'd felt so happy for Sooner. At last she'd made friends. And then Elizabeth had gone out on the veranda, and realized what they were doing. What Sooner was doing. Jigging up and down, giggling, throwing those stones. And Elizabeth had felt betrayed. As if she had been cuddling something soft and pretty to her, only to have it turn to dross in her arms.

Poor Bird. Poor crippled thing that couldn't get away.

Now, she tried to hear sounds from upstairs. What was he doing up there? Listening to some crazy explanation or other? As if there could be one. She could have told him something like this would happen, bringing a child like that into the house, into their lives—*her* life. And without having the remotest idea what kind of creature she really was.

From somewhere deep inside the voice jeered: You just can't wait to say I told you so, can you, Lizzie! Some triumph, huh?

Elizabeth immediately blanked out the voice, resenting everything, even her own sense of irony.

She hadn't heard him come down, but here Mac was, back in the office. His expression was grim, and both his eyes and his voice seemed to Elizabeth to indict her. "It's as if she were in shock," he said. "She's cold as ice, and won't say anything. You should never have left her alone."

All I've done for that child, Elizabeth thought, and when something goes wrong, he thinks it's *my* fault.

"I put a cover over her," Mac was saying. "Maybe she'll go to sleep."

Elizabeth could no longer hold it back. "Now, you listen to me, Mac. I accepted it when you brought her home. And I accepted it when Phil wanted her to go to school. But I can't accept any more. Take it day by day, you said. Well, the days have run out. I don't want her here, Mac. I just don't want her!"

"But you know it's not like her to do what she did. It's not in her nature!" His voice roughened over the words.

So he didn't find it all that easy to understand, either, Elizabeth thought with angry satisfaction.

She stood up, keeping hold of the edge of the desk to steady herself. She was trembling. "I know nothing about her nature, and neither do you. Obviously! A child you'd seen twice, and you bring her home . . . for all we know, she—"

He rode over her. "You hold on a minute!"

The blue of his eyes was darkening with anger, more anger than she'd ever seen in him. The rounded contours of his face planed out as if he were dropping twenty pounds in weight right before her eyes, and he looked tough, the way people always thought a man of his build ought to look, only Mac never had, until now.

"You know damned well Sooner hasn't an ounce of viciousness in her! Or you should. My God, she's been here a month and a half. Something, somehow, went wrong, for her to do such a thing. And if you'd even as much as gone up to look in on her, you'd have seen

134

it for yourself. It's written all over her, the way she's curled up, so still on that bed."

Mac leaned forward, now, peering into her face as if he'd suddenly been presented with a stranger to comprehend, and his next words were quiet, with a sick and growing wonder.

"Elizabeth, haven't you asked yourself, just once, what might have caused this? She loved that bird! Haven't you thought of her at all?"

She could see, building in his eyes as he looked at her, all her fears come to fruit at last. The death of love. *Was it?* Despair rose silently in her, choking her, the inner convulsion of it making her shudder, making her hand swing up, palm open, as if to hit him. It froze there, and then clenched into a fist. Now his eyes showed nothing as he looked at her and then at the hand and then back at her. She willed the errant hand down to her side, watching him through the blurred lenses of the tears that wouldn't flow, aching to speak his name. To beg him to understand her, to forgive her, not that child upstairs. But she couldn't say a word.

"She will stay here, with us, until we know what happened to her," Mac said. "And until we can undo whatever harm's been done." He turned away and went to the door and stopped, but he didn't look around at her. "Meanwhile," he went on, and took a deep breath, "meanwhile, Elizabeth, I suggest you stop seeing everything only in terms of yourself, for a change."

He left the room, and the front door slammed shut as he left the house. Elizabeth sank back onto the edge of the desk, staring at the office door. Mac's last words hung in the air: stop seeing things only in terms of yourself . . . yourself . . . He'd said them raggedly, as if they bore a truth difficult for him to utter.

She buried her face in her hands.

135

Oh, stop being so melodramatic, Lizzie! the voice lashed at her. Sitting there with your hands over your face as if there was an audience to watch and be sympathetic!

She whipped her hands down. There were no tears to hide, anyway. And no one to hide them from.

"But it isn't fair!" she cried out in a soft plea, to the no one who was listening. All this month and a half, her mind went on, I've thought about her. Wanted her to have friends. Given her pretty things to wear. Tried to think of things for her to do.

You've given her what you thought she ought to want, railed that harsh taskmaster voice. But have you once tried to put yourself inside her mind? Have you once tried to imagine the images she carries in her head, or to see her new life as she must see it, or to feel as she must feel? What did happen to her this afternoon, Lizzie? You know you haven't wondered. Not once, just as Mac said.

Feeling weary and reluctant, Elizabeth drove herself out of the office, through to the living room, and up the stairs, not having an inkling of what to say when she got to Sooner, resenting the guilt Mac seemed to think she ought to feel. That she did feel, damn it all. It wasn't fair.

The door was closed. She stood a moment, her hand on the doorknob, then turned it to open. Most of Sooner was hidden beneath the silk puff Mac had put over her. But her hand was stretched out to Bird's empty perch. Her finger had been running along its base until Elizabeth came into the room. Now it held still. Her eyes were fixed on the perch, and there were no tears on her face.

As there had been earlier, outside, Elizabeth suddenly remembered. Why had she forgotten it?—that in spite of the laughter, there had been tears, too.

"Sooner . . ." She spoke the name questioningly,

136

but Sooner did not react. She just started moving her finger back and forth along the base of the perch, caressing it. Elizabeth walked to the bed. As usual, Sooner's fine hair had slipped from its barrette, and was drooping along her cheek. She still hadn't looked at Elizabeth. Out of habit, Elizabeth smoothed back the hair. She wanted to twist its silky threads into her fingers, and suddenly recognized it as a thing she'd wanted to do before, as if she could turn the hair into a kind of cord which would bind the two of them together. She sat on the edge of the bed.

"Sooner," she said again. The child paid no attention. Elizabeth couldn't abide that small finger moving like that, and she reached out and took hold of Sooner's hand. It was cold.

"Tell me why, Sooner," Elizabeth said. The hand escaped and returned to the base of the perch. Sooner's gaze did not move toward Elizabeth.

"Please?" asked Elizabeth. She reached out to touch Sooner's hair again, but Sooner moved her head slightly, just slightly, and Elizabeth didn't touch her then. Finally, Sooner spoke.

"Twern't right, what I done," she said. "I know it weren't right." Her voice was quiet, almost remote, unpitying.

She does realize, Elizabeth thought. Lord, I wonder if she heard me downstairs? A savage, I called her. Elizabeth had to swallow quickly.

"Sooner . . ." Elizabeth cleared her throat. "Sooner, can't you tell me?"

The even little voice made no attempt to excuse, or to explain, either. It was as if Sooner were spelling out a conundrum. "We was just tryin to make him fly."

"I don't understand," Elizabeth said, wanting to very much, now. "You know Bird couldn't fly."

"Yes'm. Only, they didn't. Iffen they did, they'd've figured he wasn't worth much."

137

"Oh, Sooner!" The anguish of her full understanding set free Elizabeth's tears, and they flowed down her cheeks. "He was yours! And that made him worth everything!"

Now, at long last, Sooner looked at her. Her face went stricken, and she closed her eyes tightly and began to shiver.

Elizabeth twisted around on the edge of the bed and slid in under the puff to lie beside Sooner, pulling the small body into her arms to tremble against her breasts.

"It's all right, Sooner, it'll be all right, you'll see, honey . . ." Elizabeth tucked that outstretched hand under her own arm to warm it, murmuring the same things over and over, her own tears still running slowly. But Sooner said nothing and didn't cry.

If only she would, Elizabeth thought. The shivering went on and on. Elizabeth petted Sooner's hair and face and cold arms, and drew the little girl in close to her own body, and rubbed her hand up and down the tight back.

To prove Bird's worth, Sooner had allowed him to die. That's what it amounted to, Elizabeth knew. She'd wanted friends so badly, to belong so badly, and she'd learned at school what it would take to buy that friendship. Something of worth. And all she'd had was Bird.

I could have prevented it, Elizabeth thought. It didn't need to happen.

The small flashes of perception Elizabeth had had during the past weeks now returned to her. Perceptions I ignored, Elizabeth accused herself. The eagerness in Sooner's face and in the way she ran from the house each morning as the closed groups of children went past to school. Her lagging steps when she returned home in the afternoon, alone, turning slowly in circles as she came up the walk to the house as if still hoping somebody would call out to her, would ask her to play. The way she would sit herself down at the living-room table and print again and yet again the alphabet clear through.

But she never spoke of it, and so I ignored it, was Elizabeth's agonized thought. Didn't tell Mac. Didn't even hint that there was any kind of problem at all. I just ignored it.

Come on, Lizzie, you know very well you didn't, not completely. What about the times you took her down to the drugstore for a cherry phosphate after school? And one afternoon, you made fudge together. Remember the ecstatic look on her face when she licked the pan? And the way her hair was all sticky and brown on the ends?

If only she'd cry now as she laughed then.

Only last Monday, when the curtains were finished, you started showing her how to run the Singer so that you could make doll clothes with her. And there was that time you stood at the window and watched her, stretched along the grass with her hand open and full of seed, waiting for that blue jay to come feed from her. So unchildlike, that incredible patience of hers. You were worn out with willing it to happen, before it finally did.

But when her glance moved across the window glass, I ducked back out of sight. Why? Because I didn't care enough. Couldn't? Didn't want to? What's the difference, I didn't. All the easy things to do, I did. But nothing else. I could have called people, Harriet, Eleanor . . . they'd have helped me. I could have arranged things, could have made a little party for her, and she'd have found friends. But I didn't.

Because it would have been so settled then, Lizzie? So accepted that Sooner lived here?

Sooner's shivering slowly quietened. Elizabeth tipped her head forward to see if she had fallen asleep. She couldn't tell, though the eyes were still closed.

Should she say anything? But, no. Maybe if she kept silent, Sooner would drift off. The sun had set. The shadows were long in the room, now, the corners obscure. The house was very still.

Where had Mac gone? Would he come back for dinner?

Dinner. She'd forgotten it altogether. Nothing was even started.

Sooner's breath was coming with even regularity at last. Elizabeth could feel the light flutter of the young heart, in opposite rhythm to her own. And it was as if this double rhythm were something she had known always. She wondered whether pregnant women could feel the beat of their baby's heart, and whether it was like this. All the old longings drifted on the edge of her mind, not so important now. And the questions. How would it be to carry milk and have it drawn forth by a tiny mouth? How would it be to have all that bulk inside and wonder if it would ever manage to come out? How would it be, that coming out, the struggle and the pain and the relief afterward, and the joy? Somehow, those things had lost a little of their bite.

She continued smoothing the soft hair, sometimes dropping a kiss on the crown of Sooner's head. Together, she and the child were making a cradling warmth.

MAC

Selma's house was on Geiger Street, the other side of town from Mac's, and built some sixty years before his own by old Felix Geiger himself when he'd founded Switzer. Though it was considered the town manse by everyone, it was not large, its soft old bricks hugging the land. Selma was the last direct Geiger descendant, on her mother's side, and had lived in the house all her life.

Mac stood outside it, drawn to go ring its doorbell, to go inside, to be with Selma awhile. He'd done a lot of walking; he'd had some coffee and a piece of pie at Cy's, and had walked some more; and his feet repeatedly had carried him down Geiger Street.

He thought of telling Selma he was looking for Phil. But that would be a picayune dissembling, and more self-defeating than it was worth. He knew Phil wasn't there. He wasn't at the jail, either, because his car was gone. All Mac needed was to talk; maybe talking about things divorced from himself would help. Not since he married had he needed anyone beyond Elizabeth. But twice in less than two months, now, he'd had to go looking for someone to talk to, and he resented it, along with everything else. For as he'd walked, he'd found himself wavering between furious incredulity at what he gathered Elizabeth's behavior to have been with Sooner, and uncomfortable self-questioning. How much, after all, did he share the responsibility for what Sooner had done? He remembered only too clearly Phil's warning. He'd refused to listen, at the time. He'd been so intent on having Sooner for his own.

"Do you have any notion what you'll be asking of that little girl?"

Well, maybe he'd asked too much of both of them, both Sooner and Elizabeth. He'd given neither one any say in the matter. He'd acted only on what he wanted. And afterward, had told himself that with Sooner in the house, with less time to brood, things would change for Elizabeth. He'd believed over these

141

few weeks that he'd seen signs of it. But he hadn't. Whatever had been wrong for her over the winter was still wrong, and he had no more clues now than then to what it was. She hadn't even tried to understand the child today; and for the life of him, he couldn't understand her.

So, here he stood outside Selma's, the third time he'd hesitated in passing, wanting to go in.

Time was, in high school and even afterward, the three of them, he and Phil and Selma, had talked out everything that had ever happened to any one of them, any idea that any of them had ever thought. Sometimes, the threesome became a fluctuating twosome, so that they had taken some riding about whose girl Selma really was, Phil's or Mac's. But they had known, even though in one of those years—their junior year, Mac vaguely remembered—he'd had some stretches when he wished it otherwise. It had been a bad year for him, the reasons lost now, and Selma's easy laughter had got him through it. That, and the fact that when he was with her, she seemed to forget she was Phil's girl or maybe just that he wasn't Phil. Anyway, her eyes on him, listening, her smile at him, seemed no different to Mac from the way she looked and listened with Phil. She would even reach out and touch him sometimes, so that Mac would come away from her with little guilt dreams which, quickly as he might dismiss them, nevertheless gave him excitement enough to diminish whatever had been going wrong in those days.

He let a wave of hope move him up the walk to Selma's front door. As he rang the bell, he suddenly remembered it was Selma who had caused the best wet dream he'd ever had, and was amused that it should recall itself now after so many years. Maybe those graphic materializations of Selma, creeping so

142

often lately into his mind at odd and intimate moments with Elizabeth, were just a throwback.

The door opened and Selma stood behind it, looking at him with surprise. She fumbled a hand to her throat. "I'm not dressed," she said, too taken aback at seeing him to say hello, Mac supposed. She chuckled, and held the door wide for him. "Never mind. You've seen me worse than this, anyway. Come on in, Mac."

She was in a robe, and after she closed the door, she asked if he was looking for Phil. Mac told her no; she hesitated, and then without another word led him through the dark and formal parlor, the repository of all her family history and a place impossible to sit in with any comfort, and on back to the kitchen.

"I'll get you a drink," she said, and he didn't refuse. She waved a hand at a shabby overstuffed chair, meaning for him to take it, and uncorked a new jug of corn whiskey. "Phil lays it in for me," she said with a grin.

As in most such vintage houses, this was the biggest room in the house. The ceiling was low and beamed, and the air was fragrant. Vegetable soup, Mac finally decided. From the chair and the reading lamp, and the nearby shelf of books, he could see that the kitchen was where Selma did most of her living. It had been a long time since he'd been in here.

She handed Mac two glasses, and poured whiskey for them both, then took hers to the kitchen table, where she sat down. She lifted her glass to him before she drank. He responded in kind, and took half his down in one gulp. She still asked him no questions, and Mac was grateful. But then, she'd always been so. Her discretion and grace of person were innate. He was glad he'd come. He sat back in the chair and smiled at her.

He hadn't seen her with her hair down since school days. For that matter, he hadn't seen her much at all in a good long while, not the two of them alone, any-

143

way. Usually, it was just a hello in passing, and then her ample proportions were encased in one proper gabardine suit or another, her feet in sensible shoes, her hair skinned back from her face so that her eyes seemed flattened. Now, that glorious spread of color fell below her shoulders, rippling the way it used to, like water under a breeze. The robe was bright pink, and with that fall of red hair she was such a hot profligacy Mac had to look away from her. He finished off his whiskey in a second gulp, and Selma immediately got up and poured him another, and this time left the jug on the floor by him. The robe flowed loose and soft about her ankles, and he saw that her feet were bare.

Was this what Phil found waiting for him every night? At least, every night he wanted it?

My God, Mac thought. It was Phil's chair he was sitting in. It was Phil's woman he'd come to in need. Things weren't the way they had been in those younger days; none of them was innocent any more, and Mac knew he had no business being here.

But he didn't want to go home. What good would it do? Sooner must be fast asleep by now. And with his mind confused as it was, he'd probably only take it out more than ever on Elizabeth.

"How does it go with Judge Posey?" he asked Selma, wanting her to talk so that he could listen and stay. "Still pretty much in his cups?"

Selma laughed with a small shake of her head. "Don't see how he'll get through the next campaign," she said. "I had to practically carry him off the platform three times, last election. In his office, it's all right. The poor old geezer just sleeps all day. But he can't sleep through his speeches," and she was laughing again, "though it might be an improvement if he did!"

As she laughed, a heavy sweet scent uncurled

through the warm air from her; her white skin looked luminescent in the midst of her red hair. Mac poured himself a third drink.

"What trip are you planning this year, Selma?" he asked. She never took her trips, as far as Mac knew, but she never was without plans for one, either.

"California," she said. She waved her glass expansively; she'd been keeping up with him from the jug. "Sunny California! Where all the movie stars live!"

"Go that far," Mac said, "why not go all the way to Hawaii?"

She looked at him a long moment, took a sip of whiskey, and then smiled at him, her eyes gentle. "Haven't changed a smidgen, have you, Mac. You always did let me enjoy talking big, dreaming my dreams."

The room was warm, the whiskey was warm, and a laxness was working in him. He poured another drink; was it his third or fourth? He'd lost count. For the first time, he felt no urgency to break a silence between them. He felt a coddling comfort which he was sure existed for him only in this room, with her, and with or without talk he was determined not to abandon it.

His head was leaning back against the soft chair, and without any effort his eyes could rest on her. She seemed slowly to lean toward him, her breasts swinging forward to brush across the top of the kitchen table and push their fullness against the fabric of her robe. Mac's eyes moved down to them, fed on them, and on the swollen nipples showing big and round. He wanted the feel of them in his hands.

He looked up again at her face. She was watching him, her eyes knowing, her mouth loosening. One of Phil's hounds bayed from out back. He and Selma started as guiltily as if his hands were on her. Selma caught in her breath and sat back, her gaze still holding

145

his. Without warning, she exploded into one of her full-throated laughs, and he had to laugh with her.

"Phil's a damned fool," he said. "He ought to rope you up and carry you to the preacher, if that's the only way."

"He's thought of it," Selma said. "Or at least, he says he has. And maybe it is the only way. Sometimes I wonder if I'll ever say yes to him." She finished off her drink, her face going wry. But then she shrugged, and chuckled, and stood up. "There's a lot to be said for keeping things . . . unsure, you know it, Mac? Sort of spices up the old apple pie." She came over to Mac and the jug, and poured herself another. "Phil doesn't listen any more when I talk about taking a trip. But *I* know there's a chance—maybe just a chance, but a chance even so—that I will." She went back to her chair, sat down, and looked at him overseriously. "You have to be unsure about some things, don't you? If everything, the important things, I mean, were all a foregone conclusion . . . certain, you know? . . . why, where'd be the fun in it? You'd be so burdened down, the life'd run right out of you."

Mac stared at her, taken by a significance in her whiskey-glib words she knew nothing of. Could it be that, in curious parallel, it was with Elizabeth as Selma said? He thought about the years of hope before last fall, hope he'd helped keep alive. And then had come the awful certainty. Was Elizabeth so burdened by it that she felt all the life was just running out of her? It would explain her fear. It would explain a lot of things.

"Hey," Selma said, his continued stare obviously making her uncomfortable. She dropped her eyes. "Not bad for a high school graduate, all that speechifying." She tried to laugh.

Mac had forgotten that about Selma, how defensive she had been when he'd first brought Elizabeth, the college girl, back to Switzer as his wife. The two never had become the friends he'd hoped.

"Phil'll be along soon," she said now, suddenly matter of fact. "Did you come for something special, Mac?"

He hesitated, then shook his head. It needed thinking about, not talk. "I'll stick around long enough to say hello," he said, "and then go on home."

They sat in companionable quiet, Mac picking up a book to leaf through it, until Phil arrived. He showed only pleasure on seeing Mac, and complaining with loud good humor that they were way ahead of him, he poured himself a dollop of moonshine, tossed it off, and poured himself another. Then he asked about Sooner.

Mac shrugged. "We have our ups and downs," he responded, sliding off it with a slow-growing conviction that maybe that's all today had been: one in a series of not too worrisome ups and downs. Shortly afterward, he left to walk home.

On the way, he explored the thoughts he'd had at Selma's before Phil came. What Selma had said of herself couldn't be total wisdom for Elizabeth; they were two different people, after all. Elizabeth had always needed to be able to look ahead, to count on things getting better. And Sooner was the perfect contradiction to Elizabeth's burden of certainty that things could only stay the same. Sure, maybe he had brought the child home for selfish reasons. But in so many ways, she was the fulfillment of hope for both of them. Elizabeth hadn't seen it yet, that was all. And that was his fault, too. He'd done it all wrong, with that day-to-day business. Fearful as she was of so many things, how could Elizabeth dare open up to a child who might not even be there next week?

Tomorrow, Mac thought, I'll tell Phil to set up the

hearing. It's long past time to make Sooner's stay permanent.

His steps slowed and stopped on the front walk; he looked up at his own darkened house. She'd be in bed but awake, he was sure, waiting for him, and he knew he couldn't go in to her and tell her his decision now. In the morning would be better, after a night's sleep, when she'd be calmer, more willing to listen.

He thought of her lying there, thought of that cool, slim body that had gone so earnest on him these past weeks. A picture conjured itself up in his mind of the two he'd left behind: Phil sinking with lazy pleasure into all that amiability of Selma's; Selma laughing and enfolding and not needing a million reassurances. And lust took him for what Phil had. Elizabeth seemed by contrast unappetizingly fragile and overrefined; sterile, though it would kill her to know he'd thought it.

He could do with another drink. He turned off the walk and went around and into the infirmary, and not switching on the light, found the medical alcohol on its shelf, and drank from the bottle. He rolled the liquid over his tongue. It didn't have the flavor of moonshine, but it would do. He sat down, and went on drinking.

ELIZABETH

When Elizabeth blinked open her eyes, Sooner's room was in darkness. She hadn't a notion of what time it was. Sooner was deep in sleep, as only a tired child can be. Elizabeth gently put her aside, sliding Sooner's head to the pillow, and left the bed. She went to the dark hall, drawing the door into Sooner's room closed behind her. All was silent. Quickly, used to the dark and helped by the slight glow of light from the courthouse square, she went down the stairs and to the office, but it was dark, too, and, seen from the window, so was the infirmary. The clock, in dull reflection, said it was twenty to eleven. She could hardly believe she had slept so long. And Mac still wasn't home. Probably out somewhere with Phil.

She felt sticky and unclean from the turmoil earlier, before that quiet time with Sooner. She went back upstairs and into their bedroom, and without turning on the lights, she dropped her clothes on the floor and went naked across the hall to the bathroom. Still in darkness, she ran water into the tub. As she waited for it to fill, she stood before the medicine-chest mirror above the sink, seeing the shadow of herself reflected there.

She had a bleak certainty that Mac had spoken the truth, and not only where Sooner was concerned. In all these months of worrying about what was happening to herself, had she ever given thought to what might be happening to him? She'd been afraid he might change, yes; but it was all focused on herself. What about him? What would it mean to him, to stop loving her?

The answer to that had been staring her in the face this whole month. The way his eyes would light up when the child would run to him. His unflagging good humor even with her, Elizabeth. She'd seen it, she'd avoided thinking about it, because each time there'd been that tiny spurt of resentment she couldn't admit she was feeling. To be jealous of a child was only a sign of lack of love in oneself, wasn't it? His answer had been to go out and find himself somebody else to love: Sooner. He'd filled himself up with her. That had to be the way it was, for his anger with

149

Elizabeth this afternoon could only have come from a terrible fear that the child, too, would be lost to him.

And all she had been capable of was to meet his anger with her own, and refuse him any comfort.

She reached up to the side of the chest and switched on the light, flinching away from the brightness, but then searching her own face in the glass. "You're a selfish bitch," she told the image. But she could see no difference in herself for saying it. She closed her eyes, and let her head droop.

Dear Lord, make me different, this time. First Mac and now Sooner. I can't stand it if I've frozen them both out for good.

You can't stand it. It's still *you*, isn't it, Lizzie.

Elizabeth sighed and, turning, shut off the taps and stepped into the tub, sinking her body down into the embrace of the water.

All these months, she thought, I've been afraid to lose Mac's love, but persuading myself that I couldn't help it happening. Inability to care, I called it; but all it adds up to is selfishness.

She reached for the cloth and soap and began washing herself.

She'd fallen in love with the idea of having her own child. And when the idea had been ripped from her, along with a portion of her flesh, she had determined never to gamble her love again. It wasn't that she couldn't, but that she wouldn't. There was the truth.

Elizabeth pulled the plug and toweled herself dry. She brushed her teeth, ran the comb through her hair, turned out the light, and, still naked, peeked in on the quiet and sleeping child before going back to their bedroom. She folded the white spread carefully, and got in between the sheets. The movement of the cool muslin across her skin was erotic. She hadn't felt that slow, leisurely stirring within for a long while, and she welcomed it, moving her body now and then, just a little, so as to hold on to it. So often in the last weeks when they made love, right in the middle of things the ecstasy would go from her. The search for the release would leave her depleted to exhaustion and she couldn't want anything except to forget it.

But not tonight. The consciousness of that was joyful in her.

If, tonight, anything happened at all. He'd left in anger, yes, but also in something near to dislike. Fine help all these earth-shaking realizations would be if it was too late. How much damage had she done to them both, over the winter? The saddest thing of all, Elizabeth thought, was that she really didn't know what was inside Mac any more.

She switched on the light to look at the alarm clock. Nearly eleven-thirty. She switched the light off again. He had to be with Phil. Where else? Talking, she supposed. About her? Did men, even two such old friends, ever talk like women, endlessly, pouring it all out and getting rid of it that way?

Oh, why didn't he come home? A trickle of the despair she'd felt earlier, with him, began to erode the sweet growing of desire.

Hold on to it, Lizzie. It's not been beautiful between you for so long. Maybe tonight you can return to him a little of what you've taken away.

Abruptly, Elizabeth turned on her side, curling into herself, to wait.

*   *   *

Mac's passage up the stairs was barely audible to Elizabeth. She heard him look in on Sooner, heard his hesitation, and wondered if she should get up and go in to the child, too, but then he came into the bedroom. She let him undress in silence, still lying on her

151

side, her ear laid against the pillow so that her heart-beat sounded loud and fast.

He got into bed beside her a little clumsily, but trying not to wake her up. She turned around at once, and slid her arm across his chest.

"Thought you'd be asleep," he said, but his body gave her no response.

"You smell of whiskey," she murmured, not in reproach, and kissed his shoulder so that he'd know it.

"Good old mountain dew," he said. "Has quite a kick."

But she all of a sudden didn't care where he'd been. "It's going to be all right with Sooner, Mac." Her words came in fits and starts. She needed so much for him to believe, as she had to believe, that it was going to be all right. "She—I mean, I think I understand what went wrong for her. Mac, it's so sad. She just wanted friends, that's all. All this time, she wanted friends, and I—oh, never mind about me! But tonight after you left, I did go up to her, darling. I held her, and—I never should have said what I did to you, Mac. Of course I want her to stay with us."

"That's good, Elizabeth. I'm glad. We'll talk in the morning."

He waited a moment, then turned on his side. Away from her.

Oh, God, she thought. She burrowed her face into his back, her arms still over him. "It is going to be all right, Mac. I'm sure it is."

"So am I." He caught her hand and held it, then gave it a little pat. "Let's go to sleep. It's late."

He was gentle. He was never anything but gentle, but he didn't want her, and he was telling her so. She tried not to stiffen too abruptly. Slowly, she pulled her arm away, and turned her back to his. "Sleep well, darling," she said, managing to say it without a tremble, but sick inside, and afraid as never before.

"I'll just have to show him, that's all, she told herself fiercely. He'll see, tomorrow, and the next day, and the next. But I want him to know now. I care about Sooner very much, and that's wonderful for me, and he did the right thing to bring her home.

She lifted her head from the pillow, almost saying it aloud. But his breathing was heavy and slow, and she knew the whiskey had put him asleep too soon.

She laid her head back down, making her body relax, determinedly pushing the fear down. He'd had too much to drink, that was all. There was loads of time to come; all the time in the world. And he would see. We'll work it out—all of it—*all* of it.

It was a long time before she got to sleep.

*   *   *

In the morning, Elizabeth woke first, which was unusual. Mac habitually was awake with first light, and unable to stick it in bed one moment after. She came to awareness on the tail end of a warm and loving dream, the details hazy and fragmented in her mind, but knowing Mac's arms had been around her, his body pressed close to her. She clung to the feeling of it, letting the excitement rise inside as it had the night before. She turned her head slightly to look at the clock. Twenty after eight. Later than they slept in, even on Sundays. She held quiet, then, wanting him to awaken slowly and easily, so that maybe the dream could be prolonged into reality and last night might never have happened.

There hadn't been so much as a murmur from Sooner. Elizabeth looked again at the clock. Nearly eight-thirty, now. It was odd. Sooner wasn't normally the quietest little girl in the world. Elizabeth hesitated, then heaved a sigh and swung out of bed. She pulled

153

her robe from the closet and tied it round her as she moved across the hall to Sooner's room. It was empty, the bed straightened the way she'd had to nag the child to do every morning.

Elizabeth walked to the head of the stairs. The house was quiet. She didn't like it. She thought of waking Mac, but instead ran downstairs. Maybe Sooner was practicing her letters at the living-room table. Or maybe she was out in the infirmary.

But she was nowhere. Still in her robe and bare feet, Elizabeth lingered outside the infirmary door, looking down along the alley, uncertain but yet not uncertain at all, with dread creeping through her. The animals were restive, wanting Mac's attention. She should go awaken him. But then he'd have to know about Sooner.

Know what? Elizabeth asked herself sharply. There was nothing to know yet.

Without warning, unsought, the time with Sooner yesterday evening came back full-bodied to Elizabeth. For a moment, she felt again the weight of the child lying in her arms. And then, in despair, she remembered the shivering and silence, and felt the loss of the weight like a great emptiness.

She stepped to under the cherry tree and around it. The small grave was open, the dirt piled neatly to one side, and Bird wasn't there.

She glanced up toward the house. Sooner could have watched from the bedroom window, yesterday.

Sooner gone. Mac's love gone. How could she have convinced herself last night that everything would work out? It wouldn't. It couldn't, unless Sooner came back.

Elizabeth ran on cold feet across the lawn to the house. They had to find her.

But no, Elizabeth thought. Not me. She's running away because of me. Mac has to find her. Mac has

154

to be the one who makes things right with her, and brings her back.

Oh, God, please. He has to.

MAC

"Yeah, I saw her. Matter of fact, just now got back from givin her a lift out to where she said she belonged. Had to go after some gravel out that way, anyhow."

Donovan, he'd said his name was, was leaning out the window of the dust-coated dump truck, calling across the broken blacktop to Mac. A little farther down the road, hot tar was sending up steam into the morning air, and two men were stoking up the fire for it. The WPA crew had made it down here at last, but late, in June, just as everyone had predicted.

Something in Mac's face must have got to Donovan, because he was getting down from his cab to come across to Mac.

"Say, I didn't mean no harm, mister. Is she your kid, runnin away or somethin?"

And just how do I answer that? Mac wondered. Yes, she's running away. But—*my* kid?

Donovan leaned in through Mac's window. "Cute little thing, you know? Come trudgin along, holdin that dead bird in her two hands like if it was a bowl of milk, it might spill. Said she belonged out to Black Willow Creek, so, I put her in my truck and hauled her on out there. Guess maybe I shouldn't have, huh? Or maybe took her back to town?"

He was concerned. Really worried. Funny how

just from looking at a child, people could come to care.

"No," said Mac. After all, what had the man done but be kind to a little girl? "It's all right," Mac went on. He shifted into first, wanting to go on, and Donovan stood away from the Ford. "Did she say anything?" Mac asked. "About anything? The bird, or . . ."

Donovan shook his head. "Couldn't get a word out of her, no matter what I tried. She just sat, until we got to the lane she give out to me was hers, and then she hopped off." He grinned, suddenly. "Didn't even say her thankyous."

Mac made an attempt to smile back. "Well, then, I'll say it. Thanks." He lifted his hand in quick salute and pulled away. He had to go slowly through the repair area and hold in his impatience. There was Lucy Garn's boy, perched with a shovel on top of a heap of gravel. First bit of cash that family would have this year, Mac knew. He waved at him, and then at Moss Greenley, waiting with his shovel by the edge of the road farther on down the line. The WPA didn't pay much, but it was better than nothing for a lot of county people.

Relieved to reach a clear road, Mac kept a steady high speed, disregarding the condition of the tarmac, letting the truck buck across the potholes and the hell with it.

She must be meaning to bury Bird out by the creek, he reasoned. That's all this was for. Just to take Bird back where he came from.

But then, why that business of "out to where she belonged"?

Damn Elizabeth, anyway. He'd nearly said it to her face a little bit ago, when she'd come pounding up the stairs to shout him awake, looking frightened, trying to talk but incoherent and everything jumbled up, about Sooner being gone and how she'd thought everything was going to be all right last night, but of course now it wasn't, and how could she have been so stupid and selfish, and again that Sooner was gone.

Once dressed, he'd bulled it out of the house without a thought of her coming with him, only determined to find Sooner. All the way out of Switzer, he'd kept telling himself that kids don't just run away. They run to someplace. And where else could Sooner run to but back to Black Willow Creek?

It was lousy luck that the man Donovan had taken her out there before he, Mac, had reached her. It would probably mean trouble with Mrs. Hawes. And maybe it would even make it more difficult with Sooner. He felt he'd be at a disadvantage, somehow, in talking to her. As if he were going to have to bargain. But maybe he would have to, at that. Lord only knew what Sooner might be thinking, after yesterday. Confused? Maybe. Hating Elizabeth? Maybe.

Elizabeth's face, as he'd left her, flashed into his mind. Desperate, and pleading. She had called after him, "Bring her back, please!" But did that despair arise out of love for the child, or out of guilt for what she had wrought yesterday? Could Elizabeth herself answer that?

He turned the Ford into the lane by Black Willow Creek, and drove up it beyond where he'd parked before on the day in April that seemed so long ago. The ruts were no shallower than then, but they were as dry as if it were mid-August. In sight of the cabin, he stopped, got out, and hesitated there, hearing no human noise. He knew Mrs. Hawes, at least, had to be around somewhere. But Sooner? Had she come out with Donovan and buried Bird, only to go on to somewhere else?

Mac moved toward the cabin slowly, and only after several steps did he realize he was deliberately keeping his approach quiet. As if he were stalking a wild animal for capture, he thought with a sense of shock, followed by a wry awareness that the similarity was not misplaced.

He stepped onto the stoop, unsure if the dry, splitting boards would hold his weight, and peered through the half-opened door. Empty, the room was, and so poor. If this was what the child had run to as haven, her poverty of choice was heartbreaking. The very smell of the room was a reproach. He turned away from it and went outside and breathed deeply.

There had to be a corn patch somewhere, for the whiskey. Maybe the old woman would be there. Mac walked around the cabin and discovered a thin path meandering off down toward the creek. He followed it, trying to decide if he should call out to announce his presence. Mrs. Hawes had a still, and he recalled she'd mentioned a gun. He didn't relish the prospect of a legful of shot if he took her by surprise. Even so, Sooner had come out here to get away, and he had the misgiving that she might try getting away again if he gave warning he was here. He continued to move as lightly as possible.

Weight and bulk never do have anything to do with how quietly you can move through the woods, he thought, in one of those stray reflections that can cut across a mind even at moments of concentration. It has to do with figuring out where to put your foot, and then knowing how to set it down after spying out the ground.

He could hear the old woman caterwauling as he pushed by some junipers, and coming to the edge of the small patch, he saw Sooner. She was standing on tiptoe at the mule's head and seemed to be whispering into one large, flickering ear, while Mrs. Hawes waited behind the three-blade wooden cultivator attached to the mule. She snapped the reins running along the mule's back impatiently. "Danged mule ain't worth nothin! What for's the matter with him now?"

Mac figured he could tell her, but he also figured she'd pay not the least bit of attention. The mule was old, that was all, and should have been put out to pasture two, three years ago: old, and thin, and uncared for, his scraggly coat not replacing itself when it got torn. The meager diet Mrs. Hawes apparently fed him had made sores out of scratches, which would be long in healing if they ever did, and provided a breeding home for the flies clouded about him. Obviously a miserable animal. Still, as Mac watched, the knife-sharp haunches shifted and in response to Sooner, if not to the stinging reins, the mule began ambling forward. William. That's what Sooner called him. She talked about him a lot.

They were walking away from Mac. He started into the field toward them, keeping to the rows between the new sprouts of corn. They still didn't know he was there.

Mrs. Hawes planted by the rule of three, Mac could see—the old way, and the best when there was only a woman to harvest. A woman and, no doubt, one overworked child, at least up until this summer.

Mac had reached the center of the patch when Sooner began turning William around to start back along a second strip of rows. She saw Mac. He was close enough so that he could watch as her face lit up with joy—oh God, such joy, it was wonderful—and she began running toward him faster and faster, while the old woman cried out after her, "Sooney, Sooney, you come back here!" But it wasn't this that caused Sooner's steps to slow, her joy to fade. It was something else, Mac felt sure. Second thoughts? The memory of yesterday's misery? She came to a halt still several feet away from him, her face all solemn.

Mrs. Hawes left the cultivator to follow Sooner,

159

clumsy in her haste to cross the plowed rows toward them. Mac made himself smile at Sooner, refusing to be hurried by the approach of the old woman. Suddenly feeling the weight of the arms he had extended to the child, he dropped them to his sides.

"You ready to come on home now?" he asked, trying to sound casual.

She took a step backward, dragging the other heel through the turned-up sod. A bare foot, so quickly had the shoes come off, so quickly had she embraced what she had once been.

"She done come *home* this mornin," said Mrs. Hawes, her tone strident. She halted just beyond Sooner. "Home to stay. Ain't that right, Sooney?"

Sooner made no response, other than to look down at her feet, twisting them into the loose dirt.

"I haven't heard her say so," he said, letting his distaste for the woman ring out.

Mrs. Hawes grinned. "What for did she come back, then? Iffen it weren't to stay?" Her grin disappeared, and she put on a show of righteous indignation. "What did you do to her, in that biggety town house of yourn, you and that fine-seemin lady you got? Oh, I seen all of you, when I come in oncet to talk with the sheriff. Me with my ole mule, and you in that shiny truck! Fancy livin, that's what you give to my Sooney. She got her a pretty dress and shoes, sure, but it was me she come trailin back to this sunrise. Back to her Ole Mam!" Mrs. Hawes stepped close to Mac, her voice flooding with triumph. "Maybe I can't give her no fancy livin, like you and your lady. But I ain't killed nary a one of them fool critters of hers!"

"Is that what Sooner told you? That we killed Bird?"

"Didn't you?"

Sooner was still backing away slowly. Had she lied, then? But he said, "In a way, I guess we did."

Sooner never lifted her head. Her lips tightened suddenly, and she turned and ran, stumbling across the furrows, until she reached the junipers and was lost from sight.

"I figured. She never did say it right out, but I figured," said Mrs. Hawes. "The redwing was dead, his neck broke. And it's for certain-sure it weren't Sooney done it."

Mac couldn't bear to face the self-satisfied old bitch. He stood for a moment, staring where Sooner had run to, wanting to go after her but knowing it would do no good, even if he could find her. How do you explain to a child? How do you make her understand that grownups sometimes don't understand everything either?

"You'd best leave." Mrs. Hawes' voice was quiet and it so surprised Mac that he swung back to her. The weathered face was closed up hard against him. "There ain't nothin here for you," she went on, and her even words were pitiless. "Like I said, Sooney's come home to stay."

He turned and walked across the field, feeling as he had as a little boy when somebody else had had the last word, wanting to shout, "I'll win yet! You'll see!" But he'd never done it as a boy, and he didn't do it now.

There wasn't a sign of Sooner on the way to the Ford, but he had the feeling she was close by, hidden in some copse of bushes, like one of her little critters. Before he drove off, he called out to her secret presence, "We miss you, Puss—already. I'll be back."

As before when he'd left them, once out on the road he thought: I should have offered the woman money. She'd have taken it, that's for sure. But what good would it do Sooner? None. She'll be wearing

161

rags, her hair dirty, her legs scratched up and maybe even whipped in no time.

Mac's foot was shifting to the brake to stop and go back, but then he jammed down hard again on the accelerator. If the child didn't want to come with him, there wasn't a damned thing he could do about it. Not now, today, anyway.

And what do I say to Elizabeth? It's your fault?

He remembered his outrage when he'd come home yesterday afternoon and learned that she'd left Sooner all alone. But hadn't he ended up doing the same thing? Covered her up, sure, but then he'd walked out of the house, out on her, only full of his own resentments.

We neither one of us deserve that child, he thought. Too busy with our own problem to give hers the time it needed. I misjudged things all along. Never really judged them at all, until last night.

The immense relief of a few hours ago was bitter irony now. When he'd finally gone to bed, Elizabeth's words on top of the liquor had acted in him like a shot of morphia. If he'd picked Elizabeth up on it right then; if they'd gone and waked up Sooner and told her . . . but his head had been woozy. All he'd wanted to do was sleep. And instead of things settled, permanent, *right*, the child had run away from the house, run away across the field, run away from him.

The full impact of the loss took him unexpectedly. It weakened him so that his foot forgot the accelerator and the truck's speed fell off abruptly, bringing him back to his driving. He tried to concentrate on it as if the process were unfamiliar and complex. He didn't succeed.

We missed you, that's all he'd said. When the truth was that he loved her. She was his baby, and he loved her. Why hadn't he just damned well grabbed her up

162

and told her? Was the constraint Elizabeth seemed so full of catching?

He gave the wheel a bitter jerk, turning the Ford off the main road in order to jag around it. He didn't want to return to town through that WPA gang. The man Donovan might ask questions about the little girl. And Mac had no answers.

PART III

SOONER

She listened to the truck drive away until she couldn't hear it any more. Why had Mac said what he did to Old Mam? They hadn't killed Bird. She, Sooner, had; and had made Elizabeth cry.

When Sooner had first seen Mac walking across the corn patch, she was sure Elizabeth was there, too, somewhere. But while she was running, she couldn't see Elizabeth anywhere, and she remembered how Elizabeth had looked yesterday and the words, too: *What kind of child are you?* She knew Elizabeth hadn't come. She'd never come. Even if Mac did, Elizabeth wouldn't.

"Sooney?" It was Old Mam, hollering up the hill after her. "Come on, chile, I be needin you!"

Sooner sniffled hard. It tickled her nose, and she rubbed it with the back of her hand as she started down to the hollow. It must be getting on to time for school, she thought, and she suddenly pictured her stripey rope and wished she'd brought it away with her.

They cultivated about half the corn that day. They quit when Old Mam declared she was plumb wore out with it. William was, too. Toward the middle of the afternoon he got so that Sooner could hardly talk him into moving at all. After Old Mam unhitched him, she told Sooner to give him his feed, and she went on up to the cabin, and so Sooner was able to mix up some mealies with water into a mash for him. It wasn't the feed Old Mam meant, but any more, William's teeth just couldn't grind the rough fodder, and there were times when nothing at all reached his belly. It was while she was holding the bucket for him to suck it up from that Sooner looked down at herself and saw her dress. William's sweat had streaked it all over with dust, and the white collar was brown where she'd had to lean against him to whisper at his ear and get him to haul on the cultivator. If Elizabeth did come— only she wouldn't; she wouldn't—but if she did, she'd most likely start crying again, because of the dress. It was hot in the sun, but Sooner shivered anyway. She'd made Elizabeth cry once; she didn't ever want to make her cry again.

William had his fill, but the bucket wasn't half empty. Poor William, he couldn't take much at one time, no matter how she crooned over him.

"I'll be back, William," Sooner said, and then she left him alone and went down to the creek. She took a kind of a long way around, because she'd buried Bird high on the bank where the sun always was, near the shagbark he used to perch in, and she didn't want to go by there. It would make her remember how he'd felt, dead in her hands, stiff and hard.

She hadn't figured it out yet, how it could be that she'd seen what those gravel stones were doing and still had let it happen. Had *made* it happen. Every time she thought on it she had to swallow against throwing up. It was the first thing in her life she didn't want to puzzle over to understand it. Instead, she kept trying to turn her mind from it, only when she forgot to try hard enough she saw again the way Bird had looked at her that once before he had toppled over.

The creek was running clear, and low enough so that it made a bubbly sound over the rocks. Sooner could see down in, and for a while she watched some crawdads skittering over the silt. Two of them had a fight, and there was a third who'd lost his claw. Poor thing. She stepped into the water right where they were, and watched them scoot away, only it didn't make her laugh the way she thought it would. She wiggled her toes, thinking how big and white they must look to a teeny crawdad, but that didn't make her really laugh, either. She thought about Little One and hoped he'd be all right in his hole in the oak tree in Switzer. Had he watched yesterday what they had done to Bird?

A small bluegill darted between her legs. She used to bring down stale pone sometimes, crumbling it and rolling it in her fingers and scattering it across the surface for the minnies to rise and feed. She wished she could find some new little one to make friends with, but it was too late into spring for that. The critters had long since dropped their young. They'd be too wily by now. Of course, she might yet get her a baby redwing, but it'd only fly away when it was grown. Bird couldn't fly. That's what was so nice about Bird.

And she'd killed him for it.

"Thou shalt be for fuel to the fire; thy blood shall be in the midst of the land; thou shalt be no more remembered: *for I the Lord have spoken it.*"

The words rooted her in the bottom mud. She could not breathe, and then she could, gasping as if the fire already burned the air hot, and would burn her, too. She stared over her shoulder up the bank toward the cabin. Was it Old Mam with her Bible talk? But other words were coming, not Old Mam's. "Let not your heart be troubled, neither let it be afraid." Words the minister told over at the end of Sunday services in Switzer. They were from Elizabeth's New Testament. Elizabeth had said so.

There was no fire, nor would there be. To make sure, Sooner scooped her hands through the water, splashing the drops up into the air so that they fell in a shower over her head. It felt cool and good. She did it again, the drops all pretty with the sun shining through. Elizabeth's hair was like that when Sooner would look up at her out in the yard. Last week had been one time. They were digging the garden at the side of the house, and Elizabeth had those bright little papers full of flower seeds. They measured them out *so*, and Elizabeth let Sooner do the counting.

The water went suddenly cold. Sooner's hair was wet; her dress was, too. She waded across and sat on a big rock at the edge of the creek, and spread her skirt all around her like an upside-down umbrella. There was always an umbrella folded up and leaning in the corner of the hall in Switzer. It was shiny and its soft colors kind of ran into each other. Sooner was sure the rain had done it and had thought it a shame, until Mac had told her it was supposed to look like that.

Would the kids tell at school about it today? Sally, and Phyllis, and Samuel, and the rest?

The rock felt rough but warm against the bottoms of her feet. Where were her shoes? She'd left them somewhere, Elizabeth would sigh and shake her head and say, "Oh, Sooner!" That's what she'd said yesterday, when she'd cried. "Oh, Sooner! He was yours! And that made him worth everything!" It was something Sooner would have liked to puzzle over, what had been Elizabeth's meaning in that, because Sooner couldn't make the sense of it come clear. But it always carried her mind back to what had happened before. Better to skid on to what had come after: the way Elizabeth had been under the cover with her, holding her; and how it had felt lying against her, with her own cheek in that softness Elizabeth had, so that Sooner had stayed still as she could to have it last and last.

The sun was low on the bank behind her, now.

Sooner was hungry. But there wouldn't be any ketchup for supper. Maybe Old Mam didn't even know there was ketchup. Sooner had the funny feeling that maybe there were lots of things Old Mam didn't know about, and Sooner figured she ought to tell them to Old Mam. Like the smell of rose water and glycerine; and the story of Heidi and the goat boy—Elizabeth had been reading it to Sooner, lately, and sometimes Mac would read it, too; and playing Parcheesi after supper and the way you'd get excited when it came your turn and one of your men was almost home.

Sooner stood up and waded back across the creek, lifting her skirt high to keep it dry as if Elizabeth were there telling her to. It would have been nice, she thought, if the apple tree were still in bloom, but all the flowers had already gone to green. She heard a screech from up in the thorny locust. She looked, and there was a redwing just like Bird. The redwing screeched again. Then he flew away.

*   *   *

Old Mam smacked her lips over supper, It didn't seem to Sooner she'd used to do that. Then, her plate clean, Old Mam sat back and belched.

"Elizbeth says that ain't—*isn't* polite," Sooner told her.

"Elizbeth and Mac, Mac and Elizbeth! You been talkin nothin else the whole time we done et!" Old Mam sounded and looked mean. But then she snorted a little, and shook her head, and said, "But I suppose when you was with them, you took on just as much bout your Ole Mam. Ain't that right, Sooney?"

Took on about Old Mam? Sooner couldn't recollect it. In Switzer, at supper, there was always talk about school, or Mac's sick critters, or plans for the picnic on Saturday. But she nodded her head yes, anyway, because Old Mam seemed to be waiting for her to.

"I reckon," Old Mam said, pleased. "Well, maybe you done lived in that biggety house and all, but you ain't never been to Flordy with them two, have you?"

"Flordy?" Sooner had forgotten all about Flordy. It was that place Old Mam said once was south a ways. "No'm, I ain't."

Old Mam hitched herself forward to the table. "I done decided, Sooney, spite of that sheriff not doin right by me. Wintertimes any more, I can't seem to get these ole bones of mine warm no matter how I stoke up that fool stove. So I be goin to Flordy, come harvest. And iffen you've a mind to it, you can come along."

South a ways. Far? Sooner put down the piece of corn bread and sweet drippings she was sucking on. It didn't taste right, all of a sudden.

Old Mam was still talking. "I been cogitatin and cogitatin on it, Sooney. And I got me a plan. Jim Seevey, he come out not long back, and tole me he can't sell no more of my likker to that there CCC. Seems like the sheriff, he done turned plumb mean. But Jim Seevey's give me his promise to sell the seventy gallon I got left over to the fair, plus my last run yet to boil up, and it'll bring near to three hunnerd dollar. All I got to do now is talk him round to buying my raw whiskey after harvest all to oncet, stead of through the winter. It'll have to go cheap for its not bein aged, but seein as you and me won't be needin the mealies, nor William no fodder, I ought to get me way morn'a hunnerd gallon this year iffen the crop weathers good, so it'll all balance out. And with what I done put aside from my mushrat pelts and all, I reckon we'll do just fine down there in Flordy."

It was always confusing when Old Mam got to talking about money and whiskey-gallons, and all those days in school with double numbers didn't seem to help Sooner any. Old Mam went so fast, Sooner just couldn't keep track. Anyway, it plain gave her an ache in her middle, all this going on about Flordy.

"Is it far," she asked, "to Flordy?" She meant but didn't ask: so far, that if Elizabeth did come and they'd gone, Elizabeth would never be able to find her. Instead, she seized on the thought of William. "Cause iffen it is," she said, "I don't know as how William'll get there so good."

"William!" Old Mam threw back her head and laughed. "Sooney, if you ain't a caution! We ain't a-goin to Flordy in no mule cart! We be goin by bus!" And she laughed some more. Then she sighed and began clattering the plates together. "Go take the bucket and get some water, chile. Time to be riddin up."

Sooner did as she was told, worrying it around in her head so that William and Elizabeth and the bus got all mixed up and she didn't know where she was at. Maybe the crop wouldn't weather right, and none of it would ever happen. Once, it had rained and rained the summer long, and the corn went bad.

As she toted the bucket up from the creek, the water slopped as it always had onto her feet, and the bucket grew heavy under her hand. Her fingers itched to reach for those taps in Switzer and have the water pour forth. She searched the sky. No clouds at all. But maybe there would be tomorrow—or the day after. Anyway, even if there weren't, the bus to Flordy might be bigger than the one she'd seen in Marengo for that school group. It could be, Sooner thought, if Flordy was farther to go than Marengo. She'd have to ask Old Mam about that, because if it was, then the bus might be big enough so that William could ride, too. But if it was that far, then what of Elizabeth? Hastily, an answer came: anyway, anyway, if Elizabeth did come . . . sometime . . . and they were gone

173

to Flordy, why, Sooner couldn't make Elizabeth cry again. And that'd be all to the good. Wouldn't it?

*　　*　　*

When they finished cultivating the next afternoon, Old Mam said she had that one last barrel of ripe mash she wanted to run. She sent Sooner up to the cabin for a packet of bacon and corn bread to keep her going awhile, and to bring her shotgun, and then she went on down to the still. It would take close to three days to boil up the beer, though Old Mam said it used to be much longer until she got herself the doubler and could get her whiskey all in one boiling. Except to carry some food down off and on, Sooner stayed away as much as she could because the doubler made such a funny noise. Old Mam liked to call it the thump-keg. Sooner had heard her tell tales about how a still could sometimes get clogged up and explode and throw boiling corn mush all over the county.

But it was all right with Old Mam if Sooner stayed away. She wouldn't trust anybody but herself to feed the furnace so the temperature stayed just right. And she said it always gave her a feeling of comfort to know Sooner was up by the cabin somewhere, keeping a watch for revenuers. There hadn't ever been any revenuers, at least not that Sooner could remember, but Old Mam called it a comfort even so.

Sooner was on the creek bank, near the road culvert, looking for sour grass to chew on, when she heard a motor and looked up to see the blue top of Mac's truck turn into the lane. Her heart gave a thud. She stood up from her crouch but couldn't see but just below the top. The truck drove on up the lane. Sooner followed after, coming up the bank slowly and always with the weeds high about her. She got to where the apple tree boughs drooped nearly to the ground. The

174

truck had stopped. Now she could see in through the window. But only Mac was inside.

Sooner drew back in among the leaves. Mac got out and glanced around and started for the cabin. She let him go, and then turned and silently moved back down to the creek. When he began to call her name, she scootched herself down and covered her ears and watched some ants being busy so as not to hear him. She stayed that way a long time, sometimes looking away from the ants up toward the lane, watching for the truck to leave, but it didn't. She was still like that when the boom came.

It came from upcreek, and all her scootching down with her hands over her ears hadn't dulled it much. It had happened at last, Sooner was sure. The still had blown up. Except there wasn't any hot mush splattered around that she could see. And where was Mac?

She headed up the creek, hurrying, scared of what she'd find. She'd reached the sycamores when the second boom came, this time very loud. And right after, she heard Old Mam.

"Oh, it's you. Sneakin up on me thataway, it serves you right! Next time, I'll aim more careful."

Sooner smelled gunpowder. She ran on through the sycamores to where the still was. Old Mam had her shotgun up to her shoulder, and it was pointing at Mac. But he just looked mad; he wasn't bleeding anywhere.

"You've fired both barrels," he said to Old Mam. "That's all you've got, so put the gun down."

Old Mam glared at him, but she lowered the gun. "Don't like nobody trespassin on my place, and I done tole you yesterday to clear off!"

"I came to talk to Sooner, and I'm not leaving till I do," he said. And now he looked at Sooner and smiled.

"You want he should, Sooney?" Old Mam asked.

Sooner looked from one to the other, scared to answer anything. She'd brought a whole bag of shot when she'd brought Old Mam the gun. Old Mam could reload in a minute.

"Please, Sooner," Mac said. "I'd like to explain . . . or try to. About Elizabeth, and—and everything." He shoved both hands in his pockets and gave a quick shake to his head. "I—we want you to understand, Sooner."

But Sooner already knew why Elizabeth hadn't come. Would never come. "I unnerstan," she said.

"Well, you done heard her. Go on now. Get!" Old Mam gestured with her gun.

Mac looked from Sooner to Old Mam and back to Sooner again. He took a deep breath. Sooner watched his chest grow big with it. "We wouldn't have to talk, honey. We could—could go fishing, maybe. In the creek."

Fishing. With Mac. It would be fun. But Old Mam was standing right there with her shotgun.

"If not now, maybe next time," he was saying. "How about it, Sooner? Next time when I come back."

"Ain't no need for you to come back," she answered. Next time, Old Mam would aim better. She'd just said it. "Ain't no need at all."

There was a silence. Mac's eyes blinked as if touched by the sun, only the sun never came through enough to bother, down in the sycamores. He opened his mouth, closed it, turned and walked away.

There wouldn't be any fishing, for Mac wouldn't be back, Sooner knew. Bird was dead. And the Lord had spoken that Sooner be remembered no more. Elizabeth would never come.

"I sure hope that bus to Flordy's a big one," she said. "Cause iffen it ain't, poor William won't never get there!" She spun around and ran from Old Mam's sight, the tears in her eyes making her stumble. Dumb tears! Couldn't see for anything! And then she tripped hard and fell and just lay there and cried.

MAC

Mac dreaded telling Elizabeth about Sooner. The child had made it so final, down by the still. And Elizabeth's reception when he'd returned to Switzer alone yesterday morning had driven home the new conclusions he'd reached about her at Selma's.

Elizabeth had been watching from the kitchen for him, and she'd come running out. "Couldn't you find her?"

When he'd told her what had happened, it was oddly as if she would rather Sooner were still missing, for there could be hope that way. As it was, he watched the hope die in her eyes, her face go quite still; with a renewal of that certainty that was like a dying inside for her, he was sure. So that now, when he once again had to report failure, this time with no plan to return to the creek, no remotest sign of encouragement from Sooner, he didn't know what to expect from Elizabeth. He was afraid for her and that his own distress might prompt words from him better left unsaid.

But as he finshed telling her, she merely nodded and said, "It's over." She went up the stairs. "I'll have to call the school," she added, and then he heard the bedroom door close quietly behind her. He stood at the foot of the stairs, listening, wishing he would hear a storm of weeping. There was only silence.

The night Sooner had run away, Elizabeth had said she cared about the child. But did she? He remembered the words that had puzzled him the day he'd brought Sooner home. "Is this some kind of test or something?" And, "Were you thinking that all you have to do is force on somebody the opportunity to love, and she will?" It kept him standing there, that memory—and the suspicion that arose from it.

When she finally came down to fix dinner, she still had nothing to say. But her face was so without color that she looked as she had last fall, just home from the hospital, helpless, and half ill. Without thought he was out of his chair, putting his arms around her, hoping to pull her into him, wanting the comfort only each could give to the other, but her body was ungiving. After a moment, she stood back from him.

"You seem all right," she said, her voice even and remote.

"I'll do," he said. "What about you?"

She dropped her eyes and walked past him toward the kitchen. "Dinner will be ready soon," she said.

Sitting there in the living room, listening to the rattle of pans, he felt the beginning of bitterness and let it grow. It wasn't just that he wasn't allowed to share his own sadness, but that she refused to share hers with him. He felt closed out, not only by the child but by Elizabeth, too.

That night set the pattern for many days to come. There was politeness, and that was all. They still shared the same bed; they still shared the same house, and sometimes the same room at the same time; but they were together in nothing, and Sooner's name was never spoken.

Sometimes the conversation between them at the end of the day would continue long enough to include the news that Harriet had called them for bridge on Saturday night, or that the monthly potluck supper at the church was this coming Wednesday. And when the time came, they'd go, and smile, and talk to others, and come home in silence.

When he tried to reach her, to tell her that this separateness was intolerable for both of them, she would only look at him as from a long distance so that he wasn't sure she understood even the words he was using. Or she would push a quick smile across her face and ask for the second time how his day had gone. Once, when he reached for her, he caught some longing in her eyes, or thought he did. But then she turned away.

Sometimes, he would come home to find the house untouched since morning, and they'd have to go to Cy's to eat. Elizabeth never wanted to, saying she wasn't hungry, but Mac always made her. She was getting so thin. Her fine skin was taking on the tiny lines about the eyes and at the corners of her mouth that shouldn't have appeared for another ten years. And because they weren't the natural signs of age but signs of the spirit setting itself to accept the unacceptable, they were sad and not pretty.

Other days he would come home to find a great farm dinner underway on the stove, the house scrubbed, and an iced three-layer cake on the table, as if she had had to expend a frantic energy every minute all the day long.

Evenings, she would read—an endless series of books —and while the pages didn't always turn with regularity, her withdrawal was complete.

Only one thing was removed from the pattern. No matter how Elizabeth behaved inside the house, she was making the garden flourish as never before. It seemed the blooming of her flowers was her only balm. Or perhaps it was the labor itself, the digging and transplanting, the clipping and thinning. She would kneel for hours, her hands working and grimy, her

179

face engrossed but tranquil, the only time Mac saw those new lines smoothed away.

All these things made the absence of Sooner in the house the more painfully defined for him. He found memories cropping up in his mind that he hadn't realized he'd been storing away. He missed the heavy clatter of her shoes on the stairs. He missed her delight as he'd pushed her higher and higher on the swing. He missed coming into the house late in the afternoon to find the two of them, Sooner and Elizabeth, bent over pencil and paper at the living-room table, both engrossed in the slow awkward scrawls they called "Sooner's writing," Sooner with her tongue peeping out at the corner of her mouth, Elizabeth looking around at him with a return of that bright gay pride he'd always loved in her.

Of course, Phil had to be told. When Mac went down to the jail, he found him in the corridor of the cellblock, overseeing two boys who were scrubbing out one of the cells. The air smelled of Lysol.

When Phil saw Mac, he came into the front room, closing the door to the block. "Couple of CCC boys," he said. "Got into a drunk fight last night, and I had to bring 'em in, and they got sick all over the place."

He'd gone to the coffeepot and was pouring out two mugs.

"Jim swears he didn't sell the booze to them. I guess I believe him. But I sure wish I knew who had." He held out one mug to Mac, nodding toward the cells. "They aren't talking. Matter of honor, I suppose," he chuckled dryly.

Mac took the mug, still silent, still not sure how to say what he had to. Phil eyed him expectantly, then went to sit down behind his table and set about lighting up a cigar.

Mac took a deep breath. "Sooner's gone back to the creek," he said.

Phil stared at him, forgetting to draw on his cigar, and the lit match burned his fingers.

"You warned me," Mac pushed on, "and you were right. You said it was asking too much of her, and—you were right."

Phil kept his face expressionless, and struck another match, this time working at the cigar until it smoked nicely.

"Have you tried talking to her?" he asked.

"It's no go," Mac said. If Phil comes on with sympathy, he thought, I'm leaving.

But Phil said nothing for a long moment, didn't even look at Mac again.

"Elizabeth called the school, so I guess this finishes it, doesn't it."

Phil glanced at him with sharp eyes. "For you, maybe," he said, but mildly. "Only, what do I do in the fall when school starts? Now that the old woman's brought Sooner to my attention . . . I don't know. Maybe she should be made a ward of the county, after all."

"No, Phil," Mac said. The possibility appalled him. He moved closer to the table, set his untouched coffee down on it. "Don't do that. An orphanage would be hell for her." He leaned on the table toward Phil. "Look, if money would help . . . I mean, that's what Mrs. Hawes wanted, wasn't it? Well, tell her it's county money, and I'll give it to you."

"I'll think about it," Phil said. His eyes went distant. "Could be, something else might work."

"Phil—"

Phil hauled in his breath against Mac's urgency, and Mac straightened back from the table.

"Okay," he said. "You're right again. I haven't the right to tamper with her life any more."

"I didn't say that." Phil smiled at Mac, one corner

181

of his mouth turning down with it so that it was wry and sad. "I said I'll think about it."

Mac nodded, and he couldn't have returned Phil's smile if his life had depended on it. "Well," he said, "I've got patients waiting." He turned abruptly and went out. He got into the truck he'd parked at the curb, and suddenly realized what he was going to miss the most. It was having a little girl on his lap. He'd miss the fragrance of her, and the plumpness that had begun to cover all those skinny bones.

Sooner had become a part of so much in such a short time. Nor could the infirmary provide him the usual refuge, because she was missing from there, too. Always, he could hear her giggle, her croon as she had cajoled some sick creature to eat or to swallow its medicine. As the summer hottened up, Mac's practice underwent a major shift. The infirmary emptied. Cats, hounds, pet guinea pigs, and parakeets recovered and were dismissed into the care of their owners, and their cages remained untenanted. Mac explained his refusal of new small animal patients by saying he was too busy. And he was, with a farm stock practice that took him farther and farther afield, more and more often, until, with the exception of a few neighborhood pets whose young owners he couldn't bring himself to turn away, the infirmary became only the place he showered and changed clothes in at quitting time.

One evening, the secretary of the Fair Board came to see him. It was a formality that had to be gone through, complete with cookies Elizabeth had baked, and coffee. It always seemed a total waste of time to Mac, going over once again all the requirements for the stock exhibitors, perusing one by one the health regulations, the immunization requirements, the rules of sanitation laid down by the state, as if he'd not been in charge of the animal barns for the past eight years, or that the fifty-dollar fee for the five days' work was any higher than it had ever been or could possibly recompense him for the time lost from his practice. Still, it had to be formally offered, and he had to formally accept; for the record, the secretary always said, all the while ruining Elizabeth's good black coffee with milk and two lumps of sugar.

As usual when time for the fair grew close, Mac found he had a bunch of nervous stockmen on his hands, each of them hoping for a ribbon. Both old man Dunkle and Jackson with his hogs cured of anaemia expected miracles, but they'd left it too late to push up the milk production of Dunkle's cows, or to fatten up Jackson's barrows, either. Even Cy Crawford was getting nervy about the fair now that his trotter was back to normal. And of course, there was Harvey Drummond on his neck, though that was all right. Royal Master was one animal that stood a real chance at a blue. And so, Mac was constantly on call, during the night and on weekends, too.

But busy as he was, it wasn't enough. Always, he had to come home: home to Elizabeth and loneliness. He felt, as July came on, and then August, that they were both held perpetual prisoners in one of those periods of indecision which most people know only for a few hours or a few days, and the alienation frightened him more and more as it lengthened on.

During warm humid nights, he lay awake next to her, and felt her body as remote from him as the rest of her. He would touch her with purpose, with invitation; she never responded. Maybe she perceived a compunction in it. He didn't know; but he was left plenty of time to think about it.

Sex had always held more for Elizabeth than the pleasure in it, he knew that. It had to mean everything, be loaded with the tender significances of love, or the joy wouldn't exist for her. Before Sooner had run away, Elizabeth had been trying too hard with him,

183

as if scared that less and less of the meaning could be found. Now, she wouldn't try at all. He had to conclude that the animal satisfaction alone would be a repugnance to her, and didn't insist.

But something had to change, he didn't know what or how, and his inability to come up with a solution produced a restlessness in him, prodding him out of the house to flee her silence even in the evening. He did a lot of walking, and no matter in what direction he started out, he would end up outside Selma's.

He'd stand there on the walk and fight with himself to keep from going in, both wanting and afraid of the arousal he had experienced with her in June. The night he gave in and went to her door, she surprised him by answering the bell from around the corner of the house.

"We're out back," she said. "Come on and sit a spell."

He followed her between some cool evergreens to the back yard, watching the bunching rise and fall of her behind under her thin cotton dress as she walked. We, she'd said. Mac couldn't decide whether he'd counted on Phil's being here and now was relieved to find it true, or whether he was disappointed.

Selma turned toward the kitchen door. "I'll get another glass." She went inside, letting the screen door slap to after her. Mac continued on to the lawn, where some chairs and a table were hopefully set out in the open to catch any breeze, and Phil was a dim green shape, lit by the Citronella candle burning inside green glass on the table. Next to it, green-lit too, were the familiar outlines of a jug and Selma's old hand-crank Victrola.

Phil didn't appear puzzled to see him, nor the slightest bit reluctant to share Selma's company. He asked about Elizabeth with passing casualness, didn't mention

Sooner, and handed over his empty glass to Mac before he could sit down.

"You're up," Phil said.

Mac filled it from the jug. "Lord, I'd think Selma would have junked that old machine years ago." He gave Phil his whiskey.

"Still works, why should I," Selma said, coming out of the house. She let Mac pour his own drink, and sank into a chair. "Whew," she said, flapping her skirt above her white knees. "Do anything, any little thing, and you're drenched. What a summer!"

Mac lifted a record from the top of a small pile, laid it over the spindle, put the needle on, and cranked up the Victrola. The flat, tinny tenor of years ago came scratching through the tulip spiral. "Seated one day at the organ . . ." Mac swung to look at Selma. Her head was back against her chair, but it was too dark to see her expression. When they were kids, she'd sit listening to this record, her eyes lifted, transported by the sublime search for the lost chord.

"Better than going to church, huh, Selma," Phil said, teasing her.

She chuckled. "Always was. You fellas remember the day we carried the Vic down to the Blue and listened to records and found God?"

They all laughed, and Mac sat down, and the three of them were launched into reminiscences. Selma would rise now and then, or Phil would, to put on another record or fill up a glass from the jug. But they didn't drink heavily. It was too hot. Windows were open in the neighboring houses, and there was the sense of life all around. Crickets singing, and tree frogs, a stray fragment of female chatter as if over dishes, a dog barking, a radio dance band suddenly turned down, a father hollering his boy in to bed. The Citronella candle spiced the air.

They talked about old football games when Mac

185

played halfback, old track meets when Phil ran the mile. The hour lengthened into two, and Mac recognized growing in himself the same lust for Selma as before. Her bare legs were stretched before her and separated for coolness, with her skirt gathered to her thighs. The night had brightened as if the air had cleared enough for the stars to shine through. Mac could see her features, now, could see that she was echoing what he felt with the very languor of her body; in the way she turned her face to listen to Phil but left her eyes on Mac; in the way she held the rim of her glass against her lower lip to run the tip of her tongue along it.

If he could see it, so could Phil. The question hit Mac: What are you playing at, you damned fool? What are you chancing? If Selma doesn't care, you ought to.

But Phil was showing no sign of having noticed. Even as Mac shot a glance at him, Phil rose. "Past time for patrol, and I'm on, tonight," he said. In addition to his county duties, Phil alternated with his deputy to keep the peace in Switzer. "Don't get up," he said, starting for the street, but Selma accompanied him anyway. Before they quite left the yard, Phil hesitated and called back to Mac. "Meant to ask. Anything new about Sooner?"

Mac shook his head, then realized Phil probably couldn't see, and replied, "Nothing new."

"Well . . . see you, Mac."

Mac sat on, knowing he shouldn't. A mockingbird was sounding forth from the next yard over, going through its repertoire in some secret, precise order, every song repeated three times or five, and always with the same slight imperfections so as to tell listeners what he was.

Selma returned into the green light. "That Phil," she said. "He never gives up. Has he told you what he wants? Me to take in that kid, come time for school."

Selma? Selma and Sooner? Why not? She'd probably do a hell of a lot better for the child than Elizabeth had.

Mac heaved himself out of his chair, poured whiskey and drained it down.

"It's the last thing I need, you know?" Selma was saying. "Some kid to tie me down. And that's exactly what Phil's angling for."

Mac lifted the jug. "Want a drink?" he asked her. "No."

He began to pour himself another. She took his glass and set it empty on the table. "And neither do you." Her voice was low, and she looked up at him with an odd combination of question and certain knowledge and excitement. "Phil won't be back tonight," she said.

Mac's eyes were held by hers, and his breath came shallow and quick. Selma bent away. She picked up the candle and blew it out. The darkness was blinding. The mockingbird fell silent. Selma groped for his hand and raised it to her breast, pressing it into her and moving against it like a cat creating a caress. Her nipple went hard in his palm. He slid his hands to her back, down to the full rounds below her waist, and pulled her to meet his own hard rising.

"Come upstairs," she whispered.

Suddenly it was something not happening, but going to happen; an episode to be arranged, to find a place for. Mac let her go. He could see the light of her dress move toward the house.

The last thing I need, to be tied down, she'd said.

This wasn't a product of simple desire, not for either of them. She was using him, as he was ready to use her. And when the time came that she most needed to declare her independence from Phil, one way or another she would let him know about this night.

187

The realization should have cooled Mac off, but it didn't. Selma was standing by the screen door, waiting, and he still wanted it with her.

"I'll use her, and she'll use me, and Phil'll use Sooner; he accused me of that, but he's no better. The refrain jiggled through Mac's mind in ugly burlesque rhythm.

He found himself crossing the yard to Selma. "No," he said. It was involuntary. Where did the word come from? He tried to gentle it. "I'm sorry, Selma."

He sensed the shocked tightening of her body as she straightened from leaning against the door. "I'm sorry," he said again, and meant it. Helpless, he headed for the street.

She'd think it was because of Elizabeth. He felt disgusted and ridiculous to be running from seduction like a virgin girl, and angry that it wasn't because of Elizabeth. He looked down at himself and hoped to God he didn't meet anyone before he reached the house.

SOONER

It did rain some during the long summer days out at Black Willow Creek, but never too much, never enough to harm the corn. Old Mam was real pleased because the weather did just right by her. Still, Sooner didn't ask if the bus to Flordy would be big enough for William. Inside, she knew the answer anyway. But if she didn't ask so that Old Mam couldn't tell her no, there could be times when Sooner could pretend and not have to worry it over.

The corn got too high for the cultivator, but not

high enough yet to keep itself clean. Along with the tomatoes and green beans and the little bit of sweet corn Old Mam put in for the table, it had to be weeded by hand. At first, Old Mam worked the rows with Sooner, but as the days came in hotter and hotter, June going into July, and the nights never cooled off at all as the August sun held the humid air close to the earth so it got hard even to take breath, Old Mam would rock on the stoop and fan herself, and Sooner did the garden weeding alone.

When it had to be done, she did it in the early mornings, thinking of the nasturtiums and hollyhocks she had planted with Elizabeth, thinking of how different it would be to be weeding Elizabeth's flowers instead of Old Mam's kitchen garden. Elizabeth had said that the hollyhocks might grow even taller than Sooner. When Mac had tried to get Elizabeth to plant some tomatoes, she had just laughed at him. She was a city girl, she said, and she'd buy her tomatoes in the store.

In the humming quiet of afternoons, Sooner would go sit in the creek and let the water move around her in running coolness. The best place was way upcreek in the shade of the wild grapes. The broad silvery leaves hung down, with slender tendrils weeping toward the water like a willow. Before long, the tiny sweet-sour fruit would be ripe enough to eat. As it was, she could sit and reach from where she was the blackberries lining the bank and touched with red, reach and pick one at a time so that they could explode in puckery sweetness on her tongue again and yet again.

Sitting there in the creek, letting her hands turn and flow with the water while a bobwhite called from somewhere up the bank, Sooner would ponder over some things, not meaning to, but the thoughts came and went. Sometimes they were bothersome, and then she was grateful when the kingfisher with a white ring

189

around his neck would dive into the water nearby to catch a shiner, or when a slim, mottled-like-mud snake would glide by her, swimming upcreek against the current.

The memory of how Old Mam and William had looked the first time she'd seen them down in the corn patch that morning she'd come back from Switzer was one of those thoughts. They had seemed two strangers: William, thin and old and ugly: Old Mam, just a funny-looking lady with a streaked skirt and untidy hair and a puckered-up mouth. It was as if Sooner didn't know them, until the world gave a sort of tremble and suddenly they were the same Old Mam and William that Sooner had always known. But that first moment of seeing them had seemed to last a long time, and the memory of how they looked then kept returning like a picture in a frame. Once, days after, when Sooner was climbing the bank up to the cabin, it had suddenly looked strange, too. She had been all set to tell Old Mam that something had happened to the cabin to make it lean so, until she got inside and saw that everything was in its place and just the same, and there was that tremble again, and she knew the cabin was as it always had been.

She'd stopped naming herself something besides Sooner. It seemed a silly game now, especially since she knew Old Mam would never call her anything but "Sooney" anyway. So when bothersome thoughts came, and the kingfisher or the snake didn't happen to do it for her, she had to switch her mind to something else on her own, like wondering about Judith Ann. Now that school was out, would she be up at Bead's Knob, jumping off the fence like last year? In a way, Sooner would have liked to go up there to see. But she never had found her shoes again, and her dress was getting kind of raggedy, and Judith Ann would just giggle at her in that way she had.

After supper and ridding up, there wasn't any Parcheesi with Old Mam, nor even the talk Sooner yearned for. In the big house in Switzer, when they were three together, there had always been lots to say. But Old Mam just sat on the stoop evenings, slapping at mosquitoes, hoping for some coolness before bed. All the bugs and frogs around lifted their noises to a din so loud that Sooner suspicioned it couldn't be broken by a single voice. She tried, though, offering up things seen and tasted and smelled in Switzer, little gifts of words that never seemed to strike Old Mam's ears at all. And then, one in that long summer march of nights was otherwise. Heat lightning flashed silent on the darkening sky, and Sooner said, "Know what? Moon's just the same there as here. Ain't that somethin?"

"Same where as here?" Old Mam asked her. It startled Sooner. Old Mam leaned forward to peer out from under the roof. "Ain't no moon showin," she said, and she smacked a mosquito hard and smeared the blood away from her neck.

"Switzer," said Sooner. "Moon's the same there as here. I stayed up oncet and saw."

Old Mam sniffed.

"They's a song I done learned," Sooner said, hopeful now. "Want to hear it?" She started to sing.

> "Are you sleeping,
> Are you sleeping,
> Brother John,
> Brother John?

"Now you got to do it," she said to Old Mam.

"What you talkin, Sooney? I don't got to do nothin, cept sit and rock and try to cool off, some."

"No, I mean you got to sing what I just done finished with, and I sing something else, and it goes together real pretty."

Old Mam just sniffed again, and rocked.

Sooner thought maybe if she went on singing, Old Mam would see and join in.

> "Morning bells are ringing,
> Morning bells are ringing!
> Ding, dang, dong!
> Ding dang, dong!"

But Old Mam didn't join in, and the bugs and the frogs seemed louder than ever when Sooner finished the song alone.

"Know what?" she said again. "They's a machine they got in Switzer, you can talk into it and hear somebody a-talkin back at you. And I done saw that there big river, the Ohio, and Kentucky on tother side. And I done found out what pitch is, too."

"Hush up, chile. It plumbs tuckers me, you carryin on so in this here heat."

Sooner jumped to her feet with a fierce longing to be heard.

"But I done found out! Over to Marengo, down in that cave. It's an underground river, that's what it is. Cause you can still see the streaky marks it done left behind on the ceilin!"

"Pshaw, Sooney! Tain't no such a thing." Old Mam slapped another mosquito dead. "Underground river's same as any other river. And them streaky marks you done seed . . . just lamp black, more'n likely."

"No," Sooner said, shaking her head at Old Mam, feeling suddenly bereft. "No! Cause the man who told us, he *said*. Without no lights, it's black as pitch down there!"

"Water's water, underground or atop," Old Mam said. "I swan, chile, them folks in Switzer, they sure done changed you unseemly. Like to talk my ear off ever since you done come home. Now you hush up, hear?"

Sooner didn't feel changed, nor unseemly, either. She stepped down off the stoop into the flickering darkness, stumbling with her hurry to get away.

Maybe that cave river wasn't pitch, but she wasn't changed. The only difference between now and when she went to Switzer was she didn't have Bird any more, nor Little One. But she wasn't changed. Old Mam was different, maybe, but *she* wasn't.

"Sooney? It's near to bedtime," Old Mam hollered after her.

Sooner paid her no mind. She went around the cabin and back to where William was tethered in among the weeds. She put her hand on his back, and leaned into him, and rubbed her face against his side. He whickered at her.

"That bus to Flordy, it won't never be big enough for you, William," she said.

She moved along his side to his ear twisting for the sound of her.

"You hear me, William? It won't never be."

She wrapped her arm under his neck, and pulled gently at his mane. It was full of burrs.

"We ain't goin to Flordy, William. What need we got to go? Ain't none. We be stayin here, you and me. Ole Mam, she can get on that bus of herself withouten us. And come winter, William, I'll feed you all the mealies you can want."

She turned her head down and rubbed her face against him again.

"We'll do just fine, you and me. Just fine."

ELIZABETH

"Pass the bread, will you?"

"What?" Elizabeth looked up from her bowl of soup.

"The bread," Mac said.

She looked at him a moment more, still blank. "Oh," she said, then reached for the bread plate, closer to her than to him, and handed it across the table.

She'd been thinking about Little One, and wondering if she had enough peanuts to put out for him tomorrow or if she should go to the store for more.

She looked back down at her soup, cream of tomato out of a can. The spoon in her hand was still clean. How long had she been sitting there, not eating? Mac's bowl was empty, she saw now, and he was buttering a last slice of bread. She spooned up some of the soup. It was almost cold and tasted tinny.

Putting out food for the chipmunk was a habit she'd got into since Sooner had left. It was almost a compulsion with her, as if by leaving Little One here when she'd gone, Sooner had given over a trust. Sometimes, Elizabeth would waken at night, unable to remember whether she'd put out the peanuts that day or not, and then she'd worry for what seemed like hours, though she knew it was silly of her. It was summer, after all, and Little One was quite capable of looking after himself, so she never mentioned to Mac that she was doing it. The peanuts were always taken by Little One. She'd watch until they were gone, and she'd feel relieved, and the day would seem lighter for it.

Mac got up from the table and left the kitchen, and she heard him go into his office.

I didn't even ask him what kind of morning he had, she thought.

She set down her spoon and followed him to the office. The door was open, and she looked in to see him unlock the gun rack and take down one of his father's rifles. He didn't see her. He opened the breech of the gun, checked it, closed it again, then moved to the desk and took some cartridges from a drawer.

It isn't hunting season for anything, it is? Elizabeth asked herself. Anyway, Mac doesn't hunt any more.

Dropping the cartridges into his pocket, Mac turned around from the desk to find her in the doorway.

"Sick hog," he said. "The farmer won't be too happy about it, so I asked Phil to go out with me."

A car horn blew from the street.

"There he is," Mac said, and he started past her for the front door.

Elizabeth felt an excitement stir. She didn't give herself time to think about it. "Mac?" she said, walking after him quickly. He looked back at her from the living room, waiting impatiently as Phil blew his horn again. "Leave the keys to the truck, will you? If you're not taking it . . ."

She saw the question in his eyes. She rarely asked for the truck. He was waiting for her to say something. She didn't, and he reached into his pocket, pulled out his keys, tossed them on the living-room table, and went on out of the house.

She crossed to the table and picked up the keys. She hardly dared think about what she was going to do. She wouldn't think about it; she'd just do it.

She went up the stairs, moving quickly now, almost running up them, and went straight into Sooner's room. She hadn't been in it, except to dust, since Sooner went away. The baby doll was still sitting on

195

the dresser, but Bird's perch was gone. She'd thrown it out the very next day.

I'll take the doll, Elizabeth thought. The doll and some of her clothes.

When she opened the closet and the drawers in the dresser, she saw many more things than she'd remembered. She began to collect them, until, in the bottom drawer, she caught sight of the blue sunsuit. She pulled it out, recalling how Sooner had relished the red apple stitched to the pocket and how pretty her little-girl legs had been when she'd worn the suit. Elizabeth skimmed the shiny chintz of the apple with her fingertips, feeling instead that other silky smoothness beneath her hands when she'd bathed Sooner.

Pain took Elizabeth by surprise. Was this why she had kept out of this room? But she had lived with failure the summer long, she thought with wonder; and had accepted it as *her* failure. How was it that she should feel pain now? Only, she suddenly knew this was nothing to do with conscience. It was something else entirely.

She picked up the sunsuit and held it to her face, as if to catch the smell of the child who'd worn it. There was a residue of the cedar-lined drawer it had lain in for so many weeks, no more than that.

She caught in her breath against what was swelling inside her, and hastily tumbled things back from where she'd taken them, all but the sunsuit. She tucked that beneath her arm, and picked up the doll. In the small top drawer were the extra doll clothes. She grabbed them up in a little bundle, slammed the last drawer shut, and went down the stairs and out of the house without a glance at the dirty lunch dishes, only with a terrible pressing hurry. But she refused to wonder at it, or at herself, any more.

She got into the truck and set Sooner's things, precious good-luck charms, carefully on the seat while she started the motor. She'd never been out to Black Willow Creek, but Mac had told her where it was, once, and she'd be able to find it.

*   *   *

It took a while for the dust to settle after she stopped the truck on the lane. The air was hot and sultry, the sun glancing off the polished metal of the hood of the Ford so that she had to squint against it, and she tasted the dust on her lips.

She'd found the way easily enough, hardly thinking about landmarks. What would Sooner say? Would she want to come back? But every time her thoughts wanted to project an answer, she blocked it, trying to block the wild soaring of hope, so that the questions ran again and again unanswered through her mind.

From the seat she looked through the window across the dirt waste to the cabin. It was awful. Falling down and dreary and awful, as she'd suspected it would be. That had been one of her excuses for not coming before. To see what Sooner had run back to could only make it worse.

Then why was she here now? She'd clung to excuses the whole summer, afraid that with a decision to go see Sooner, hope would be born. Anyway, she almost never had the truck these days, with Mac gone so much. Nor could she tell him she wanted to come; she'd imagined too often what his reaction would be. "Leave her alone, Elizabeth. Haven't you done her enough harm?"

Elizabeth leaned abruptly on the handle and thrust the truck door open. The chance had come; and without predicting, against all resolution, she'd grasped it and she was here. Never mind the why.

Her heart beating high in her throat, feeling oddly as a woman must when embarking toward an illicit

197

assignation of love, Elizabeth slid from the seat to the ground. Little puffs of dust lifted about her feet. There wasn't a sign of life in the hot midday. Should she give a call?

She started across the yard and was caught there in the furious August sun, halfway between truck and cabin, by the old woman coming out onto the stoop from the dark recesses within.

How had Elizabeth been so stupid, not to have realized it could come to this—that she might have to confront Mrs. Hawes instead of the child? Oh, God, the woman was atrocious in her filthy dress, and terrible with the strength of an old root rising brown and stubborn out of the earth.

The sun beat through Elizabeth's hair, through her skull. Light shimmered all about her as if preparing to explode. The woman's black gaze, flat, rejecting, pinned Elizabeth under the driving sun like a nightmare of nakedness on a spotlighted stage.

"I want—" Elizabeth had to clear her throat. She'd spoken nearly in a whisper. It was a wonder to find speech at all. "I want to see Sooner," she said.

"Wouldn't have no inklin where she's at," Mrs. Hawes said.

The sneering county twang reduced the woman to what she was. "Shall I call for her, or will you?" Elizabeth asked, the firm sound of it startling her.

"Twon't do you no good," Mrs. Hawes said. Slowly, she smiled. "More'n likely, she's hidin out over in them bushes. Watchin the bothen us. Listenin. Iffen she wanted to see you, she'd come out, of herself." She moved forward to the top step of the stoop and spread her feet to stand with her arms akimbo. All that Elizabeth had seen in her to begin with was there again: the immutability, the sureness, the dire force of her. "Get," she said, no smile now. "You done harm enough to my Sooney."

Elizabeth fell back one step, two, recoiling from the words. She had dreaded hearing them from Mac, and was hearing them anyway.

Unable to help herself, she looked around at the brush encroaching on the packed dirt. Was Sooner there, hiding somewhere, watching? Hiding from her?

Elizabeth bolted for the truck, climbed in, started it, and somehow turned it around and out onto the lane without looking toward the cabin again.

"Oh, Sooner," she murmured, and she went on murmuring it over and over, her right hand not on the wheel but on the red chintz apple, petting it as if it were a beloved live thing.

Even after she left the lane, its dust seemed to surround her, coating the windshield. Her eyes were unclear. It was hard for her to see the road, but she had a need to go very fast, and the bumps made the steering wheel whip in her left hand as if it wanted to spring free.

She wished that it would. She wished for something to happen outside herself that wouldn't be her fault and that would finish it once and for all. She kept the touch of her fingers on the smooth and shining apple.

The dust blew in through the window, gritting between her teeth; the sun turned the tar ahead on the road to wavering mirage lakes; she felt the back of her dress go damp with her sweat against the leather seat; she felt the sweat run in lines down her legs from under her skirt; and her damned left hand went on fighting with the wheel, holding the speeding truck straight and safe.

MAC

When he'd gone out to the car, Pop's old .30-.30 in his hand, Phil had leaned over to the passenger window and eyed him a little quizzically. "I can take care of it, if you want," he said, patting the pistol at his hip.

Mac laid the rifle on the back seat, and got in beside Phil. "You've been seeing too many of those Westerns over at the Regent," he told him. "The rifle'll do a better job."

Phil started driving. "Up to you," he said. "But I know it's not exactly your idea of pleasure."

"No. No pleasure," Mac answered. He slumped down onto his tail in the seat. In spite of the shortness of his words, he felt a gratitude to Phil. All Elizabeth had said when he'd told her was, "Oh." Time was, she'd have known how low he felt, having to kill a domestic animal. She'd have wanted to know why. She'd have touched him and said she was sorry.

"However," he went on, "your pistol might come in handy for Detweiler. Never saw a man so angry. You got the warrant?"

Phil nodded. He was relighting his burned-out cigar, as usual. "You going to lose him as a customer over this?"

Mac gave a wry chuckle. "Already have. And by the way, don't let me leave his place without warning him. He won't get his stock by me at the fair unless he has health papers dated as of this week."

Phil grinned. "How to make yourself real popular, huh?"

Mac shrugged, looking out the window. "Nothing for it," he said.

The fair was only one week away, and Mac had spent all day Friday of the week before with one of his new farmers, Ray Detweiler. Detweiler was a Duroc breeder, a fine one. His hogs were always among the top ranks at every county fair in southern Indiana, and at the state fair as well. His land was clear to the Orange County line, and Detweiler had always used the services of Dr. Moore up in Paoli. Why he'd switched to him Mac didn't know, but he had been delighted, until Friday, when he'd seen that ailing sow. He'd had a very good idea what they were in for, but he'd taken a blood sample to make sure. On Monday, he'd had to give Detweiler the bad news. It was brucellosis. Detweiler's whole herd ought to be retested and certified healthy. Certainly it was a must for the breeding swine he planned to enter in the fair. And the sow would have to be slaughtered.

Slaughtered! Mac had thought for a moment Detweiler would have a heart attack. Instead, he'd torn into Mac. He'd be God damned, he'd shouted, if he'd slaughter his prize breeder! He'd isolate her. She might recover—hogs did, sometimes—and McHenry could retest the rest of the herd to a fare-thee-well. But he'd be God damned if he'd slaughter that sow!

Mac had told him he had no choice. Sure, maybe hogs could recover, but cows didn't have such an easy time with it, and neither did people. In fact, he'd strongly recommend that Detweiler have himself and his family tested for undulant fever at once. The brucella could spread just from being carried around on a farmer's boots.

At which point, Detweiler had fired Mac and kicked him off the farm, and Mac had had to call Phil. Maybe Detweiler would calm down and see reason in time, but there wasn't any time. The poor fool could lose his entire herd, and if it jumped farms, the county could have an epidemic. Phil had figured they'd better make it as official as they could, with a warrant and the sheriff's car.

They both fell silent after they left town. Detweiler's farm was a pretty far piece, mainly over graveled roads. The woods close and green, the high yellow corn cut the breeze so that the dust they raised hovered about the car like its own private cloud. Occasionally, a break would come when the land cover opened for a farmhouse, and the air would trail the dust away from them for a passing moment. The farmer, sitting in faded coveralls on his porch out of the sun, would wave. Or a woman, stirring a kettle of soap over a fire in the yard, would raise up wearily and look at them from under her poke-bonnet.

They turned east when they reached the county line. "Not far now," Mac roused himself to say. Their shirts were sticking to them by this time, and Mac's handkerchief was a sodden mess of sweat and dust from mopping his face with it. He didn't see things getting any cooler, either, with Detweiler's quick temper. He took a deep breath and slid himself up in the seat. One lousy day, that's what it was.

* * *

Mac knew his man, all right. Detweiler went ugly, and it took every bit of authority Phil could muster to shut him up: badge, warrant, *and* pistol. Finally, Detweiler shouted at them that by God if they did the slaughterin' they could damned well do the buryin', too, and the shovels were in the barn. After which, he stomped into the house and slammed the door.

At least he had isolated the sow. She was in a small pen to herself, lying stretched out, as weak and sickly as yesterday. It was never an easy thing for Mac to do. Today it was bitter. His sweating fingers slipped

202

as if oiled on the cartridges, so that loading the breech seemed to be something done on slow-motion film. The sow panted helplessly in the sun, weakly lifting her massive head one inch, two, only to have its weight slam her back down into the mud. She grunted with it, with her desire for life.

Mac sighted along the .30-.30 toward the great skull and fired. The heat, his sweat, his fitful nausea, something or all of them together blurred his aim. He had to eject and fire again, his hands shaking from the pained and fearful squealing of the sow. The death stillness afterward was blessed. But the job was yet to be finished. They had to find a place off a ways, dig a hole, drag the dead sow into it, toss in some quicklime, and cover her with dirt. More than two hours of labor, and the only control for Mac's recurring nausea was to feed up an ire instead. By the time they were done, he was near to boiling over with it. But Phil was good-humored, though he did allow as how this wasn't the kind of duty he had in mind when running for office.

"Digging graves isn't exactly what I trained for, either," Mac snapped. Phil lifted an eyebrow at him, but Mac couldn't rise to humor right then, nor did he feel like apologizing for it. Without another exchange, they scrubbed in the barn and while Phil went to wait by the car Mac went to the house to speak his piece about the fair.

Detweiler heard him out in stony resentment, as if by having diagnosed the disease Mac had been the cause of it.

"Hell'll freeze over afore I show my hogs to your friggin fair, McHenry!" Detweiler burst out. "You trumped this whole thing up anyways, just so's I'd pay you the damned fees for recertifyin em!"

"Think what you like." Mac's voice came tight but held even, somehow. "Use any vet you want. But get your hogs recertified, because I've got to notify every fair board in the state your health papers are invalid now." He turned to leave, his anger unrelieved.

"Butcher! That's all you are, McHenry! Nothin but a son-of-a-bitch butcher!"

That did it. Twisting around, Mac grabbed Detweiler by his overall strap and hauled him off the porch into the hard punch coming up clear from Mac's heels. It threw Detweiler sprawling back on the steps. Blood trickled from the side of his mouth. Mac started toward him, but suddenly Phil was at his side, holding on to Mac's arm.

"That's enough," he said.

"He's hurt," Mac said, "I hurt him," and he tried to shake Phil loose to go help Detweiler, but Phil hung on.

The front door opened and Mrs. Detweiler stood looking down at her husband. "Detweiler," she said, sounding utterly disgusted, "you're an old fool." But she went to him, and knelt down by him. He wasn't unconscious. He had a hand to his mouth, and was trying to get up. "Son of a bitch," he was mumbling, "that's what he is. Son of a bitch."

Phil shoved Mac off. "Wait for me in the car," he said. Mac halted, half turning back, and Phil glared at him. "Will you get out of here? You want to file charges?"

From the car, Mac watched Phil and Detweiler's wife help him into the house, and then he waited what seemed one hell of a long time while none of his own rage abated. He hadn't socked anybody since grammar school, but he could remember that then he'd felt some better afterward, the mad kind of wiped out by it.

Not now. And the least reason was that he knew damned well he'd have to come back out here and eat crow and blood-test every one of that bastard's Durocs for free.

He rubbed at the knuckles of his right hand. They weren't skinned, just reddening up some.

Nobody'd ever called him a butcher before. Christ. Nothing came easy or simple, these days. God damn it, not even killing a sick hog.

Phil jerked the car door open and whipped in behind the wheel. "He's all right," he said, not looking at Mac. "Just cut the inside of his mouth some."

He turned on the ignition and swung the car around and down the drive quickly.

"I told him he provoked you into it and that I was witness. You're off the hook." He said nothing more, but they hadn't gone half a mile when he pulled over to the side of the road and stopped. He got out, went around and opened the trunk, and came back with a jug of whiskey.

"Always keep a little on hand for medical purposes," he said. "I figure Detweiler can supply his own, but you look in need." He uncorked the jug, grinning now, and took a long swig before he handed it to Mac. "Be my guest."

Mac recovered from his surprise, but couldn't quite make it with the grin. He could sure tilt the jug all right, though, and God but that burning rotgut went down smooth. Phil got behind the wheel again, not starting the car. Mac sat with the jug between his knees, staring at it.

"You sure have the look of a man fixing to tie one on."

Mac looked up at Phil. He forced a smile and passed over the jug. They sat like that in quiet for a few minutes, just letting the whiskey travel back and forth between them.

Mac's anger was still riding him hard, still a-building. A fury, almost: at having killed a fine, young, productive breeder like that sow; at Detweiler's stupidity; at just about everything in his life, including Elizabeth. Sitting there, this noon, picking at her food, with never a glance for him to know he was alive in the house with her.

Phil lit up a fresh cigar. "Year ago, a thing like this, it wouldn't have riled you so. Couple, three months ago even, it wouldn't. Not so's you'd haul off and hit a man." He waited, just leaving it lie.

But Mac could make no answer. Only, he knew suddenly that he wasn't going home alone, not for one more evening with that silent woman in that silent house.

"How about taking supper with us?" he said. Trying to lighten it, he added, "Might make it up to you for all that digging back there. And for getting me off the hook."

Phil slid the jug across the seat to Mac and reached for the key. "Another time," he said. "Told Selma I'd treat at Cy's tonight."

"Bring her along," Mac said. He kept his eyes forward not to meet Phil's, wondering what the hell kind of demon had pushed those words out of him. "Yeah, sure, why not?" The demon was pushing harder. "We can pick her up right now." He took one long last swallow, corked the jug, and turned his head to find Phil watching him doubtfully.

"Kind of short notice for Elizabeth, isn't it?"

Mac swung the jug over to the floor in the back, and put an end to it. "I'll call her from Selma's," he said.

Phil started the car and they were on their way to Switzer again.

What he'd done, inviting Selma along, was plain foolish. Worse, it was reckless. He'd walked away from what he'd felt with her the last time. He doubted he would, or could, again. But what the hell. He'd use them—Phil, and Selma. He'd be the son of a bitch Detweiler said he was. He wanted company for tonight, and now he'd have it. Shove the rest.

ELIZABETH

"Mac? Mac?" The line was dead. She wanted to cry out again, "Oh, not tonight, please!" She wanted— It was too late, he was gone. She hung up the phone and stood over it, her eyes closed.

The despair that had remained at bay all afternoon swept up in her, to turn into anger against him, for not listening, for not knowing. She straightened slowly, and opened her eyes, and saw in front of her the wilted glads in the vase by the phone. How long had they been that way? Days? A week? Just like everything else. No good.

The sob broke out of her, hurting her throat, and her hand flew up and smashed the vase to the floor. The foul water splattered and began seeping toward the rug. The brown petals were fallen off the stems and lay everywhere. Elizabeth looked at the mess, and sat down on the floor half in the water by the broken pieces of china, and cried as she'd not done in a long while, giving forth more harsh sobs than tears, like a child hoping somebody would hear. All she'd wanted when she got home was to go to bed and sleep. She was ready for sleep. She hadn't come directly to the house from Black Willow Creek. She'd stopped the truck outside of town near the new overlook, unable to face going home, worn out struggling with herself over everything. There were woods below the overlook, pine woods that looked cool and dark, a place she could hide in. She'd walked them, her mind empty; she'd sat down on the carpet of fallen needles, the sun barely dappling through the high branches of the lodgepoles, and she'd leaned back and closed her eyes and smelled the piney fragrance, and the afternoon had passed.

At last she'd returned up the steep hill to the truck, had driven carefully the rest of the way into town, and had just entered the back door when the phone rang. She'd rushed to answer it, a wifely reflex in a vet's household, dropping the bundle meant for Sooner on a chair. Now the sweet baby doll smiled at her from on top of the red apple and mocked her. She could still see that terrible old woman and hear her words.

Sitting there on the floor, Elizabeth couldn't find her handkerchief, and ended by rubbing her nose with the back of her hand. Just like Sooner. The tears which had been drying up wanted to flow again. She sucked in a ragged breath and got up. She rocked a shard of the vase with her toe. Nearly every day Sooner had been in the house Elizabeth had been after her to be careful not to break anything. She hadn't except for a saucer which she'd dropped while helping Elizabeth dry the dishes, and it had been cracked, anyway. No, it took Elizabeth to destroy Mac's mother's prized Haviland vase. And all she'd accomplished with her fit of temper was to make one more thing to do before the company came. She went to the kitchen for a rag and the broom and dustpan, and swept up the broken flowers and china.

Mac had suggested baked potatoes, saying they'd buy some steaks on the way home. They'd be here soon. She stood for a moment, the full dustpan in her hand, thinking of the lunch dishes still on the table, and felt panicky about what to do first. The doll and its clothes; she had to get rid of them. She picked them up and took them upstairs, and at the top of the landing turned sharply away from Sooner's door and went into the sewing room, where there was a blanket chest. She opened the lid and dropped the things in, and stared down at them. She'd taken them with her as an added inducement for Sooner, she admitted it, now. And she hadn't taken everything because she'd wanted to hold something back, in case she had to go out there more than once to talk Sooner around. She admitted this, too.

Well, there wasn't going to be another time. She whipped up the blankets and buried everything out of sight at the very bottom. She dropped the lid and brushed her hair off her forehead. She had to find a moment at least to wash her face. It must be streaked with all that dust and then the crying.

But first she went down to the kitchen and put the potatoes on to bake, and started washing lettuce and tomatoes for salad. What about dessert? Maybe Mac would think to bring ice cream.

She hardly ever entertained Selma, more in the early years than recently. They'd never become the friends Mac had thought they would, and Elizabeth knew that had disappointed him. But they had so little in common, with Selma single and working. More important, Selma was a Methodist, and Mac and Elizabeth belonged to the Christian Church, where his family'd always gone. Silly, Elizabeth had concluded years ago, but true: in a town as small as Switzer, some kinds of compartments in living were necessary even if artificial, because without them the interdependency of people and the lack of privacy would be stultifying. Anyway, Selma's proper bearing had always put Elizabeth off. Seeing Selma's hair bun and laced shoes, Elizabeth could hear her mother saying, "Middle-class and dull!" When she'd commented something like that herself to Mac, he'd smiled and shaken his head a little, but he hadn't pushed her at Selma after that.

So why did he have to push it tonight, of all nights? He'd been absolutely set on it, over the phone, had even hung up on her.

Elizabeth dumped the last of the lettuce into the salad bowl, collected the dirty dishes and put them to soak, and then let herself droop a moment at the sink. She was so tired. Lord, there they were. She heard them on the front veranda.

Quickly, she ran some cold water and splashed it onto her face. She was drying it on a dish towel as Mac's voice said, "Might as well all go out to the kitchen." Elizabeth glanced around wildly; she hadn't even wiped off the table. And then they were coming through the door and she saw Selma and forgot to glare at Mac.

There was no stodginess about her tonight, far from it. Her hair was only loosely tied up off her neck to hang down her back, the first time Elizabeth had seen its length; she wore a green silk dress with a flowing skirt; and sandals were on her bare feet. She was cool and fresh and buoyant. All this Elizabeth took in at one look, and was made starkly aware of her own sad and grimy state.

Selma and Phil sat down at the table, and Elizabeth had to wipe it clean under their very noses. Mac seemed totally oblivious to her turmoil. He went about getting out the pan for the steaks, setting up glasses for the jug of whiskey Phil contributed, bantering with the other two about his own domesticity.

It rather bewildered Elizabeth. She took a chair at the table, too, and willed all their bustle to go remote from her. But the only substitutes were memories of the day: the cabin, and Mrs. Hawes, and Sooner hiding.

The quiet time in the pine woods might never have happened.

"Hey!" It was Phil, touching her on the hand, smiling across the table at her. Elizabeth always thought what nice eyes he had, with a twinkle in them but never any ridicule. Now, he gestured toward her untouched glass of mountain dew. "Join the party," he said.

She took a taste, the first she'd ever had, and choked. Suddenly, the general good humor was including her, pulling her in, and she found that after that initial burning sip the whiskey tasted not bad at all. Selma's spirit was contagious, and Elizabeth was laughing with her. It shocked her. She stopped, thinking how sort of sad and grotesque it was. But before long, she had to laugh again, and something untwisted and began to ease inside.

Maybe it was only the whiskey; what did that matter? Her pristine kitchen pulsed with the red of Selma's hair, her green eyes and dress; red salad tomatoes; the yellow butter melting into the potatoes; the spurt of blood under knives cutting into rare steak. Sound and color were all about her, and the smell of her own sweat. But it wasn't just her own. The men smelled of it, too, and of the barn.

She looked at Phil across from her, and then at Mac, really looked and saw the dust in the lines of his forehead, the stained armpits; and she heard, for the first time, the edge in his voice beneath the banter. Had it been there all along? It was as if he'd whipped himself up to something.

It came to Elizabeth: that hog he'd had to kill. She watched again his heavy, reluctant movements when he'd checked over the rifle after lunch, and remembered her own lack of anything offered in comfort.

"Bunch of old busybodies!" Mac said now. "They

ought to let the county vote wet and leave you alone, Phil."

Not at all his easygoing self, thought Elizabeth. What on earth was he so vehement about? She caught back through her mind to what Phil had just been saying. Something about the local WCTU and the commander of the CCC camp, and how they'd called in the state excise, and it would sure put the skids to the sale of moonshine at the fair next week. Why should Mac be upset about that? He couldn't care less.

The afternoon must have been awful for him.

Elizabeth leaned toward him, speaking softly under Phil's reply. "Was it awful this afternoon?"

His eyes flicked to her, but there was no other response. And then, Phil interrupted himself and picked up her words "this afternoon" and launched into a tale of what had happened out at Detweiler's. He tried to turn it into an epic that was very funny, but Elizabeth couldn't laugh at it, not at Mac so beside himself he had to hit a man. Mac listened to Phil, his face impassive, and at the end he didn't look at Elizabeth, he looked at Selma. Elizabeth watched their eyes meet and hold. Selma's lips were parted and her color was high. Elizabeth knew as surely as if it were herself that the idea of Mac in a fight had excited Selma. She was suddenly aware that her own breath was coming shallow and quick.

And Mac . . . Mac's eyes were hot. Elizabeth saw them move from Selma's face down to her breasts and linger there.

My God, she thought. He wants her.

And why shouldn't he? Hadn't she, Elizabeth, turned away from him for weeks? Every time he'd reach for her, she'd thought it was out of duty. Or pity. But maybe it was plain need.

Elizabeth looked across at Phil. He shifted his gaze hastily from hers. So he'd seen it, too, what she'd seen in Mac and Selma. Was he hurt by it? He, at least, had the right to be.

"How about it, Mac? Right now?" Selma's voice was throaty and low.

Elizabeth turned in shock to stare at her.

"Sure. Come on," Mac was saying, and he stood up. "Haven't got many patients out there, but you can see what it looks like."

Elizabeth closed her eyes a moment, fighting a hysterical desire to giggle. Selma was only asking to see the infirmary.

As they went out the back door, Elizabeth began stacking dishes on the table. "We forgot the ice cream you all brought," she said to Phil, hoping he couldn't hear her voice shake. "It'll be melted."

She carried a pile to the sink, and Phil began stacking to help her. She could see out the window to the lighted infirmary. It was quiet. Was he kissing her, there? She heard Selma laugh.

She probably laughs in bed, too, Elizabeth thought, and never asked if she's loved. I'll bet she's fun in bed.

Phil was by her side, dishes in his hands. "Elizabeth," he said, and then hesitated. He set the dishes down. "Look, don't let it worry you. Those two've had a chemistry going for them off and on for years. Nothing ever comes of it."

She looked at him, knowing things he didn't know that could make this time different. Surprising both him and herself, she bent forward and kissed him on the cheek. "Want to dry?" she asked. "The towel's on that hook there," she said, nodding to it, and she began running the hot water.

She hoped Phil was right, for his sake if not for her own. She had it coming, whatever did happen this time.

Lizzie, for heaven's sake grow up, why don't you! Forgive yourself a little, and grow up!

She was startled. She hadn't heard her mind's voice since—since Sooner left, come to think of it. After the long dead silence all summer, it sounded to Elizabeth more than ever like her exasperated mother, as if it were she and not Phil doing the dishes with her.

Isn't it possible—the voice was sarcastic—that things happen for reasons that have nothing to do with you? Just like a child, that's what you are, Lizzie—thinking you're the center of the universe!

What? Elizabeth's hands suddenly went still in the dishwater. Just like a child. Like Sooner?

Mac had told Elizabeth to stop seeing things only in terms of herself. Could it be that Sooner was doing the same thing—taking all the fault onto herself?

Sooner's stricken face on the pillow that day in June when Bird was dead flashed into Elizabeth's mind. The face going stricken only then, when at last she, Elizabeth, had understood, and had said so, and had herself begun to cry.

Could it be that Sooner hid from her today not for fear of being hurt herself, but for fear of hurting Elizabeth? As Elizabeth had hidden herself away from everyone the summer long?

Why not, Lizzie? Everybody does things for reasons of their own. Sooner . . . you . . . everybody.

Then nobody can be to blame for *every*thing. Nobody. Not even me.

She could have told herself that a million times in the last year; she didn't know whether she had or not. Maybe it was because of what Phil had said about Mac and Selma and the past; or because she could begin to understand, really understand Sooner, now, and herself a little bit, too; or maybe just because she was ready. But she believed it. She wasn't to blame

214

for everything. And Sooner . . . she and Sooner were two of a kind.

The low rumble of Mac's voice came through the open window. He and Selma were returning to the house.

Mama? Elizabeth wanted to call out. Mama, what should I do about Mac?

Now, Lizzie. Elizabeth heard a dry chuckle. Lizzie, you aren't *that* much of a fool!

"What?" It was Phil.

Elizabeth looked at him blankly.

"You laughed. And then you said, 'Oh' . . . as if you'd just struck gold down in that dishpan," he said.

She didn't have to answer because Mac and Selma came in. And shortly after that, Phil was saying they'd better leave.

At the door, over their goodnights, Elizabeth saw Selma lean into Phil sort of in passing, and he quirked an eyebrow at Elizabeth and winked. It was obvious where they were headed, and he was letting Elizabeth know. Elizabeth glanced at Mac. He knew it, too.

Elizabeth watched Selma go down the veranda steps to Phil's car, watched the flesh moving unrestrained under Selma's skirt, watched Phil's hand drop from Selma's waist to rest possessively against her hip. Elizabeth felt a tightening inside.

When Mac turned from the door, she was leaning against the hall jamb into the living room. He halted on seeing her there, surprised, and then puzzled, and then hesitant. She never looked away from his eyes, and stepped forward toward him, meaning to glide gracefully into his arms, lifting hers to embrace him. But she went too fast and landed on him heavily.

Damn, she thought.

"You aren't tipsy, are you?" he asked.

She leaned back, her arms around his neck, looking up at him. She couldn't tell whether he was amused or not. She drew a finger along his cheek toward his mouth. "No," she answered. She slid her hand to the back of his neck, and lifting on her toes, she kissed him. His hesitation held. Her tongue went between his teeth, and suddenly, with a shuddering sigh, he became the aggressor, his tongue hard and forcing hers back into her mouth, bringing her in to him with his hands cupping her behind. As he rose against her, she felt the wonderful, weak giving-way feeling deep down, felt her stomach muscles grab, and then they were on the living-room sofa. She could never remember how they got there.

It was fevered and, except for the sounds of their breathing in the quiet house, it was silent, and over quickly, both of them exploding against each other.

Afterward, he lay panting with his head on her breast, and the beating together of their hearts was like that other time when it was Sooner's head resting there. But now, with Mac, the tips of her breasts were aching with a need to be sucked, and she felt again the sweet anguish of this afternoon, up in Sooner's room, and pain and joy were one and the same. Hardly daring to breathe for wanting it so, she took Mac's head between her hands and turned his mouth to her, and his tongue curled around her, and he drew her in as if thirsting after her milk. And the fever was in them both again, and they rolled to their sides and lay like that for a time, their hands and their tongues giving each other no rest. She felt him huge and hot against her stomach. She wanted him inside her, but her hands wanted to caress him, too, he was so beautiful. Until the waiting became unbearable and she guided him home. As slowly, slowly he entered full into her, it groaned out of him, "Elizabeth . . . Elizabeth . . ." A few moments they remained that way, locked and unmoving, as if this alone were fulfillment.

How simple, she thought. What else were we made for but to fit together like this?

It seemed that her whole body enfolded him, and that she was at once his victor and his slave. As they moved, and built it into one thing, and burst through it as one, she exulted that he was pouring himself into her, only her, not anyone else but her, Elizabeth. She felt triumph at his helplessness and, knowing her own helplessness beneath him, it was at the same time a glorious surrender.

There had been no words of tenderness, no words at all except the twice he'd spoken her name. Spent, still entwined, Mac had gone off to sleep at once. Half on the way to sleep herself, she realized she hadn't once asked if he loved her. She hadn't needed to. She'd given, instead: her deliverance was come.

* * *

She awoke in the half-light of dawn, alone on the sofa. She saw where her dress was fallen to the floor in a jumble and her underpants, too. She stirred a little, and looked down at herself. Her bra and slip were bunched together around her waist. The place looked like a bordello, herself included, and she was amused that she wasn't disgusted by it.

She started to sit up, and saw Mac standing in the dining-room doorway. He was watching her with curiosity. His trousers were on him, only partly buttoned up, and he had a bottle of milk in his hand. As their eyes met, he ducked his head and took a long drink. Almost, it was as if he were shy.

Elizabeth wrapped her arms around her knees, hiding herself. "Can I have some, too?"

He hesitated, surprised maybe that she'd drink it from the bottle, and then he brought it over to her. The milk was cool and smooth and sweet.

"I was on my way up to get a bath," he said.

She smiled up at him, still swallowing some milk, and nodded.

Abruptly, he rubbed his hand over his head and started for the stairs. He stopped and looked back at her, studying her. "What came over you, last night? I mean—did you like it?" He sounded so . . . wondering.

Suddenly very unsure, Elizabeth stared back at him. "Didn't you?" she asked.

He let go his breath with a whoosh, and shook his head. "Elizabeth . . . Elizabeth, I don't think I'll ever understand you! Not ever!" He went on up the stairs.

She felt abandoned, somehow. And then, she was taken by a wave of indignation, and set the milk bottle down hard on the floor, wanting to hear it bang, but of course the rug was right there and it didn't.

Damn him! How could he make her doubt last night and what had been so good?

She jerked herself to her feet and scooped up her dress and panties, and hauled down on her slip. She was still thirsty, so she finished the bottle of milk. She stood there, looking down on her bare breasts, not full and eager now, but limp, with the nipples gone soft. Pathetic, standing there in the gloomy living room alone, pathetic, that's what she was. But she hadn't felt pathetic last night. She'd felt . . .

She gave a little laugh. Just the memory of how she'd felt was making her nipples crinkle up. She spun around to the stairs, wanting to shout after him, "You don't have to understand! It's all right, you don't have to!"

Rejoicing, she had to laugh again. She'd had one night when she hadn't thought, she'd only been. And not even the question, would it happen again? could mute the marvel of it. It had happened the once; and that made everything possible.

SOONER

As it came on time for the fair, Old Mam dug out her aging barrels from under the shock, and she and Sooner jugged up the whiskey and carried the jugs to the stoop. It was hard work, toting them. Old Mam could carry two gallons together, her fingers hooked through the loops of the earthen jugs, but Sooner could only manage one at a time. And then, on the day Old Mam said the fair was to open tomorrow, late in the afternoon Jim Seevey drove up in his big black hearse.

He got out, nodded at Sooner but didn't wink, looking at the jugs piled high. "Quite a load of whiskey you got here, Mrs. Hawes." He didn't sound as if it pleased him.

Old Mam's eyes sharpened on him. "Iffen you can't cart it all to oncet," she said, "you can just come back. Did you bring that sugar and malt, like you promised? Be needin it pretty quick, now, with the harvest comin on." And she peered through the curtained window into the back of the hearse.

Jim Seevey pulled out a big hankie and mopped his face. "Mighty warm day. Mighty warm. Sure could do with a little touch of your brew, Mrs. Hawes."

But it was as if Old Mam didn't hear. "Ain't no sugar in there! Nor no malt, neither, not that I can see!" She stepped over to Jim Seevey, her face going set. "Jim Seevey, we got us a deal, you and me. Somethin more than three dollar on the gallon for the likker here, along with sugar and malt enough for after harvest. Where's it at?"

"Now, Mrs. Hawes," said Jim Seevey. "You just keep calm, now. We got us a little problem."

"What's your meanin, a li'l problem!"

Jim Seevey cast his eyes again toward the jugs on the stoop. "Don't suppose you could spare me just a touch?" He wiped his hanky between his collar and his neck, looking back at Old Mam. "No," he said, "I don't suppose you could."

Old Mam just waited, glaring at him.

"You see Mrs. Hawes . . . well, it looks like we won't be sellin your whiskey over to the fair like we thought."

Sooner watched Jim Seevey grimace as he watched Old Mam. When Sooner looked too, Old Mam was turning from red to white.

"What you mean, Jim Seevey! What you mean! We been sellin my whiskey ever year since twenty-nine over to that county fair!"

Jim Seevey shrugged. "The sheriff come to see me. Truth to tell, he come to warn me, and I'm grateful to him, and so should you be. He says the commander out to the CCC complained, and the excise from Indianapolis'll be in Switzer. Says these fellas, two of em seems like, are comin to walk the fair the whole four days, and if any bootleg turns up there's prison in it sure, for you and me both."

"That sheriff!" Old Mam was sputtering. "Allus it's that sheriff givin me trouble. And him drinkin bootleg ever bit as much as the next!" Her eyes narrowed. "How're them revenuers to know where the whiskey's at? Your dis-play's allus been good enough afore."

Jim Seevey just shook his head. "Phil says he'll be checkin and if he finds any moonshine on the grounds he'll have to pull us in. Says it could be his job if he don't. And he knows better than most the use I put those back coffins to, at the dis-play."

Old Mam's eyes were getting narrower and narrower. "You been lyin to me, Jim Seevey. You done tole me you weren't sellin to that CCC no more. What's the commander got to complain for? You got somebody else moonshinin for you cheaper than me, Jim Seevey?"

Though Jim Seevey shook his head and tried to say something, Old Mam wouldn't be stilled. "Now you listen here. I got me a plan, I do! Ain't never been no trouble to the fair afore, and you be lyin to me, that's what. And you're gonna take this here whiskey, and you're gonna sell it and bring me the cash for it, and sugar and malt, too! And then you're gonna buy my next year's run all to oncet and age it for yourself. Cause I aim to be where it's warm, come winter!"

It seemed to Sooner that Old Mam sure was getting herself overfussed at Jim Seevey. Could it be that Old Mam might not be going to Flordy after all?

Jim Seevey had been staring at Old Mam throughout her spilling of words. Now, in the quiet afterward, he chuckled a little. "With no market for us over to the fair, why, where'd I get the money to do all that? Mrs. Hawes, you're not talkin sense. I'll take your whiskey off your hands a bit at a time through the winter, and maybe by next year things'll ease up with the excise. But I sure can't buy it all at once, Mrs. Hawes!"

"Liar!" Old Mam's voice went so high it cracked. "Get outa here!" She pushed Jim Seevey toward his hearse, and then she rushed to the stoop and hefted up a jug. "Get on out, or I'll bean you good, so help me!" Jim Seevey didn't waste any time. He tumbled in behind the wheel, jerking the door closed behind him. He started the motor and then called through the window. "You'll calm down, Mrs. Hawes. And

I'll be back." The wheels of the hearse spun, and he left.

Old Mam stood there panting; then she uncorked the jug, tilted it over her shoulder, and took a long swallow from it. "Liar, that's what he is, Sooney. Nothin but a liar."

Sooner was keeping very quiet, unsure what was to come. Old Mam sank to the step and took another swallow. "Well, we ain't givin up Flordy cause of no liar, Sooney. No, we ain't!" She took a third, long, long swallow, and then corked the jug and set it down beside her with a bang. "We'll cart the whiskey to the fair ourselves, that's what. Pile some of William's fodder on top so's folks'll think we're come with feed for the stock, and take all the profit to ourselves. Just might come out so far ahead, the harvest can go rot."

Sooner heard her in a growing alarm. She could feel even yet in her arms the heaviness of those jugs from toting them yesterday. She spoke out helplessly. "But—but William, he can't never haul them jugs clear to Switzer! He just can't!"

"Course he can. Let's get to loadin up." Old Mam got to her feet. "We got to get an early start, come mornin."

Sooner didn't budge. If she wouldn't go to the fair, then William wouldn't go either. Not with that heavy a load. He wouldn't even try. "Ain't goin," she said.

Old Mam swung around on her so fast Sooner thought for sure she was going to get hit, but it was only to study Sooner a moment. Old Mam placed her hands on her hips and grinned. "Hoo-ey," she shouted, "ain't you the uppity one, though!" She calculated a moment more. "Seems to me, Sooney, you'd be just itchin to get to the fair. Ain't never been, have you? And that McHenry, he's sure to be there, him bein the only animal doc here bouts. He's sure to be."

Sooner looked down at the ground. It was a hard

thing, but there was William to worry over. "Don't care," Sooner said.

Old Mam just laughed, and then she let her voice go all wheedling, the way it did sometimes just before she laid the switch to William. It always made Sooner uneasy, her sounding like that. "Iffen they knowed you said so, they'd be mighty sorried by it. Why, he come clear out here just to see you. Come twice, he did." Old Mam was speaking very softly. "And she come, too, Sooney. Only this past week, it was."

Elizabeth came? Sooner looked back up at Old Mam, as the thought struck. "You didn't take out after her with that gun?"

Old Mam laughed again. "That fancy one? No need! She'd've gone harin outa here if I'd no more'n said boo! But she come, right nough, drivin that there blue truck all by her lonesome. Wasn't no point in her waitin round none, though, and I tole her so, you bein off somewheres." Old Mam folded her arms, watching Sooner, and there was a glitter to her eyes that was hateful. Old Mam wasn't just wheedling, Sooner knew. She was telling the truth.

The cry was torn out of Sooner. "Why didn't you call out for me? I'd've heard! Why didn't you?"

Elizabeth had come! She had come, and Old Mam had said nary a word! Staring up at her, Sooner's thoughts came all of a rush. About how Old Mam was with William, switching him, and how sometimes she'd do the same to Sooner, and how that switch could sting, and how sometimes those little critters in Old Mam's traps'd be left just to die. And Elizabeth had come and Sooner never knew.

All at once, words she'd heard at the jail came screaming out of her. "You mean old bitch!"

Old Mam's hand came flat across Sooner's face.

"*Shut your mouth!*" Old Mam paced out the words evenly and almost in a whisper, her eyes round and hard like marbles. "You're a-goin with me to the fair. And you're gonna get that mule to haul my whiskey for me. Cause iffen you don't, I'll lay into him so, he'll wish he weren't never born!"

She turned away then, and picking up two jugs started around the cabin. "Now help me load up!"

Old Mam had hit hard. Sooner's eyes were watering from it, and her teeth hurt. There wasn't anything could be done. She went over to the stoop and gathered up a jug and followed after Old Mam to the cart around back.

* * *

"Ye shall pass over Jordan unto the land which the Lord thy God giveth thee!"

William was trembling like a willow in the breeze, his head drooping low, his eyes closed against the flies which wanted to crawl into them. He dragged to a halt on the small hill and lurched back a little with the weight of the cart. Standing with her hand on his headband, Sooner couldn't find it in her to urge him forward any more, no matter what. Finally, she made herself look over her shoulder, hoping the look alone would hurry Old Mam into throwing on the brake, or else poor William was going to be pulled clear back to the bottom of the hill and it would all have to be done over again. But Old Mam was just sitting there on the seat, the jug of whiskey in her lap, her eyes closed the way William's were.

"A land that floweth with milk and honey!" Old Mam had been talking her Bible talk almost ever since they'd left Black Willow Creek. Behind Old Mam, the cart was piled high with fodder. Not a heavy-looking load, but beneath it was the corn liquor. It had taken them a good long while last night to finish loading it up. And then, this morning early, they'd started for Switzer and the fair.

Up until now, Sooner hadn't been able to look at Old Mam even once. She kept hearing over and over again the things she'd called Old Mam yesterday, kept feeling again that hard slap it had got her. And it puzzled her how, the more the hours passed, the more she wasn't sorry about it. It was almost as if, should she look at Old Mam, she might say it again, especially with the way William was laboring to pull that heavy load.

The sun was high, now. Sooner reckoned it must be close on to noon. And it was hot on the road, the tar melting and swelling up into bubbles which popped when she or William or the wheels pressed them flat. For a little while, making them pop had seemed to make the road run by faster under her feet, and she'd been glad for the holey boots Old Mam had stuffed with rags so they'd stay on while Sooner walked. But as William started to go slower and slower, and each little rise began to get harder and harder for him to climb, Sooner had forgotten the tar bubbles, pulling on William, whispering in his ear, afraid and sure that soon Old Mam would be bringing her switch across his back. But she just went on sitting there, never reaching for the switch, sipping a little from the jug, and Sooner kept thinking that if they could only get to the fair, she would find Mac and he'd make William feel better.

The cart lurched backward again, hauling William two halting steps with it. Old Mam's eyes blinked open.

"You got to put the brake on," Sooner told her, wishing and wishing that she'd hurry. "He just can't go no further. He's wore out."

Old Mam's lips tightened. "He can be wore out much as he likes when we get there," she said. "But now ain't the time. We got to get there, Sooney!

And find us a place, and put the word around what we're a-totin'."

She pulled the old straw hat with its frayed brim off her head, and rubbed her face down with her skirt, and then slapped the hat back on. Sooner stood and watched her, feeling something start up inside her—a feeling she recollected. She'd felt the same when Judith Ann Drummond had smiled at her in the way she did sometimes, and Sooner had known she didn't like Judith Ann.

Old Mam eyed her. "Iffen you can't work him, I will," she said. Now she was reaching behind her for the switch.

It wasn't right, and Sooner wanted to yell it, but where would be the good of it? Instead, she put her arm under William's neck, and grabbed hold of the worn leather cheek straps with both hands, and began pushing William ahead.

"I'm sorry, William. I'm sorry." She murmured it over and over in his ear, pushing at him all the while, his sweat mingling with her own and burning into her eyes.

William tried very hard. But the cart was too heavy, and suddenly he went down to his foreknees.

Sooner spun around to face Old Mam. "See?" she cried out. "See what you made me do?"

Old Mam climbed down from the cart all in a rush, her face set, and came to William's head and began hauling on him. "Worthless no-good, you get up and do like you're tole!"

The world seemed to Sooner to be spinning in a whirl of heat and sweat smell and flies, and the memory of Bird lying dead in the gravel got all mixed up with the sight of William down on his knees. "Leave him be!" she shouted. And she grabbed Old Mam by the skirt and tried to pull her away from William. But then, the roaring in her head turned into a car coming up the hill behind them, and it blew its horn as it swerved past. Whether it was this or Old Mam's hauling, William raised up off his knees and jerked the cart into motion and as Sooner and Old Mam stood by amazed, he pulled it all the way to the top of the hill. He rested there, his bony flanks heaving as he tried to get his breath.

Old Mam stared down at Sooner, her eyes marble-hard the way they'd been yesterday, but with something else there, too. A kind of puzzlement.

"What's got into you, any more? Allus sassin me!" She reached out and shook Sooner by the shoulder, but not very hard. "You listen a-here, girl. You want to go to Flordy with me, you mend your ways!"

She turned and stomped on up the hill to William and the cart. Sooner didn't follow after right away. *Want* to go to Flordy? Of course she didn't want to. She'd decided that long ago. But though she'd never said it to him, she wasn't really certain in her mind that Old Mam would let her stay with William. Now she knew; and lost in the sudden, queer, free feeling of it, Sooner moved herself slowly on up to the top of the hill.

She could hear, before she could see, the wheeze, jangle, boom-boom of a kind of music that was strange to her, and gay. And then, as she came to the cart, she saw in the distance the big wheel set on its edge and going round and round. Along with the funny music came squeals and screams and the full, quick-paced thrumming of trotting horses.

The fairgrounds lay off to the side of the road below. It had seemed just an open field when Sooner had passed it last in June, with a few scattered buildings all closed up. Now, a whole town was sprung up there, its little houses with canvas roofs lining a twisting dirt way where people walked, and flags flew, and big machines, glinting in the sun, bucked and whirled and turned about, and on beyond was a neat earth-red track where the horses ran. The clamor of it rolled up the hill at Sooner in waves like the heat. Altogether, sights and sounds, it seemed to her to be the most wonderful thing in the world.

Old Mam slapped William's rump, and he started forward down the hill. Sooner trailed them behind, her eyes returning again and yet again to the fair. It reminded her of something, only she couldn't get hold of what it could be. And then she figured it out. It was like one of those places out of the stories Elizabeth had read to her. The kind of place the stories named magic.

Old Mam walked alongside of William, hefting the jug up to her shoulder to pour the whiskey into her mouth. "A land that floweth with milk and honey . . . milk and honey . . . as the Lord of thy fathers hath promised thee. The promised land, that's Flordy for sure!"

William kept stumbling, and had to lock his knees against the cart pushing down on him, but he didn't fall. The thought came then, and opened a fear inside Sooner: all those people . . . how would she find Mac, in the midst of all those people? But she looked at the big wheel turning, and listening to the music sounding louder and louder, and she remembered that it was a magic place, where anything might happen.

MAC

Mac hung on the fence to one side of the grandstand, watching the time trials. The horses were running

228

slow, the way they usually did at the start of the trials, and early side bets were being taken only by the fool-hardy. The track was dry, the sun was high and getting hot, and all of it, the fast hard rhythm of the sulky horses, the jingle of rigs, the sly but good-natured exchanges of money, all of it pleased Mac exorbitantly, and seemed to have an air of expectancy about it. So did everything, this past week.

He'd thought it a fluke, that night a week ago when Elizabeth had come back to him. A fluke, or Phil's whiskey. But in the days since, he'd caught her smiling to herself at odd moments, and making plans—a shopping trip to Paoli with Eleanor, for one. And when Harriet called last night, he heard Elizabeth say that maybe she would go to the fair with her after all, she'd see. And she came back to the dinner table wistfully bemoaning that it was too late to enter her hollyhocks in the flower show. "I'd have a chance at a prize, I think," she said. "They've never been love-lier than this year."

No, it hadn't been a fluke. And it was a discovery he made anew every day, this sense of freedom, as from a weight lifted after too long a time. Elizabeth shared it, too. A couple of mornings back, she'd been dishing up breakfast, singing a song under her breath. "Frère Jacques," it had been, and she'd turned from the stove to see him staring at her. She'd set his plate before him, and bent to kiss him, and then held his head against her in a hug. "I know it's crazy," she said, "but every day I feel as though I'm on the brink of something—something . . . monumental!"

Some might call it hope, and he guessed he'd been as much in need of it as she. But where it had come from, or how, he hadn't a notion. It was, perhaps, the oddest thing of all that in the midst of this renascence they'd done very little talking.

But Elizabeth had told him what she'd done that

day last week. She'd cried, telling him, and he'd felt an anger as strong as any all summer; anger at that cruel old woman, and at himself. "I never should've brought Sooner home in the first place," he said.

"You're wrong," she said, lifting up above him on the bed to look into his eyes, hardly able to see for the tears in her own, he was sure. "You're wrong," she said again. "At least for me." She laid her head back down on his chest.

He ran his hand over her hair, feeling an immense sadness. "How long does it take, do you suppose, before a man learns? There're no easy solutions for anybody."

"No," she said, so gently. "That's not always true. Sometimes the simple way is the best. Sometimes. Oh, Mac, we have so much. We have everything. And she's left with nothing at all. I think about that—all the time, now. What does Sooner have? If only we could start over again . . ."

He'd told her then about his proposal to Phil of money for Mrs. Hawes. It hadn't comforted Elizabeth, any more than it really comforted him. He never mentioned Phil's hope that Selma might take Sooner. It would hurt Elizabeth, as it hurt him, thinking of the child in town with someone else. Selfish, sure, to be hurt by it. It ought to make him glad for her, and hopeful, too. Instead, there was guilt that it didn't. No, time enough to tell Elizabeth if Phil's plan ever happened.

Mac sighed, then swung around against the fence to face up the fairway. The Geiger County Fair was small and shabby by any standards, and he knew it. But it never seemed so when he was there, in it. A hangover from boyhood, perhaps, when everything on the grounds had always appeared several times life size, even the animals. Or was it that for everyone in these hard years any moment of simplest difference became gilded by the drabness of the days surrounding it? The ferris wheel looked loaded already. The crowd was building nicely. It would be a good opening day.

The week had been busy for all of them involved in getting things ready here, and near to frantic for Mac. If he wasn't out on calls, he was on the grounds, overseeing the cleanup of barns and stables, setting up the temporary infirmary, checking over exhibitors' papers. Or out testing Detweiler's hogs. When he'd gone back there, he'd found the apology came easy for him. Detweiler's wife must have read him one hell of a lecture, for he was as meek as a lamb, and offered to pay for the blood tests.

Mac blinked to discover he'd been staring blankly at Selma. She was directly across from him, opposite the back of the grandstand, where the county organizations had their booths: the Grange and the Scouts, the Republicans, even the Democrats. Selma was manning one of the desks, and wasn't aware of Mac's looking at her. Her hair was gleaming from reflected sunlight, and her shoulders quivered as she laughed with another woman sitting there with her. Probably talking about that trip to California, Mac thought. Had she ever tried to imagine how it would be for her if Phil got tired waiting? Probably not. Full of laughter, and fun; an easygoing sounding board for others; but she was no seeker into herself. Poor, foolish Selma.

He wished Elizabeth would come to the fair. He'd darned well take her for a ride on the ferris wheel. And buy her some cotton candy, too.

He was turning around back toward the fence when, "Did you see, Mac? Did you see?" It was Cy. He had hold of Mac's hand, wringing it and shaking it with glee. "Only four tenths off the track record, and that's just the first heat! I tell you, I'm gonna take that purse yet!"

231

"Doc! Doc!"

Grabbing Mac's other arm was Tim Hardman. "My filly's torn a ligament, I know it! Come take a look, will you?"

"Sure, Tim, sure." He started off with Tim toward the stables, but remembered to call back, "See you around, Cy. And I think it's great!"

SOONER

Old Mam made William haul the cart clear around to near the stock barns. It wouldn't look right, she said, to go anywhere else with all that fodder piled on top of the whiskey. There were some trucks parked there, and some tents and vans, too, where people were living for the time of the fair. Too full of their own business, Old Mam said, to pay them any mind. But there was no shade left over, so that William had to stand, held still between the traces, in the sun.

Old Mam shook out her skirt, tucked a wisp of hair under her hat, took a last pull from her jug, and hid it among the fodder. Watching her, Sooner had a return of that kind of sight of Old Mam, where Old Mam looked to be a stranger.

Old Mam picked up Sooner's hand and plunked a nickel and a dime into it. "Get yourself somethin to eat," she said, "but don't get lost. I'll look for you to be back here long about sundown. I got to go pass the word and find me some whiskey drinkers." Without a word for William, nary even a glance, Old Mam walked away toward where the big turning wheel showed above the barns. But this time, nothing trembled for Sooner, and Old Mam went off still looking to be a stranger.

Sooner closed her fingers over the coins in her hand, the first Old Mam had ever given her, and in spite of the hot sun and the noise from all the people so close by, she felt shivery and alone. She dropped the money into her pocket, and began wondering what to do first. William's coat was dark with his sweat and he needed rubbing down. But he needed a drink, too. Maybe first of all, he needed Mac.

She saw, by the big door into the nearest barn, a spigot dripping and with a pail standing beneath. She crossed over and filled the pail, hoping nobody'd mind, and carried it back to William. He sucked up a little, but only a little. She set it down under his nose where he could reach it when he wanted more. Now and then, he gave a shudder. Weakness or a chill, Sooner couldn't tell. She sighed, and turned toward where Old Mam had walked away. If she went that way, too, would the magic really be there? Would Mac be there?

As she stood, unsure, automatically she worked the oversized boots off her feet so that at last they could be on the ground and cool. A cow called from the near barn. Suddenly sure, Sooner crossed over again to the big door and stepped inside. Where else could Mac be but here, with the animals?

But he wasn't. She went through five barns, all in a long curving line. She had never seen such cows, so tall she had to tip her head back to spy the tops of their haunches. She had never seen hogs so fat, nor sheep with wool so thick and even, and she puzzled over it until she watched a man combing a ewe. She had never seen rabbits so lazy nor with so many colors to their fur. People walked along the lanes between the stalls, looking, as she was, or working, shifting

233

hay or watering the sheep or spreading corn for the pigs. No one paid her the slightest notice. And no-where did she see the yellow head, round and solid and rising high above the rest, that would be Mac.

The sides of the barns where the heads of the stalls were, were open to the air, and all the time Sooner walked she could hear the music and the spinning grind of the big machines and the screams that never sounded frightening, somehow. Smells came from outside into the barns, mingling with the heavier warmth of animals and hay but separate, too—of grease used too long, and of fish frying, and of something that reminded Sooner of the time Elizabeth had made sugar syrup and had forgotten and let it burn.

The fifth barn was different from the others. There were rows of benches on all sides, and in the center was an open space where a man was shouting in a kind of singsong with strange words Sooner had never heard before, while another man walked around prod-ding with a long stick at a steer so fat its legs splayed out beneath it. Everywhere around were people watching. Sooner had to push her way in and out of all those people, circling the place where the steer was, and it was all very closed in and a little scary, and she didn't find Mac. She was glad to get back to the door.

She leaned against the building for a little bit, look-ing out to the fair. How was William doing, under that sun? Where was Mac? She scratched an itch on her leg; the music banged at her ears; the big wheel kept going round and round. Down a little path be-tween the canvas huts, a man was bawling something to the passers-by, his voice harsh and deep. There was a shout of warning behind her, and she had to get out of the way to let the man prod his steer out of the barn. She moved into the sun; suddenly the sounds and smells were all about her, and someone down the path was laughing, and the magic was there again, pulling her along into the narrow path and toward where the big wheel was.

The huts she passed were all the same, yet all were different, with a counter across the front, and colored lights inside, and somebody calling every minute, voice reaching out with promises to get people to stop. Behind the counters, some had shelves of toys like stuffed bears and enormous dolls all dressed in satin and lace; some had piles and piles of dishes, and boys standing in front of the counter were trying to drop hoops over the tops of the piles; some had moving tin figures and other boys were trying to knock them over with a baseball. Around one corner, a lady was seated without a roof over her. She was digging a sharp tool into a sheet of copper while a little boy sat fidgeting. When Sooner looked closer, the lines on the copper looked just like that little boy. This was the best magic of all, so far.

The man with the voice she'd heard clear to the barn was selling mops. They must be very remarkable mops, Sooner figured. The man said they'd do everything, even wring themselves out. She thought of how Elizabeth would like one. They cost seventy-nine cents. All Sooner had was Old Mam's nickel and dime. Anyway, she was getting pretty hungry.

The path widened as Sooner followed along it until it emptied into the wider twisting way she had seen from the hill, the *really* magic way, she was sure, for here were the machines spinning around and here she could see all of the big wheel turning and see the little carts strung along it, and here was where most of the people were. The music and the screaming were very loud, sounding from all directions. The little houses were scattered farther apart, and most of them sold things to eat: hot dogs and hamburgers and banana pie and shiny brown popcorn balls and one, the one she came to first, smelled of that burned-sugar smell and inside it a sudsy froth of pink was blowing up against the glass walls. Sooner thought it was just to look at, it was so pretty; but then two girls put some money on the counter and the man inside scooped up some of the suds onto the top of a twisted piece of paper and handed it to them; and the two girls, one on each side, began to eat it, giggling. It looked better than sugar pie to Sooner. Nobody else was at the counter, so she went and laid her nickel and her dime down. The man nodded at her, and scooped up some more of the pink froth, and when he handed it across to her he only took the nickel and slid the dime back. She dropped it into her pocket, and looked at the pink mountain in her hand, turning the paper this way and that, the way she always did with an apple, wondering where to take the first bite. But when she finally did take a bite, it disappeared in her mouth like air. She couldn't believe it, and then the sweet sugar flowed on her tongue, and she knew it was the loveliest thing she'd ever tasted. She closed her eyes and took another bite, and another, licking her tongue out around her mouth to catch every last bite of the pink sweetness. She had finished even sucking the paper clean of the darker pink sticking to it and was searching for a place to throw the paper away when she saw Elizabeth.

It *was* a magic place. It *was*. She hadn't dared for a moment to hope that Elizabeth would be at the fair.

At the very same time Sooner saw her, Elizabeth turned from watching one of the spidery spinning machines and saw Sooner. The sun was catching in Elizabeth's hair, the way Sooner remembered it did, turning the brown to red. They looked at each other, only a moment, and then started toward each other. Elizabeth's face had gone very still when she first saw Sooner, but now it was lighting up as if the sun itself

were shining down through her eyes. But then . . .
but then . . . Sooner didn't know which of them it
was who faltered first, or why, but suddenly she knew
her mouth was sticky with sweat and pink sugar, and
she remembered her dirty dress and her dirty bare
feet, and she stopped before she ever got to Elizabeth.
Elizabeth slowed down, too, and stopped just a little
away from Sooner. The noise and the people were
everywhere around them, but apart somehow. If only
Elizabeth would kiss her. Sooner wanted it even more
than she'd wanted it all the summer. Would Elizabeth
ever kiss her again?

But Elizabeth didn't. She only smiled down at
Sooner, and asked, "Did you like the cotton candy?"

Oh, Sooner thought. That's how it's called.

She nodded a little, trying to smile back, and then
she dropped the twist of paper and tried rubbing at
her face to get rid of the stickiness, but she stopped
that because she knew it was only making it worse.
Elizabeth kept smiling.

"I ain't none too clean," Sooner said, and then,
hastily, "*aren't* . . . " but that wasn't right either, and
so she just went on standing there, not knowing how
to finish.

"Are you still hungry?" Elizabeth asked, ignoring
the rest. "Um . . . how—how about a hot dog—or
maybe a hamburger?" She made it sound very important.

Sooner shrugged, but she was still hungry. "Only
got me the one dime left," she said, and she rummaged
into her pocket to pull it out.

"Never mind," Elizabeth said, pulling out of her
pocket the little red money purse Sooner could remember that she always carried. "I've got lots more
than that!" And then Elizabeth smiled bigger, as if
something struck her funny. She waited, and as if she

237

couldn't help it, she reached out and smoothed back Sooner's hair. "You lost your barrette," she said.

Sooner wanted to reach up and keep Elizabeth's hand there and to say she was sorry, but the hand went away too quickly. It hadn't always done that. Sometimes, Elizabeth's fingers had stayed on Sooner's hair just a little while and Sooner would turn her head not enough ever to pull away but enough to feel the warmth in Elizabeth's palm. The day she'd lost the blue barrette came back all at once. She'd been running down the creek bank and her hair had caught in a thistle and the barrette had pulled off. She'd collected it back, but it was broken, and she'd had to work very hard in order not to cry.

"Well, come on, then—let's us both have a hamburger." Elizabeth turned slightly and waited for Sooner to come walk at her side. "We have to find just the right place," she said as they started off, and she sounded very solemn, but Sooner could tell it was only pretend, in the way Mac always did when he wanted something little or silly to be fun. Sooner gave a skip, fitting her step to Elizabeth's, and they looked at each other and this time they *really* smiled.

They passed up several stands—that's what Elizabeth called them, hamburger stands—because each time Elizabeth found something wrong. Either the hamburgers weren't big enough, or the buns didn't look fresh, or there wasn't any piccalilli laid out, so that it turned into a treasure hunt that would make the hamburgers, when they found just the right ones, taste better than ever, Sooner was sure.

It was near to the big turning wheel that they finally found just the right hamburgers and buns, just the right everything. When Elizabeth told the man behind the counter to fix them two, she said very firmly, "And we want lots of ketchup on both of them."

238

They stood where they were and ate the big juicy things, and when a litille fountain of ketchup spurted out from between Sooner's bun and exactly the same thing happened with Elizabeth's, suddenly the two of them were giggling, and they went on giggling as they wiped at each other's chins, and licked at their fingers, and said over and over how good those hamburgers were. Sooner knew this was the very best time she'd ever had in her whole life. A magic time.

Meanwhile, the big wheel kept turning. Sometimes it would stop, people would get out of the little cart nearest the ground, and more people would get on.

"Would you like to take a ride on the ferris wheel?" Elizabeth asked.

Just then the big wheel started up with a jerk, and the people in the rocking carts screamed. Almost without realizing, Sooner took a step backward. Take a ride on it? Now wouldn't that be something—but awful, too.

"I know," said Elizabeth, before Sooner could answer yes or no, "let's just walk around awhile and look at things, and you can think about it."

Sooner felt a little let down, but relieved at the same time. She nodded, and Elizabeth got the hamburger man to give them each a bottle of sarsaparilla with some straws, and they started walking along, sipping from the fizzy bottles and looking. The bottles went empty while they were watching the Octopus. Everything on it spun around, and it went up and down, too. Sooner thought the people riding on it were mettlesome as could be.

There was no place to leave the empty bottles. Both Sooner and Elizabeth found it out at the same time, and they were giggling again. Then Elizabeth put her finger to her lips, and peered at the man who was stopping and starting and speeding up the Octopus. When he was being very busy she took Sooner's bottle and tiptoed up behind him and set the two bottles down by his feet. Sooner thought it was so funny she hugged herself, and bent over with what a huge joke it was when Elizabeth ran quickly back to her and turned again to watch the Octopus with her eyes opened wide and her face looking as if she'd been standing there like that all the while. And then they both doubled up with their laughter, and it was just the way it had been last spring in the kitchen sometimes, when they would make fudge together. Elizabeth was laughing so hard tears came to her eyes. When she rubbed the tears away, she left streaks on her face, and that made Sooner laugh all over again. They both looked alike now, she thought. She and Elizabeth—just alike.

Now, Sooner remembered the mop.

"Have you got money a-plenty?" she asked.

Elizabeth looked amazed. "You mean you want to ride on the Octopus?"

Sooner shook her head quickly. "It's somethin else," she said, "iffen you got the money."

"Well, I've got plenty," Elizabeth said, her voice excited. "Why?"

"Come on," Sooner said, and she started away down the twisting lane toward where the narrower lane was, looking back over her shoulder to be sure Elizabeth followed. When they reached the man, still bawling about the mops that would do everything, Elizabeth was right behind her.

"Lookit there!" said Sooner, "ain't it somethin, though? Figured you'd want one of them for sure! Seein as how it wrings itself out and all."

The man must have overheard, because he stepped right up to Elizabeth and said, "The little lady's ab-so-*lute*ly right, ma'am! It surely does wring itself out!"

Sooner waited for Elizabeth to pull out her red money purse, knowing she was giving Elizabeth some-

240

thing remarkable—ab-so-*lute*ly remarkable—and she felt herself quiver inside she was so glad. Elizabeth blinked, and moved back from the man a little, and looked at Sooner.

"Well," she said. Then she smiled. "You figured just right, honey. I sure do want one!" She got her purse from its pocket and opened it. "How much?" she asked the man.

Sooner saw the man's eyes flicker from Elizabeth to her and back to Elizabeth again. Couldn't he remember how much?

"Dollar and a half, ma'am," he said.

Sooner stared up at him, all her gladness gone. "But you said only seventy-nine cents, afore!"

Elizabeth and the man looked at each other in the eye, and Elizabeth wasn't smiling any more. Then she poked around in her purse and counted out three quarters and four pennies and held it out in her hand to the man. "One mop, please," she said.

The man ducked his head, shrugged, and smiled sidewise. "Seein as how it's for two such good-lookin gals," he said, and he handed over a mop to Elizabeth and pocketed her coins so fast Sooner could hardly believe it.

Elizabeth looked at the mop all along its length very carefully. "My," she said. "It's certainly a remarkable mop!" And Sooner almost jumped up and down with the return of gladness.

"*I* know, *I* know, Elizabeth! I still got me that dime left, so can we go ride on the ferris wheel now?"

"We sure can," Elizabeth answered, and they walked back all the way they'd come, Elizabeth with the mop resting over her shoulder and keeping step with the boom-boom of the music. She reminded Sooner of the soldiers they'd seen in the Memorial Day parade in Switzer, only Elizabeth was funny doing it.

Elizabeth had never been like this before, Sooner thought to herself, the thought coming to her for the first time since they'd met at the fair. At least, always before, Elizabeth had never been like this for very long. It was as if . . . as if Elizabeth were suddenly become a little girl. As if Elizabeth were happy that way. But of course, this was a magic place. That was why.

When they got back to the ferris wheel, not many people were in line so they didn't have to wait long for their turn. And that was good, because as the carts jerked upward and people screamed, Sooner had a kind of uneasy feeling about it. Then, before she could change her mind, they were walking through the gate. Elizabeth shoved the mop at the man there, saying, "Keep it for me till we get off, will you please? It's a very remarkable mop!" He grinned, and holding the mop in one hand he lifted the bar for them to sit down in the red and gold cart, clicked the bar in place, and the cart gave a jerk. Suddenly, they were swinging up and back and free of the ground. They had been the last in line, and the turning wheel made no more stops. The cart rocked and the ground fell away and Sooner felt herself swooping up and up and over the top. It was how the yard swing had always made her feel inside, only bigger. She couldn't help it; the scream was pushed out of her by the rising inside, and she closed her eyes and held on tight to the bar. And then, through the whirlingness of it all came Elizabeth's voice.

"Hey, I'm here, remember?" The voice was full of laughter, but it had a comfort in it, too, and a kind of pull. Sooner felt Elizabeth's arm about her shoulders, pulling her, pulling her, and Sooner turned and grabbed Elizabeth around the middle, and buried her face in the softness above that had never been forgotten. And suddenly, both of them were screaming

242

and laughing and Sooner dared to open her eyes, and the wheel swooped them out and down again, and round and round. All about them, the world went round and round, too, and sometimes when the cart would tip, the ground became the sky and the sky was beneath their feet. As they circled in the air, the music rose and fell like a breathing. And because Elizabeth was there and it was happening to them together, it was like flying and like falling and it was wonderful.

The wheel slowed down as they were coming up the curve and stopped. "I wisht I was called Elizabeth!" Sooner's heart skipped a beat with having said it.

"What? Why—why, that's very nice, honey. But everyone has to have a name all their own. And Sooner's a fine name. A beautiful name, just because it's yours!"

It was like what she'd said about Bird: *worth everything because he was yours.*

William was Old Mam's, but she called him worthless and no-good.

Suddenly, the cart started up and topped the curve and stopped again, rocking over hard. And in the unexpected upside-down quiet, all that was wonderful inside rose and poured out of Sooner's mouth and into Elizabeth's lap—sarsaparilla, hamburger, ketchup, even the corn pone from morning. No feeling of sickness afterward. Just the mess she'd made on Elizabeth.

"Oh, Sooner!" And then, so very quickly, "It's all right, honey. It doesn't matter a whit! We'll be getting off right away. Just never mind, now. Never mind."

But how could she never mind? The smell of what she'd done was all about, even as the cart moved down around the great circle. And the sound of that: *Oh, Sooner!* had been so familiar. Hadn't it been with her all summer, every time she remembered Bird?

Every time she remembered how she'd made Elizabeth cry?

She pulled loose of Elizabeth and looked up at her from what was in her lap, not wanting to but doing it anyway, and saw what she knew would be there: tears, not of laughter but the tears she'd always known that someday she would make Elizabeth cry again. Bird lying dead in the gravel. William down on his knees with the flies crawling on his head. William standing in the hot sun, maybe dead by now. And then she'd have killed *him*, too. Because she hadn't found Mac.

They were closing with the ground again. Sooner could feel Elizabeth's hands fluttering at her hair, her face, touching, wiping, reaching. The cart stopped and the man clicked up the bar. Elizabeth rose, was lifting her skirt to make a kind of hollow with it, was saying to the man, "We had a little accident . . ." But Sooner pushed past Elizabeth and her skirt, and ran out through the gate.

There was a great bunch of people, more than had been on the dirt lane before, and she got herself all mixed in with them. A man knocked into her, paying her no attention, saying, "Horses sure are runnin slow. Maybe it'll pick up later in the week."

Horses. Sooner remembering them, running on a track, and the track had been beyond where the lane ended. Mac would be there. He had to be there.

She set herself against the current of people, while through their noise, and through the noise of the music, which was loud and wheezing and with a boom-boom that seemed endless now and could be felt up through the bottoms of her feet, she could still hear Elizabeth calling and calling.

"No, Sooner, don't! Come back! Oh, Sooner!"

ELIZABETH

Elizabeth stared into the throng of people pouring down the entertainment strip from the race track. Sooner had been so quick, just dodging into the crowd like that. Elizabeth had no idea which way she'd gone. Or where she would go to.

She looked down at herself. Why didn't I use some sense? she thought. What did I expect? Feed a child a whole bunch of stuff and put her on a topsy-turvy ride she's never tried before and of course she's going to throw up! Oh, God, everything was going so well. They'd been having such a good time, a silly, happy time.

For a moment, Elizabeth was afraid she might be sick, too. She'd called Harriet on the spur of the moment this morning to say she'd meet her at the fair, and then, Sooner was just standing there as if waiting for Elizabeth, her bright eyes lighting up with shared joy. Her face was smeary; her hair was summer-bleached and fell unrestrained across her forehead; no shoes, dirt-streaked and mosquito-bitten legs, scrubby dress—Sooner had looked as flawless to Elizabeth as any child ever dreamed of.

It was the perfect end to this week of rediscovery, the talisman of a real beginning, and Elizabeth didn't want to bungle it. She'd had care not to press, to take things slowly. What a wonder it had been when Sooner had finally thrown her arms around her, when she'd held her little girl close. Only to frighten her again with those stupid tears.

There in front of the ferris wheel, her skirt clutched up in her hands, Elizabeth knew, and fiercely, that this time she would not be turned aside. This time, Sooner mustn't be let to run off and lick her wounds alone like a hurt animal. She needed Elizabeth. And Elizabeth was going to find her.

She shoved the hem of her skirt all into one hand and headed for the public toilets. While she sopped the front of her dress and rubbed at it with paper towels, she tried to figure out how to go about it. She could get Mac's help. He was around the fair somewhere. Probably over at the track checking the horses after the races. And he had the truck, in case they had to go out to Black Willow Creek after Sooner. But if he wasn't at the track, she'd have wasted time. No. First, she'd walk the fairgrounds. She was supposed to meet Harriet at the 4-H Building, where her children were working, but Elizabeth couldn't worry about that.

Out on the step of the toilet house, she hesitated, the noise and the crowd on the fairway threatening to stop her before she got started. The laughter and the manufactured fun seemed flaunted, now, almost an affront. It was such a gigantic hodgepodge. There was no place to begin.

Well, there was the ferris wheel. Maybe Sooner had come back there, looking for her. Maybe she was there, looking, hoping, right this minute.

She wasn't. And the man running it hadn't seen her, or at least that's what he said, impatiently. There was no sympathetic glint in his eye, now that Elizabeth wasn't interested in buying a ticket. He didn't really seem to remember the little girl who'd got sick. But maybe there were a lot of children who did.

The mop was still leaning against the entrance booth. Elizabeth had forgotten all about it. She picked it up, and didn't at all want to carry it the way she had before, but there was no other way, she found, except over her shoulder.

She looked indecisively up and down the strip, finally just turned and started along it. She had to zigzag out of the road of a small boy who was very determinedly transporting to somewhere a white leghorn almost as big as he was.

Elizabeth was suddenly quite sure where to go first—the only place Sooner would run to in the midst of all this. To the barns.

She started with the auction barn because the path she took led her to it. She was appalled by the number of people, by having to pick her way through them, and then it occurred to her that Sooner would have been appalled by the same thing. She wouldn't have come here, Elizabeth was sure, or if she had, she wouldn't have stayed. But the rabbit barn? Yes, of course. She loved little creatures, and it was always quiet in there.

But there was no Sooner. Nor was she in the sheep barn, which came next. Nor with the pigs. Nor with the cattle, either.

As she reached the door at the other end of the cow barn, Elizabeth was thinking with dread that now she would have to go back and search that crowded fairway. She was hardly aware of the sounds of quarreling coming from somewhere outside the barn. But when she stepped outside, a high and angry county twang slapped at her ears and stopped her cold.

"Excise! Ain't nobody here from the excise that I seen. In cahoots with Jim Seevey, that's what you are. Tryin to do a poor ole lady outen what's due her!"

The woman, that awful old woman, Mrs. Hawes, was standing by a mule cart, screaming her invective at Phil.

Sooner would be here. Where else? She had run

to the woman before. Elizabeth started toward Mrs. Hawes.

"The excise're on the grounds, I'm telling you." Phil was sounding at the end of his patience. "I don't even know what they look like, but I do know if you don't get this whiskey out of here now, I'm confiscating it. And you'll end up in federal court."

Elizabeth searched everywhere as she neared the cart, around the corner of the barn, over toward the caravans, even under the cart's wheels. She couldn't see Sooner. The cart was piled high with corn shucks and, from what was said, probably corn whiskey, too. Sooner couldn't be in there.

"I can't get William to move, not by myself!" It sounded almost like a whine. Closer now, Elizabeth could look into the shadowed face beneath that incredible hat. Mrs. Hawes was peering up at Phil with a mixture of calculation and uneasiness. The dread Elizabeth had felt of the woman out at her cabin, and afterward remembered, dissolved.

"You stubborn old—" Phil heaved a sigh. "If that's the way you want it. But it's a lousy shame. You brew the best damn corn liquor I ever drank." He reached for her arm. "You're under arrest."

Mrs. Hawes jerked back from him, fear opening on her face.

"Mrs. Hawes, where is she? Where's Sooner?"

But Mrs. Hawes barely glanced at Elizabeth. She shoved Phil aside, and grabbed the mule's harness, muttering, "Ain't never around when she's wanted." She began pulling at the mule's head, trying to force him forward. He balked.

Poor old thing, he didn't look as if he could budge that cart as much as a foot, Elizabeth thought. Then she turned to Phil.

"Have you seen her, Phil?"

He tossed a blank look at Elizabeth, his eyes re-

248

turning immediately to Mrs. Hawes. But after be-thinking himself, he said, "Sorry, Elizabeth. Sooner, you mean . . ." He was shaking his head. "No, I haven't seen her." He stepped to the other side of the mule. "Here—I'll get him moving."

Mrs. Hawes slapped his hands away. "You keep offen my mule!"

"Mrs. Hawes . . ." Phil took a deep breath, but she didn't wait to hear him finish. She moved to the cart, reached into it and picked up a—a switch of some kind, Elizabeth saw it was—and laid it with a snap across the mule's back. Dust rose from the rough and streaked coat, and the mule started abruptly into motion. But he didn't go on for long, and the switch whistled down on him again, and again, and again, while the mule kept straining at the cart. The flies, leaping into life from around the mule's head, lifted up, spread out, and some of them tried to settle on Elizabeth. It was hot and sultry, and the flies were thick and sluggish, and no one was giving a damn about Sooner except herself. An island of ugliness, the scene hung before her eyes like a mirage, wavering in a haze made almost tangible by the slanting rays of the afternoon sun. The mule's spare, knobby body shook with a massive trembling, and slowly, like a pile of overbalanced inanimate objects, he toppled.

"William!" The old woman howled it, rushing to his head to try to haul him up. "Get up, William, you hear?" She swept the hat off her head and whipped it down and about his neck and ears and soft nose. The flies whirled above them in a cloud. Phil was moving, Elizabeth assumed to pull Mrs. Hawes away, when there sounded a piping cry of "William!" Elizabeth swung toward the barn, and coming around the cor-ner, pulling Mac urgently by the hand, was Sooner.

She broke away from Mac, running pell-mell for William, crying his name again. Elizabeth tried to intercept her. Whatever the mule's condition, and Elizabeth had a sad certainty that if he wasn't already dead he was dying, it meant more unhappiness for the child. But Sooner was too quick for her. She fell to her knees by the prostrate animal, and with her small arms tried to cradle his head.

Mac slowed as he reached Elizabeth. "She turned up over at the stables. Said she'd been looking to find me for William and then, for a while—well, she said she just forgot." He looked and sounded puzzled.

Elizabeth felt as though she'd taken a blow to her stomach, and all of a sudden the mop which had become a part of her, unnoticed like a third arm, recalled itself by having the weight of a ton on her shoulder. Oh, God, she thought, if the mule is dead . . .

"You can see for yourself, sheriff." It was Mrs. Hawes, whining again. "I can't get my whiskey offen the grounds. I can't! You wouldn't be goin to rest me even so? You wouldn't do it, would you, sheriff?"

"What's all that about?" asked Mac.

Elizabeth shook her head quickly, impatiently. "See to the mule, Mac." She looked up at him, pleading more for Sooner than for the animal. "Do something for him—something?" Sooner was looking around at Mac now, pleading in her face, too. Mac's eyes shifted to Elizabeth and he hesitated a moment, grim, as if he already knew; and then he walked over to William.

Mrs. Hawes was still working on Phil. "Me and Sooney," the whine went on and on, "we be goin to Flordy, and iffen you take my whiskey and jail me up, I ain't never gonna get where it's warm!"

Elizabeth felt herself go sick inside. She was going to take Sooner away? Away from her to where?

"Florida!" Phil stared at Mrs. Hawes. "So help me, old woman, I swear I'd take up a public collection to get you out of here. Send you to Florida, to anywhere, just to be shuck of you!"

Mrs. Hawes blinked up at him, her expression again shifting between fear and calculation. Phil cast a covetous glance toward the cart.

"Why not? If I'd be shuck of you for good . . ." There was a twinkle in the eye he cocked at Mrs. Hawes. "You're on, Mrs. Hawes. Even if I have to turn bootlegger to do it, you'll get your money to go to Florida."

"Oh, Phil!" The cry came out of Elizabeth in a whisper. "What about Sooner?"

"Now will you get out of here? Go on home!" Phil finished.

Mac was bent over William, one hand resting on the jaw under the ear, the other reaching down to the animal's chest. Now, he lowered his head to where that hand was, listening, Elizabeth was sure. Sooner strained across William toward Mac, her eyes never leaving Mac's face, her mouth open.

Mrs. Hawes stepped close to the mule and nudged his rump with her toe. "He don't get hisself up and walk, he'll do me outa this year's crop. No-good mule never was worth nothin!"

Mac glanced up at the woman in disgust, then sighed and raised his head to look at Sooner. "Puss . . ." He got no further. Sooner didn't let him.

"He *ain't* no-good! He *ain't* worth nothin!" she cried to Mac, as if by convincing him she could stop the words she knew he was going to say.

"Sooner . . ." Mac began again.

But Sooner poured the words out. "Don't you see? It don't matter none that he can't pull so good no more!"

Mac's head went down, as if bludgeoned by the protests.

Sooner's voice was quieter now, but the solemn pleading continued. "You see, Mac, iffen there's somethin belongin to you, why, it's worth *everthin*—just

251

cause it's yours!" Sooner swung around to look up at Elizabeth, desperate with need to keep William alive. "Ain't it so, Elizabeth? *Ain't it?*"

"Yes!" Elizabeth almost shouted it, in anguish for the child, and triumph, too. Damn it, she would *not* show tears. Not this time. "Oh, yes!"

Mac turned Sooner firmly back to face him and kept hold of her. "Sooner . . . Puss, I'm sorry—but William's gone. He—he's dead, Sooner."

No outcry, no frozen shivering, only silence from Sooner. And then, a small nod of her head. "Just like to Bird," she said, as if she'd really expected it. "I killed em both."

"No, Puss!" Mac said, and Elizabeth reached for her. But Mrs. Hawes pushed between them with a snort and grabbed up Sooner's hand, yanking her to her feet and away from Mac.

"Talkin silly, like allus. Never did see such a chile for it. William was old, is all. Would've been dead years afore this, iffen you hadn't coddled him so."

Sooner stared at her in shock. The old woman gave Sooner a swift shake by the hand she was holding, and her voice was sharp. "You think I didn't know all the time bout how you was wastin my good mash on that fool mule?" And she turned, starting away, hauling Sooner with her. "Come on. The sheriff says we got to get." She called over her shoulder, "But don't you forget, Sheriff. That's mighty fine corn likker in all them jugs, you done said it yourself. So I'll be lookin for a good price from you to get us to Flordy!"

Sooner was letting herself be pulled off without argument, without a backward look at Elizabeth, or Mac either. Elizabeth ached to tear after them, to smash the old woman to the ground, to snatch up Sooner and run, run. But if the child wanted it this way . . . Elizabeth felt Mac's hand on her arm. She couldn't look at him. His hand slid down her arm to take her hand in a tight grasp, and she clung to it.

Two aberrant figures, the woman dragging the child stumbling behind her, diminishing in size the farther away they went. A horse trailer stood in their path. They'd veer around it, and disappear.

Oh, Sooner, don't go!

The child suddenly dug in her heels and tried to twist her wrist free.

Had Elizabeth called the words aloud? She hadn't thought to.

Mrs. Hawes let go of Sooner and peered at her. "What's the matter with you, anyways!" Exasperation pushed her voice high and carried it back to Elizabeth. "I done tole you, we got to get!"

"I ain't goin," Sooner said, her voice high, too. Elizabeth held her breath. "I done decide afore. I don't want to go to Flordy." Now there came a quaver into what she said. "I figured to stay here, with William, and see to him. Only—" Her hands went to her face.

Even as Elizabeth let go of Mac he was taking the mop from her, and she started running.

"Well, what you snivelin for?" Mrs. Hawes was saying. "I never said you *had* to come, did I?"

But Sooner was already turning back, turning toward Elizabeth. "Only, William's dead!" she wailed, and she threw herself into Elizabeth and cried.

Elizabeth went to her knees, the better to hold her close, and Sooner's tears released her own, but she knew it was all right, now. "Little love," she whispered, "my little love." She raised the hot and wet and quivering face and kissed it. Sooner flung her arms around Elizabeth's neck and went on crying.

"Go back to bein a forrester chile, iffen that's what you want. You allus was a one for foolishness, Sooney." Elizabeth looked up from Sooner's tousled head toward Mrs. Hawes, ready to hate her. But the old woman's face held no reflection of her scoffing words. Could it possibly be a yearning Elizabeth saw there, and a sadness? But no. Mrs. Hawes' mouth quirked down in scorn. "That mule never was worth nothin, like I said." She jerked her hat down on her head and walked away.

Mac was at Elizabeth's shoulder, now his face tight with wanting what she did, and yet with doubt. "Things could go wrong again, Elizabeth," he said.

She smiled at him, and sniffled up the last of her tears. "Things probably will," she answered. She looked beyond him and found Phil. "That hearing, Phil—right away?"

He grinned. "Sure as you breathe, Elizabeth. Right away."

She lowered her face into Sooner's hair for a moment, and tried to get up from her knees, but the child was heavy to lift. But Mac was helping her up and taking Sooner into his own arms. The three of them started for the truck. Elizabeth picked up the mop from where Mac had dropped it, and thought, Good heavens—Harriet. She's still waiting for me.

Harriet'd be just the person to ask about getting Sooner into 4-H. Why, Sooner'd love to raise some rabbits. Or, if we could catch one . . .

"Mac?" He glanced at her, still walking, "Can a raccoon be housebroken?"

Mac looked surprised, and then he started to smile, and then he was laughing. Sooner pulled her face out of Mac's shirt and rubbed her arm across her nose.

"I know lots bout coons," she said, still having to gulp a little. "What's housebroke mean?"